LEGEND OF THE DRAGON SLAYER:

THE HIGH ORDER OF KNIGHTS

ISBN: 978-1515372912

Acknowledgements

To Gretchen, for the countless hours spent with the red pencil, all to make me a better writer

To Kristen, for all your insight and advice—and for making this possible

To Mom, for your honesty and valuable critiques, all to make this book something worth reading

And last of all to my wife: for putting up with me while I spent hours upon hours typing away, for being an ear to bounce ideas off of nearly every day for four and a half years of writing, and for being the encouragement I needed to publish this book

Legend of the Dragon Slayer:

The High Order of Knights

By Jonathan Dorr

Part I

Chapter 1—The Vision

"It is here!" shouted a man running down the city street, arms flailing. "The dragon is here!"

Windows burst open then shut, doors slammed, curtains were drawn. In the streets people screamed as they ran for cover.

"Run! The terrible beast is upon us!" the man continued shouting as he raced around a corner.

In the purplish-blue evening sky, closing in on the outskirts of the city, was a great dragon. It was enormous, even by dragon standards, and its outstretched wings seemed to fill the whole sky. With olive-gray scales, sharp claws protruding from its leathery wings, and teeth like sabers, it flew straight for the fleeing citizens.

Suddenly, it changed course. Veering to its left, it flew towards a man standing fearlessly on open ground. Young, but with the heart of a courageous warrior, the man wore no armor, only a cloak, a shield, and a glimmering sword.

Once it landed in front of him, the dragon spread its wings to their full, glorious span. Its throat started glowing as it prepared to unleash its fiery weapon. The man held his ground and stared directly into the beast's black eyes. When the dragon spewed forth its fire, the man held his shield up high. The flames hit the metal but did not melt it. Instead they bounced off of the shield and back towards the dragon.

The dragon moved to its right and circled the man. Turning, the man drew his sword and challenged the great reptile. Each stared at the other for a moment. Then the dragon lunged forward. Too quick for the large animal, the young man darted out of its way, rolling onto the ground before springing back to his feet again.

Before the dragon could react, the man swung his sword at its leg. But the dragon's scaly armor was thick and strong, and the sword barely cut it. Even so, the dragon's eyes blazed in anger as it faced its bold challenger.

"You do not frighten me, dragon!" shouted the man. "I will not let you pass."

The dragon then pointed its wings to the clouds. Lightning ripped across the sky. A deafening clap of thunder echoed throughout the city. When the man looked back up at the dragon, it had a crown upon its head. Its eyes looked almost human as it stared down at him with intense ferocity. Then it spoke.

In a voice that resembled the thunder seconds ago, it said, "I do not fear you, fool! When I return you will not be able to stop me, even if every man in the world stood with you!"

With that, the dragon flapped its massive wings, disappearing into the darkening sky. But the great dragon soon returned. Still wearing his crown, it led an army towards the city.

The young man shouted a warning to the people in the city. "We must flee! The dragon and its army are upon us! Follow me to safety. I will protect you!"

The people were terrified. Many refused to listen. Some hid in their homes, covering their eyes to the approaching terror. The rest of the people, though still trembling in fear, followed him. With sword raised to the sky, he led them into the mountains until they were out of sight of the dragon. Meanwhile, behind them, the dragon's soldiers surrounded the city so no one else could flee. The giant dragon flew high overhead. Rearing its head back, it opened its mouth to release its fire on buildings and townspeople alike. The consuming fire roared forth, almost drowning out the screams.

***

"Leandros, what did you wish to speak to us about?" asked Elarom, a man with silver hair.

8

Five other men joined Elarom in looking expectantly at Leandros. All were dressed in embroidered tunics. They sat in a circle of chairs in the center of a spacious, well-lit room.

"My fellow knights," said Leandros, "I experienced something that you as elders on this council must hear. I can hardly believe it myself."

They leaned forward in eager anticipation.

"I have had a vision."

The other knights shifted nervously in their seats. "A vision?" asked the bearded knight named Balkar. "Are you sure? There hasn't been a vision since—"

"I am certain," interrupted Leandros. "I cannot explain what I saw in any other way. It was too real to be a dream, yet it was dream-like. And what I saw, well, you will agree with me, I could not ignore it."

"Tell us," said Elarom again. "Let us hear and decide as a council what this means."

"Yes, of course," answered Leandros. He looked around the room as he began. "I saw a dragon—a huge dragon—and it was wearing a crown. It was not just any crown...it was the crown of the Emperor."

"The Emperor of Malakron?" interrupted another knight.

"Yes, Celdron. There was no mistaking it. He came to attack a city, but a man stopped him. A young, fearless warrior challenged the dragon and warned it to leave. The dragon heeded his warning and did not advance immediately, but returned stronger. It came with an army that looked very much like the army of Malakron. The young warrior led many to safety in the mountains while the dragon and his soldiers overtook the city."

The knights were silent until Elarom spoke. "It is not unlike the visions the ancient prophets had long ago. What do we make of this, gentlemen?"

"It must be a sign, a warning," said Celdron. "Our secret society of knights has watched the Emperor of Malakron for many years, waiting for the day when he would lead his armies against the kingdoms of Albantria. The prophecies have foretold this terrible time, a time which may very well be near. The Emperor has grown powerful in recent years, and his army is growing every day. The time of his great rise may be coming sooner than we first thought."

"And what of this young warrior?" asked Balkar.

"I think we all know who he is," answered Leandros. "The Prophecies tell of several who will challenge the Dragon and his armies. This man is one of them. He will slay dragons and soldiers of the evil empire, and then lead many thousands to safety as the Emperor's armies march across the Albantrian continent. I want to find him. Surely he won't know of his importance, so I will teach him about the prophecies and train him in our ways. He must be prepared for what awaits him."

"If this young man is indeed the Dragon Slayer as the vision suggests," said Elarom, "then we must keep this between us for now. We cannot share the news with the other knights until we are absolutely certain. If he is who we think he is, there will be a clear sign."

"I agree," said Celdron.

"Very well," said Leandros. "If the elders agree, I would like to leave soon to begin my search for him."

"Leandros," said the oldest knight again, "if this was really a vision, which I do not doubt, then you will not need to find him. He will find you."

Chapter 2—The Slaves

The Valencian Desert was a vast, sandy wasteland, stretching all the way to the great Western Sea. Nearly fifty slaves marched across the scorching sand. They followed four men on horseback while a slave driver swung his five foot whip through the air, yelling.

"Come on, you worms! What is slowing you down?! You aren't even halfway there yet!"

A quarter of these slaves had been picked up by the slave-train several miles back. One of these new arrivals, a young man, looked as if he had met his match in a fist fight before joining them. Bruises on his face, and one eye swollen nearly shut, he stumbled across the hot, cracked sand. Despite the condition of his face, he looked nothing like the rest of the slaves. His clothes were neither tattered nor old, his body was strong and healthy, and he looked as if he had been eating three square meals a day.

The slave driver walked up beside this young man and glanced at his wrist, which had the numbers 614-11 tattooed on its underside. "What's your problem, Eleven? Get beat up pretty good before you got dumped off, did you? Well, I don't care. You keep up with the rest of us."

The slave driver marched faster to address a slave further up the line, cracking his whip as he moved.

"So long's you stay on your feet and keep moving, you'll be safe from his whip," said an older slave next to the young man. He had graying hair and bronze, wrinkled skin. "If you fall, though, you'd better watch out."

The young slave did not respond to him.

Once they had all stopped for a short rest, the older slave looked at the young man and asked, "What's your name?"

After hesitating, the young slave finally said, "Why does that even matter?"

"Easy, boy. Just trying to—"

"You can call me Eleven."

"Leven?" his neighbor said, not realizing he had told him his number.

In no mood for a lengthy conversation, Eleven conceded. "Yup. It's Leven."

"I'm Harron," the older slave continued. "This here is Karmur behind me, and the man in front of me is Norden. We've been marching together through hell four days already." He waited a moment longer to give Leven a chance to speak, but Leven said nothing.

"Yup," said Karmur, the slave with a hideous scar above his right eye. "It's a terrible journey to make. Many don't finish it. Ya gotta do what ya can to keep your mind off of it all. If you let yourself start thinking about the heat, the thirst, your feet—"

"Nothing's going to get my mind off of this," said Leven dismally, staring into the distance. "I'm a slave now. My life is over."

"That's what you think at first, but you'll get used to it," said Norden. "I've been a slave four years in one of the southern camps. I was just sold to these men."

"What's your story?" Karmur asked Leven. "You don't seem the right sort to be cast the same lot as all of us."

"Obviously I am," Leven muttered.

"Right," Karmur said, raising his eyebrows. "I meant you just don't see boys lookin' like you ending up slaves. Get rid of those cuts and bruises, and I'd say you were once a nice-mannered, clean-shaven boy—nothin' like Norden or Harron, eh? Only the roughest sorts get sent to the slave camps, or the ones they want to make disappear. So what happened to you?"

Although Leven had heard him clearly, he did not answer. His story was something he did not want to even think about, much less talk about. It was all too fresh. Besides, he felt like he was dying. He was nauseous and his legs were weak, so why would he waste what little energy he had to talk about something he desperately wanted to forget? How could anyone *ever* get used to the knowledge of being sentenced to a life of pain, misery, and suffering?

Soon the whip cracked and the slave driver prodded them forward again. On they marched under the blistering desert sun.

Hours later they stopped again for a rest in a small cave, escaping the heat for as long as their slave masters would allow them.

"So, Friend," said Norden to Leven. "Are you going to ever tell us what you did to end up here?"

Leven looked straight ahead, ignoring him.

"Really, you don't say!" Norden snickered.

A couple of slaves around him laughed. "Talkative that one is," said one of them.

"Might as well confess your crimes now," continued Norden. Laughing again, he added, "It'll make you feel better, boy!"

"Yeah, let's see," said Karmur, looking at the men immediately around him. "Lareck here sold stuff that he stole. Norden owed debts to too many men he couldn't pay them back. And old Harron here was a burglar a long time ago, and he—what else did you say, Harron?"

"I was no ordinary burglar!" Harron said defensively, a smile crackling his aged skin.

"Oh no!" said one of them. "Don't get him going again about his stories."

Harron looked back at him, smirking. "You don't even know my whole story. I was not just a burglar. I did other people's dirty work— important people's dirty work. They paid me damn well, too."

Perhaps that explained why the old man's speech was clearer and more intelligent than the other men's. Leven wanted to look him over again but resisted.

"Yeah, yeah," said Norden. "Paid you good money to snoop and steal things, right?"

"And I was the best," said Harron.

"That's why you got caught," quipped Karmur.

"I got caught because I had no idea what I had gotten myself into until it was too late."

"And what was that?" asked Norden.

"You really want to know?" asked Harron. "Can you bear to hear the old man ramble on with another one of his stories?"

"That's why I asked," Norden retorted. "Go on, tell your story. Whether we believe it is another thing altogether."

Harron smiled at him. "I'd done work for politicians before, men in *very* high places, but the job that got me here...it was different. It was a long time ago, during the political war in Albakran. Bardane had just taken the throne after his father's death."

For the first time, Leven looked over at Harron with curious eyes. "How long ago was this?" he asked.

Several looked at Leven with surprise.

"More than fifteen years ago now," said Harron. "Why?"

The interest on Leven's face dimmed as he looked away and waved Harron on.

Harron shrugged his shoulders and resumed his story. "Even though it had been some time since the Grelleck bloodline had lost power in Albakran, they were still after the crown. Lord Pharon became lord of the Grelleck estate after his ill father died and his brother was killed in battle."

Norden waved his hands, his face twisted. "Now how do you know all this?"

"I gained the confidence of many to learn everything I could. That was my job. A dangerous job! But the payoff...if Pharon came to power..."

"Nonsense," Karmur muttered under his breath.

"Ah, hush!" Harron said. "Like his father, Pharon also wanted the crown. His grandfather had sat on the throne for a short while during the War for the Crown. Everyone learned quickly he was terribly corrupt, a ruthless king. He was overthrown near the end of that war and a new king took over Albakran. After regaining the trust of his people, he eventually passed the crown down to his son, King Bardane, who still rules Albakran now."

"What's any of this political nonsense got to do with you?" asked Norden.

Ignoring him, Harron continued. "Since his own grandfather once ruled Albakran, Pharon felt that he had a claim to the throne. Because King Bardane had no children, only a younger brother and a nephew, Pharon was encouraged only more to seek the crown. And that's where I came in."

Again Leven looked over at Harron, but this time only briefly, and he dropped his gaze when Harron noticed. "Pharon had everything to gain from learning about the members of the Albakranian Royal Council—and having any influence over them that he could. You see, King Bardane's wife had died during childbirth, and he had no direct descendants. If Bardane died or abdicated, he would have appointed a successor—in all likelihood his younger brother. Since he had no son to appoint, the Royal Council would have to vote to approve his choice. If the majority did not approve, they could reject him and vote on another candidate for king."

Harron stopped. "You following this, boys? It does get somewhat complicated."

"What're you looking at me for?" asked Norden. "I understand what you said...I think. Pharon needed a certain number of the councilmen under his control so he could get even closer to sitting on the throne."

"Exactly," said Harron. "And digging up dirt on politicians was my specialty. I was ordered to find everything I could about four of the Royal Councilmen. I went to Albakran and spent several months there. Paid handsomely for what I found, they gave me my next task: finding more about Lord Baldorn, King Bardane's younger brother. I followed him and his family, sneaked into the castle, recovered letters from his study, and learned all I could, including the type of wine he drank before bed!

"Then everything changed. King Bardane's brother, Baldorn, who I had learned enough about to fill an encyclopedia, suddenly died. Baldorn's physicians suspected poison, but there were dozens of rumors. His wife died also, leaving their son, Rallden, orphaned. I believe the poison was meant for the boy, the next in line for the throne after his father. Somehow his mother took it instead. As soon as that happened, the boy was rushed off to the royal palace for protection. It was a miracle he was not killed, I realized later." He paused, gazing above their heads, his mind going back to that time.

"Is that what got you here? They accused you of poisoning the brother and wife?"

"Aye, no. I would've been a dead man if that were the case. After the king's brother and his wife died, I realized what I had done...I had helped them kill Baldorn. I was a thief, a criminal, but I was not a murderer. I wanted nothing more to do with the plot. But I also knew it was too dangerous to simply move on. You don't quit working for men like that and expect to live. I decided I would have to play it smart and wait, and then at the perfect time I would vanish. Dumb plan. I waited too long. Before I had the chance to disappear, they sent me here. I suppose I am fortunate they spared my life, knowing what I knew."

"If you call this life fortunate," said Karmur.

"Involved in a plot to overthrow the king of Albakran!" said Norden. "I don't know if I believe it."

"I know I don't," said Karmur. "But you tell some good stories, even if you do make 'em up."

"Suit yourself," said Harron shrugging his shoulders. "It's the truth, but believe what you will."

Leven listened to it all while trying to hide his interest. He had questions, but he could not ask them now.

"Move out!" bellowed the slave driver, cracking his whip in the air. They shuffled back out into the burning sun and sand.

After some time passed, the slave immediately in front of Leven fell to the ground. Halting the line, a slave near him said frantically, "Get up!"

"Oh no," muttered Karmur. "Here comes the bear."

"Who?" Leven asked, wrinkling his sweaty forehead.

Karmur nodded towards the approaching slave driver. "He's as big as one, and he's just about as hairy, too. I've called him The Bear ever since I first saw him."

When The Bear raised his whip, Leven could tell the fallen slave was too weak to stand on his own. He could not stand to watch. Instinctively, he reached down to help him to his feet. Before the slave had regained his balance, he collapsed again.

"Leven, don't!" hissed Harron. "Let him be. You'll get whipped good for that!"

"Get back!" The Bear shouted to Leven.

16

Leven ignored the order. He reached under the fallen slave's arm, trying to pull him up again.

"Fool!" The Bear shouted.

He rushed over to Leven. Then the whip came hard and fast across Leven's back. Leven clenched his jaw as he fought the urge to cry out. But seeing the slave still on the ground, he tried a third time to help him. The whip sliced through his shirt again, stinging his ribs and lower back. This time he muffled a cry and fell to his knees.

The other slaves watched with wide-open eyes. Ready to deliver one more for good measure, The Bear stopped suddenly. He heard one of the horsemen shout, "That's enough! You've made your point. That slave is worth too much money to me." Turning to Leven, he added, "Back in line."

The horseman looked at the slave who had collapsed and, shaking his head, said, "Cut him loose. If he cannot rise even with help, he cannot go on."

The Bear pulled out a knife to cut the ropes that bound the man to the others in line.

The slave whimpered, trying in vain to push himself up. "Please, no! I can do it."

"Move out!" The Bear swirled his whip in the air and snapped it over their heads.

The line moved forward, each slave staring ahead. Leven didn't move until the man behind him shoved him, making him stumble forward. Leven looked over at the slave on the ground, who reached a hand out toward them.

He started to crawl after them. "Please, don't leave me!"

"Stay down, you fool. Don't move," Harron muttered with a look of disgust. "If the heat doesn't kill him, the sand serpents surely will."

Leven spoke loud enough so only Harron could hear him. "At least he'll soon be free from misery. I'd rather be dead than alive in this hell."

"You say that now, but I doubt you'd want to die like that, boy," said Harron. "You don't know suffering until you die a slow death in a place like this."

Leven met the fallen slave's dying eyes as Harron's words echoed in his head.

"Why did you try to save him?" asked Harron.

"Why did I?" asked Leven, confused. "Why wouldn't I?"

Harron was silent.

"He needed help," continued Leven. "I couldn't just stand there."

Harron smiled with only his eyes. "You are certainly not one of us, that's for sure. I would love to know exactly how you ended up here, though."

Leven pretended not to have heard him. He trudged forward, trying to think of something to take his mind off of his fresh wounds.

Chapter 3—The Helderan

It was afternoon. The bright rays of the desert sun blazed relentlessly on the hard, cracked, earthen ground. Rippling waves of heat emanated from the surface in every direction, making the horizon seem almost a mirage, wavering, shifting in the distance. And still the slaves marched on through this hellish oven.

"Where are they taking us?" asked Leven. It was the first time he had spoken to them all day.

"Kelishran," said Harron. "Capital of the Valencian Empire. They have a huge slave market. Buyers come from all over the world."

"Yep," said Norden. "Noblemen looking for servants, merchants looking for help, but most of us will build in the city. Hard work all day under the hot sun. It's brutal."

"I'm sure that's where I'll end up," Leven muttered. He marched on in silence, feeling the heat from the baked ground through the soles of his thinning shoes as he forced himself forward with each labored step.

Later, the terrain changed. A thin layer of sand covered the desert floor and grew deeper. "Sure does burn the ankles when you sink in, but...at least it's softer on the feet, eh?" the slave in front of him sneered sarcastically.

Leven was about to reply when he heard a terrible noise. The slaves in front of him shouted. The slave masters' horses whinnied frantically as they reared up in a panic.

"What is going on?" Leven asked as he felt what the others had: a slight trembling in the ground.

What happened next, Leven could scarcely believe. About ten yards before him, the ground began to disappear. The sand that was present moments before sank into a rapidly growing pit. Hissing came from inside the pit as its diameter rapidly doubled in size.

"Run! Get back!" one of the slaves shouted.

There were shouts and screams, and words uttered in many different languages. Leven recognized only one of the words: *Helderan*. He had heard of this desert creature that lived below the sand in its hidden traps, waiting for unsuspecting prey. He had never been certain of its existence—until today.

A number of men had already fallen into the pit, and many more were now screaming as they struggled to keep from the edge of the growing hole. Sand continued to fall into the expanding pit, and men everywhere were quickly slipping, losing their footholds in the shifting sand.

Leven backed away from the pit, as did Harron and the slaves behind them. He went as far as he could go, but the slave he was tied to had already started sliding into the pit.

"Help!" Leven shouted. "Help me!"

Leven fought to dig into the ground with his heels, but it was no use. He was moving closer and closer to the opening. He caught a glimpse of Harron shouting at one of the riders. The man on horseback cut Harron's and Karmur's ropes, freeing them so they could help Leven. Grabbing onto his wrists, they tugged on him. For the moment, he stopped moving, but he could feel the weight of the other slave pulling on him.

"Pull!" Harron shouted. He and Karmur both pulled Leven back from the pit, inches at a time.

The other slave tied to Leven was being pulled up also. Eyes wide with hope, he shouted, "Keep pulling!"

Once Leven was far enough from the pit to be safe, the horseman ordered The Bear to cut Leven's ropes. "Save as many of the healthy ones as we can!" he cried.

The Bear used his knife to cut the rope that bound Leven to the slave in front of him. This freed Leven but sent the other slave—who had just started thinking he would be saved—falling backward into the pit.

Leven was relieved he was safe, but he felt his stomach turn as the other slave slipped back into the pit. He turned, unable to look into the man's horror-filled eyes.

Shrieks of agony echoed from the pit, sending shudders through all the survivors.

"Let's move this way!" yelled one of the horsemen.

As they moved on, the victims' screams faded until they were almost inaudible, but they could still hear the echoes of their shrieks in their heads for hours afterward.

Thirty five slaves walked in line, heads down, not sure if they were thankful to be alive.

"Look! Ahead!" yelled the leading horseman from atop a sand dune.

As the slaves climbed over a sand dune, they saw it, too— something rising out of the infinite flatness around them. Far in the distance was the magnificent desert city of Kelishran.

The slaves marched under the blistering sun. With each step they took, the buildings grew taller and multiplied in number.

When the slaves reached the city gates, they marched through Kelishran's crowded streets.

"They're taking us to the slave market where we'll be sold," said Harron.

"And there I'll begin the next phase of my pathetic life," murmured Leven.

"Aye, the next phase," replied Harron reassuringly. "But who knows what will happen? Maybe you will be sold to a wealthy household and be used as a house servant, fetching wine or something. You could have a better life than most free men!"

Leven did not smile. He did not even look up at Harron. "No, I won't be that lucky. I am destined to live a miserable, lonely life."

Harron frowned and shook his head. "I hope you're wrong, Leven. I hope you're wrong."

The next morning, the slaves were corralled like swine into a pen. A man came in and placed a tag with a price around each of their necks. Next, they were ordered into the viewing area. Although the auction would not begin until later that day, they were placed on view early to whet the slave shoppers' appetites. Prospective buyers stared, some asking the slave masters questions about their prospective purchases.

Kids also stopped by the fence and jeered at them. "Hey slaves! Come over here! We've got to show you something!" exclaimed one of them.

Then another added with an obnoxious laugh, "Oh wait, Jekra, they can't! They're tied up!"

They erupted into laughter while they continued to point and stare.

Harron looked at Leven to see his reaction, but he seemed not to have heard them. He looked straight in front of him with a blank stare.

Once the time came, they were prodded into a tent and arranged in a line. Leven was placed last. One by one they passed through the tent flap until few remained.

When Harron was next, he turned and bid him farewell.

Leven had known this man only a few days, but as he was his only friend in the world, he was saddened by the thought of never seeing him again. "You have been a good friend to me, Harron," Leven said. "I'm sorry this is goodbye."

Harron nodded just before he disappeared out of the tent.

Leven waited anxiously, his stomach turning. With not a glimmer of hope in his future, he solemnly turned to face the tent flap. When the time came, Leven slowly stepped outside. He looked out from atop the platform into the hundreds of faces staring up at him. Several men holding signs raised their hands.

A man just off the center of the stage said loudly, "One twenty."

"One forty!" said another.

As the bidding continued, Leven noticed Harron being escorted behind a tent with several other slaves. Breaking his concentration, he heard the auctioneer next to him yell sharply, "Sold!"

Leven was prodded down the steps and around the corner of the tent, and then dragged towards a wagon already filled to the brim with slaves. After Leven climbed into the back of the cart, he looked dismally into the mob of filthy, putrid men. He felt sick. The finality of his fate was now indisputable. He was a slave.

Despite the terrible lot he had been dealt, he was relieved at what he saw next. Small and weak though it was, a smile formed across his face as he saw Harron turn towards him. Though Leven still felt the same sickening stomach twisting from before, he was happy to see the only man he knew in this inhospitable place.

"Against all odds we meet again," Harron said.

Chapter 4—Life as a Slave

The next morning they were wakened an hour before dawn. "Welcome!" said a cold, unwelcoming voice. The man who spoke was a short, stocky man with black, piercing eyes and light brown skin. "You'll work for me until you are of no more use—either too old or dead. Work hard and cause no problems and you'll get water, food, and a bed to sleep on each night. Test your slave masters and you will suffer for it. Each morning you will wake before dawn and catch your wagon so that you arrive at your worksite by daybreak. Are there any questions?"

Giving no time for any of them to speak, he began to assign each a wagon. Much to their surprise, Leven and Harron were assigned to the same worksite. Leven was certain this would surely be the last good news he would ever get.

The work was difficult, especially excruciating in the heat of the desert air. The sun rose quickly just as Leven had expected, but the heat was worse than he had anticipated. This work required constant movement, as well as strength and concentration. As most of them found out that day, asking for water or stopping without permission, even if for a moment, resulted in a lashing.

"Get moving those beams!" shouted the slave driver behind Leven. A thick, brawny man, the slave driver stood a full head above Leven. His dark tan skin glistened with sweat, drawing more notice to the rippling muscles of his huge arms, shoulders, and back. His name was Bellok, and Leven hated him the moment he laid eyes on him.

Leven's partner was a lean, bony man, barely capable of lifting a small tree branch let alone the heavy beams they had been carrying all morning. To get the job done and avoid a lashing from Bellok,

Leven had to lift more than his fair share. When a slave fell nearby, Bellok was upon him in no time. Leven cringed as the whip sliced through his partner's back, leaving a deep line of raw flesh exposed to the broiling sun.

The hours passed, and the heat worsened. Leven felt the wrath of the desert sun intensify as the rays baked his skin. He looked enviously upon other slaves resting under the shade of a tree.

"He doesn't let us rest for more than a minute," said Leven's scrawny partner as they dropped their beam by the carvers. "I'm not going to last if he doesn't let us rest again soon."

"We've got only one more beam to move," said Leven, trying to encourage him.

"I'm not going to make it," groaned the man.

As they started to move the last beam, Leven's partner slowed down with each step they took. His arms and legs began to shake. Leven knew this man might not be able to finish moving another beam, and if he collapsed while carrying it, he could easily get crushed under the weight of it. The moment they dropped their beam in the pile, Leven called out to the slave driver. "This man needs rest!"

Bellok glared fiercely at Leven as he marched towards him. "What'd you say to me, slave?!"

"I said that he needed to—"

"Shut your mouth!" Bellok growled. "I'll decide when you rest and work. What's the matter with you?"

"But he'll collapse before—"

Suddenly, a forceful sting jolted Leven's body. It sent a deep, throbbing pain that started at his back, but moved to the inner core of his body. The whip had sliced through much of his skin. Leven stifled a cry of pain by biting his lip.

"Now move on to those beams over there!" shouted the slave driver. "You both keep on working. No break yet. That will teach you for next time."

Leven stared at the man in disbelief. When Bellok stared back and cracked his whip, they wasted no more time in moving to the new pile of beams. Leven once again carried most of the load. His arms nearly gave out while carrying it, and he started to feel nauseous. A throbbing headache and cruel thirst plagued him. But on he pressed, as his partner's legs started to wobble again.

When they started moving the second beam, Leven wished to die. There had never been a feeling like this, and the sheer pain from the lashing was only the half of it. There was no reason to endure this unbearable torture. Yet, something inside him told him to continue on and not give in.

Then his partner dropped to the ground. When he landed, the beam fell on top of him, rolling over his neck. Leven used all of his strength to move the beam off of him, but it was too late. The man did not move.

Bellok raised his whip to lash him, but when he saw the man was not breathing he stopped himself. "Over here! We've got another!"

Leven shook with anger at Bellok's callous response. Seething, Leven clenched his teeth and turned away from him.

The next week passed with each day like this first one. Each night Leven felt as if he were sorer and weaker than the day before. Bellok continued to work Leven's group of slaves harder than the rest, relishing the power he held over them. Despite this, Leven pressed on. He often thought that it would be easier to give up, to allow his body to give in so that he would no longer suffer; but he did not. There was some inner force that kept him fighting despite everything.

With each new day, Leven found himself dwelling more and more on the events of his recent past. While squeezing under the shade of a tiny tree during one of their breaks, Harron looked over at Leven.

"You are thinking of your life before, aren't you?" Harron said.

Leven sighed, "It haunts me all the time. I try to forget it, but I simply can't."

"Sometimes it is all we have to keep us sane. Tell me about it. Keep us both sane."

"It's a long story."

"All the better."

"My father..." Leven said slowly. "My father, Lanellon, was a commander in the army of Kallendria, the small seafaring nation south of Albakran. After my mother died, he took a new position...I think to start over and get away from the pain of losing her. 'We're going to the capital of Albakran, the city of Balankor, Amaran,' he told me. My real name is Amaran, Harron. I never told you before."

"Amaran," repeated Harron.

"My father was assigned to Balankor for an eight year post," Amaran continued.

"After the war?" asked Harron. After seeing Amaran nod, he added, "I know of this."

Amaran went on to explain how the end of the war between Kallendria and Albakran resulted in the signing of a peace treaty. As part of the terms of the agreement, each nation conceded to open up its larger cities, including the capitals, to several regiments of the opposing nation's army. The regiments would be stationed there eight years to ensure stringent adherence to the pact.

"I was there in the Balankor palace when the two kingdoms came together for the first time. That's what I will tell you about. Maybe you'd like to hear what became of the King's nephew who almost died?"

"The one I knew of? Whose parents died because of what I was involved in?"

Amaran nodded.

"I can't believe this!" Harron exclaimed. "No wonder you listened so closely to my story!"

"Just wait until you hear the rest of my story. Just wait...."

Part II

Chapter 5—Inside the Palace of Balankor

"Grab some breakfast quickly, Amaran!" Lanellon shouted into the other room. "We'll be off to the Balankor Palace shortly."

In full uniform, Commander Lanellon wore a form-fitting metal helmet with a protruding white plume. A deep purple jacket covered his back and shoulders, and underneath was a silver vest centered with a row of finely crafted buttons. His white trousers extended down to low black boots. Lanellon was a handsome man with dark, piercing eyes; a strong jaw line; and chestnut brown hair—though salted with a few specks of gray.

"I'm ready, Father," Amaran said, snatching the last of the bacon and bread off the table and heading to the door. Amaran resembled his father quite closely. His hair and eyes were both dark brown like the commander's, and it was obvious he would one day inherit his father's handsome face.

"Very well. Let's go, son," answered Lanellon. "We must reach the palace shortly."

Soon, they were riding through the Balankor streets alongside a dozen other Kallendrian officers. "Do you realize the opportunity you have here today, Amaran?" Lanellon asked his son. "It is going to be an exceptional experience—something most commanders' sons would *never* have the opportunity to see. You might not realize it now, but you will when you're a little older."

"Yes, it will be interesting," Amaran said unenthusiastically.

"You won't be allowed to sit in with us during the meeting, of course," Lanellon continued, paying no attention to his son's bland reply, "but you will see the inside of the palace and meet some of the Albakranian leaders. You'll witness firsthand a friendly greeting between two enemy nations."

A short while later they passed a group of young Albakranian soldiers at an intersection. The soldiers eyed the Kallendrian officers closely. Amaran swallowed deeply as he felt the cold, hard stares upon him and his father.

"Why do they have to stare at us like that?" Amaran muttered.

"It'll take some time for everyone to adjust," Lanellon said matter-of-factly. "It's only natural that you feel a little afraid. We all are, the Albakranians included. You will be safe here...as long as you follow the rules about leaving the barracks."

"I will," Amaran promised.

When they finally reached the palace, a man dressed in a white and blue robe greeted them. With him were two officers of the Albakranian army. "Welcome, gentlemen!" he said warmly. "We are most glad that you are here! I am Lord Grairon, and with me are Commander Relledren and Commander Ardonell. Please, come inside."

Lanellon thanked them, speaking for the Kallendrian officers accompanying him.

They followed Lord Grairon up the front steps. Massive, wooden doors with lustrous silver handles opened before them. Amaran stayed close to his father, his heart beating rapidly, staring in amazement at all the sights of the splendid place.

Once inside, they stood in the center of a huge room with a marbled floor. Towering pillars—each etched with a different carved picture—rose to a ceiling that seemed to reach the sky. At the pinnacle of the ceiling was a large domed skylight letting in the bright morning sunlight. The walls were decorated with paintings of scenes of Albantrian life. Amaran was so captivated by a scene of a knight fighting the infamous beast called a malken that he almost did not notice the call for his father's men to enter the meeting room.

After Lanellon and the other Kallendrians followed their escorts into the banquet hall, Amaran plopped himself down on a bench by the doors. A servant walked up to him, carrying a large silver platter full of delectable appetizers. Amaran's eyes opened wide and his smile doubled in size when he saw the enormous heap of sweet biscuits drizzled with a cinnamon-honey glaze. There was also some juicy mangala fruit cut into perfect cubes and a sampling of succulent shrimp, deviled lobster cakes, and steamed oysters.

Amaran graciously took the whole tray, much to the surprise of the servant. Shaking his head, the empty-handed servant turned and left the foyer. Amaran smiled down at the appetizer tray that was now all his to enjoy.

While the Kallendrian and Albakranians discussed the terms of the treaty, Amaran waited outside the meeting hall. After two hours, he was as bored as one might expect an eleven-year-old boy would be under the circumstances. He decided to play a game to defeat his boredom. Having just finished his goal of stepping on every black marble tile in the hall, he started his journey across the hall while stepping on only the white marble tiles.

Concentrating intensely, he carefully balanced himself so that he did not accidentally touch the black marble with the edge of his foot.

"Hello there!"

The voice behind him startled Amaran so much he lost his footing and fell sideways onto the floor.

"Sorry, I didn't mean to scare you quite like *that*," said a boy roughly the same age as Amaran. He quickly outstretched his hand to help him back to his feet. "My name is Rallden. What's yours?"

"Amaran," he answered, looking at a boy who was far better dressed than he.

"What are you doing here? Who do you know?" Rallden inquired.

"Well, my father is a Kallendrian commander. He's in charge of the troops in Balankor. He's meeting with a bunch of important men—his own men and your military commanders, too." Then, imitating his father as best he could, he added with a smile, "To discuss the protocol for the troops while in Balankor and what the future holds for our two countries."

"Ha!" Rallden laughed. "Sounds like a fun time for you."

"Yes. Very. I was so lucky to be able to come with him...and wait here...until the very end of the meeting." Amaran rolled his eyes.

"So you're Kallendrian. That explains it. I did think you were dressed somewhat...differently. How long will you be here? In the city, I mean?"

"For the full term. About eight years."

"Wow. That's a long time to stay away from home, eh?"

"Yep. Although I guess this is our new home...for now," Amaran said with a sigh.

Rallden looked sympathetic. "I sure would not want to have to live in one of *your* cities for eight years. To leave everything behind...."

Amaran stared at him hesitantly at first, but then a smile of relief gradually spread across his face.

"Hey, Amaran, I've got an idea." Rallden turned and headed for the huge staircase in the center of the foyer, as he spoke over his shoulder.

His feet fixed on the floor, Amaran looked skeptically at him.

"Come on, you can trust me. You may be Kallendrian, but I'm not going to lead you into the dungeon."

"I know," Amaran said with a laugh. "All right, I'm coming."

They flew up an impressive staircase and ran along the upstairs hallway. When they reached the end of this corridor, they found a large, ancient-looking door. Rallden opened it. "This way."

They ran up a narrow, spiral staircase. A few feet up, Amaran stopped at a window.

"Look at that! You can see the entire city from here!"

"Come on, Amaran!" Rallden shouted. "Don't look yet. Wait until we get to the top!"

He followed Rallden to the top, waited for Rallden to open the door, and followed him into a small, circular room. Rallden stood in front of a large, open window.

Amaran slowly approached. As he got to the window, he looked out over the city. From there the buildings were even smaller than they appeared through the first window. Specks—people, horses, and carriages—moved about in the streets far below them, looking like toys.

"It's something, isn't it?" Rallden said proudly. "You should see it when a storm is on the horizon."

"It is incredible," Amaran agreed. "I think I can even see where the barracks are from here...right over there, in that corner of the city."

"Yeah! That's close to the Eastern Gate. There's a good fishing place not too far from that entrance. Which gives me another idea...." He paused momentarily before finishing his thought. "What do you say we go fishing sometime?"

"Really?" asked Amaran, raising his brows.

"Down the road there is a perfect spot in the woods. I've been there a few times before. It's only a few miles beyond the city walls. What do you say?"

"Well, I don't know...."

"Oh, come on, Amaran! It will be an adventure."

"I'm not allowed to sneak out. If I got caught, my father would be furious!"

"Are you serious? A chance for adventure and you're afraid of getting in trouble? I will show you how to sneak out without getting caught. It's easy," Rallden said, grinning. "I promise."

The next day Amaran made his way to the spot where Rallden had told him, watching the sights of the busy city along the way. He was so distracted he walked right past the blacksmith shop where Rallden had instructed him to meet. In fact, he walked right past Rallden himself.

"Hey! Where're you going?" shouted Rallden.

"Oh! Hey, Rallden. I wasn't paying attention." Amaran turned his head and, as if he were a marionette being jerked back, stopped himself mid-stride.

"All right, here is what we're going to do. See all the carriages going through the gate there? We're going to find the right one, one with good cover, and jump in. It'll take us right out of the city."

Amaran could feel his stomach rise into his throat in anticipation of the daring plan. "Okay. If you think it will work, let's go!"

Rallden motioned him towards a carriage driven by an old man with a gray, bushy beard. The cart was full of baskets and barrels, all covered by a single blanket. Once it started to pass them, Rallden whispered, "All right, here's our chance. Now or never!"

With a grunt, Rallden reached for the sidebar of the carriage. Grasping it firmly, he very cleanly swung himself up and over the side of the carriage. Amaran followed suit. Without delay, Rallden adjusted the blanket to make sure they were both covered.

The carriage stopped at the gate's checkpoint, but only for a few seconds. Amaran peeked through the carriage's sideboards as it rolled across the drawbridge, over the moat, and onto a narrow dirt road that meandered into the wooded countryside beyond. After a few minutes, Rallden spotted the bridge ahead. He caught Amaran's eye and nodded. The boys simultaneously slipped out from beneath the blanket, hopping off the back of the carriage. The oblivious driver rolled onward.

While Amaran scouted out a suitable stick to fashion a fishing rod, Rallden moved into the shadows underneath the bridge. "I hope it's—there it is! Good," he said to himself. Then he disappeared entirely into the darkness. A moment later, he reemerged from under the bridge dragging a boat from its hiding spot. Amaran helped him carry it to the water's edge.

"This boat is so light!" Amaran remarked.

"It's made of Grall wood, so it's incredibly light—though strong as anything," Rallden said proudly.

He hopped in and Amaran followed. Before long they were floating down a narrow channel lined with thick reeds and overhanging tree limbs. Rallden paddled past a grove of purple-leaved trees.

Amaran narrowed his eyes as he focused in on something along the edge of the water. "Look! A faragrin!" He pointed to a large-eared, pig-snouted creature with shaggy brown fur.

"Yeah, what a nuisance they are! They dig huge tunnels all over the place, even into farm fields. The farmers hate them."

Suddenly, both boys pulled backed from the boat's edge. Swimming close to the boat was a two foot long water centipede with nasty stinging tentacles.

Eventually the stream emptied into a pond, and this was where they stopped. After a bit of fussing with the lines and hooking the bait, Amaran asked, "So who are you anyways? You know who I am and why I'm in Balankor, but why do you live in the palace? You never told me yesterday."

Although Amaran was not entirely sure, he thought he noticed a slight shifting of Rallden's eyes. "I am a ward of the king, looked after by him and one of his advisors—because my parents died when I was a little boy. For my protection, they do not allow me out of the palace without an escort. Like you, I would be in a *lot* of trouble if anyone found out I came here."

Raising one eyebrow, Amaran stared at Rallden. *Who was he? Why would he need protection?*

Rallden noticed the curious expression on Amaran's face. "You really don't know, do you?"

"Know what?" Amaran asked, irritated slightly.

"Of course, how would you know? It's not too big of a deal, really. It's just that I'm not used to having to tell people, because everyone already knows who I am."

"Tell me what?" Amaran pressed. "Who are you?"

Rallden drew in a deep breath before beginning: "I am an orphan. My father and mother both died when I was young. The physicians couldn't save them. Now I live in the palace with King Bardane. He is my uncle."

"Your uncle?!" Amaran replied incredulously.

"Yes, my uncle. My father was the king's younger brother."

"Your uncle," Amaran repeated, shaking his head. "I am sorry about your parents. My mother died, too, and not too long ago. Do they know how they got sick?"

"At the time no one would tell me. Later I learned that it was poison. King Bardane's own guards came and took me to the royal palace. I've lived there ever since, learning the ways of the kingdom—and about becoming a king."

"King Bardane has no children?" Amaran asked.

"No. His wife died some time ago, and he never remarried. They had no children, and so he has no direct descendants to succeed him. My father was the king's only brother."

"So then you'll be king!" Amaran exclaimed.

"Well, possibly."

"Possibly, but not certainly? Why not?"

"Pharon," was all Rallden said in reply.

"Pharon? Who's that?" Amaran asked, thoroughly intrigued.

"It's a long story," Rallden said with a sigh.

"So? We have all day."

So Rallden told him all about Lord Pharon's family history: how Pharon's grandfather took over the throne before then losing the crown to Rallden's grandfather. Rallden told Amaran about how Bardane then assumed the throne, leaving Pharon hungry to regain the crown his grandfather once wore.

"So," finished Rallden, "since King Bardane has no direct descendant, Pharon has made it no secret that he feels he deserves the crown next. And, according to just about everyone one of my uncle's advisors, he is a ruthless man. He will stop at nothing to get what he wants."

Chapter 6—The Dream

It was a clear day towards the end of summer when both boys were nearing thirteen years of age. The light breeze gently persuaded the treetops to sway from one side to the next.

"You'd be dead if this were a real sword!" Rallden shouted to Amaran after dealing a successful blow.

Just then, a man with a pale face, but hair as black as night, appeared at the top of the steps of the palace courtyard. "Rallden, the king is waiting for you. You are expected in the main foyer *immediately*."

Rallden sighed. "Okay, Murken."

Murken began to slink away, but then stopped and turned halfway around, adding, "Oh, yes, and the Kallendrian boy may come, too."

Amaran followed Rallden up the steps. "He doesn't like me much, does he?"

"Are you kidding? Murken hates you!" laughed Rallden. "You are Kallendrian after all, and he is the royal advisor my uncle chose to watch over me—and to prepare me to be Albakran's next king! He despises you being here in the palace with me."

"But your uncle doesn't mind me."

"And that's all that matters," said Rallden, patting Amaran on the back. "My uncle cringed at the thought of my leaving the palace unguarded again to have another adventure. And he really likes the idea of us being friends—a good image for the kingdom, he says. I heard Murken grumbling about it one day. He thinks my uncle agreed to let you visit weekly for no reason other than for politics."

When they entered the main foyer of the palace, they saw a somewhat tall, but very round, man standing with a woman and a girl. Rather homely, the man's cheeks and bulbous nose were bright red and his head bald save the wild wisps of hair growing from his temples. The lady and the girl standing next to him, however, were both quite pretty. Obviously of noble blood, the woman was elegantly dressed. The young girl beside her had dark brown hair with lustrous curls framing her face. Her large brown eyes shimmered brightly when she first saw the boys, but she bashfully retreated behind her mother, batting her dark eyelashes as if to hide her curious eyes from them.

"This is Councilman Haldegran from the Southwest Province; his wife, the lady Aragelle; and his lovely daughter Elle," said the king. "This is my nephew, Rallden. And the boy with him is a good friend of Rallden's named Amaran."

The boys both bowed, but Rallden demonstrated the more courtly and well-practiced bow of the two. Councilman Haldegran bowed, too. His wife nodded pleasantly, smiling at both boys, but her eyes rested on Rallden thereafter.

Elle curtsied, staring the two boys in the eyes only briefly before looking away. Her glance shot back at each of the boys again shortly afterward, but she kept her stare fixed on Amaran slightly longer than on Rallden.

After the councilman and his wife and daughter were escorted to the guest wing of the palace, the king said, "Rallden, the councilman and his wife will be traveling while attending to some important matters. Elle will stay here during that time. You will be kind to her and make her acquainted with the palace."

After dinner that night, they all left the dining hall. "Let us show our guests the quickest way to their chambers, Rallden," said King Bardane. "Amaran may come, too."

As they all continued down the hall, the Councilman and his wife fell behind the rest of them. Only Amaran, walking behind Rallden and Elle, could hear what they said.

"I am going to miss her so much," Lady Aragelle said, her eyes tearing up. "To know that we won't see her for quite some time…."

Haldegran put his arm about his wife as she began to cry. "She'll be in good hands here," he assured her.

"I know she will be well-cared for," Lady Aragelle replied, "but I can't help but think about how fast she is growing up. The next time she comes back here it will be for a wedding…."

That night, Amaran fell asleep almost as soon as he pulled his covers over himself. He dreamt he was in the forest on a beautiful, clear day. He and Rallden were playing a game where they were knights battling an army of goblins. Murken was there with the guards that often escorted them out of the palace.

"Hey, Amaran! Look at this!" Rallden called from a few yards away.

Amaran came running around the bend only to stop dead in his tracks. "Whoa!" he exclaimed.

"Yeah, tell me that isn't a weird-looking tree!" said Rallden. He was staring at an old, dead tree with gnarled roots, white bark, and a trunk nearly three times the diameter of the next biggest tree around them. It seemed to not belong in that forest.

"How have we never come across this tree before?" asked Amaran. "After all the times we've come out here…."

"I don't know, but—" Rallden did not finish. There was a noise—a terrifyingly loud noise—that stopped him. It was unlike anything Amaran had ever heard before. It sounded like a fierce gust of wind, but also not.

When the boys heard it again, they looked upward. It had come from the sky. It was even louder the second time. Whatever it was had to be close.

"Rallden!" Murken shouted. "Boys! Come quickly!"

Amaran saw it first. It was a huge dragon, flying over the treetops. He tried to tell Rallden, but he could not speak. When Rallden saw it a moment later, his jaw dropped. Neither boy could move.

Finally Rallden looked over at Amaran and shouted, "Run, Amaran! Run!" He dashed into the bushes.

Amaran was still unable to move. Sensing someone else there, he turned. His father appeared next to him. King Bardane was there, too. Some of Amaran's Kallendrian friends from home appeared. Then Amaran saw his mother. It made no sense, as he knew none of these people had come to the woods with him that day, but nonetheless there they were.

Remembering the dragon, he looked up again. It was flying directly over him. He saw the beast's sharp talons tucked underneath its massive body. Its huge wings flapped with such force he felt the wind hit his face. He had had no true reason to fear until that moment, however. The dragon moved its head—and looked straight down at Amaran. Its eyes fixed on him. It seemed to be looking into his soul. It circled around and flew back towards him, getting lower the closer it got to him.

The people that had appeared beside Amaran moments before started shouting and running. But Amaran still did not move. He was terrified, but he felt compelled to stand his ground. The dragon honed in on Amaran. Its fearsome snout opened. Smoke started spilling from the beast's nostrils. The dragon was almost upon him...

Amaran awoke with a start. His heart was racing. His body was still trembling.

"It was a dream!" he said aloud, trying to calm himself. Yet something, what he could not say exactly, made him feel as if it had not been a dream. It was obviously not real. He had just awoken. Still, it seemed too real to be a dream. The images had been remarkably clear, not fuzzy and distorted like a dream. The sounds in the forest had sounded so real, and the dragon had certainly looked real.

He told his father about it at breakfast. Not knowing how to explain the lifelike nature of the dream, he simply told him the order of events.

"That would be something!" his father said with a laugh. "Dragons haven't been seen in these parts in I don't know how long."

"What if there was one, though?" Amaran asked.

His father seemed to notice how serious Amaran was. "I don't know, son," Lanellon answered. "All the dragons have been asleep for well more than a century. If there really was a dragon, it would mean nothing good. Nothing good at all."

Rallden loved hearing about Amaran's dream. When the councilman's daughter Elle joined them for a ride in the meadows later that week, Amaran told it again so that she could hear it. The more Amaran described the dream, the less real it seemed to have been and the less it consumed his thoughts. Soon he had nearly forgotten about it.

Months passed. The three children became good friends. They often rode together into the woods and meadows beyond the city whenever Murken arranged the armed escort. On one sunny, but chilly winter day, they made their way out into the forest that lay east of Balankor.

"We've not been out this far before!" Rallden said excitedly to the others.

"No, so you won't go far, will you?" said Murken sternly.

"No, Murken, we won't," answered Rallden. Turning so that only Amaran and Elle could see him, he rolled his eyes. They tried to suppress their smiles.

The children left their horses with Murken and the royal guards, while they headed for the nearby woods.

"Not too far!" shouted Murken. "You will never leave the palace again if you don't heed my warning!"

"Yes, Murken!" shouted Rallden again over his shoulder. "We'll stay close!"

They heard the crunching of the frozen ground and snow beneath their feet as they moved farther into the trees. Turning to Elle and Amaran, Rallden said, "Let's go that way! Look at how thick the woods are!"

Elle hesitated. "It looks pretty dark in there."

"It's safe," said Rallden.

Elle was not convinced.

Amaran held out his hand for her. "Come on, Elle. Rallden's right. It's safe. I promise!"

Elle looked up at him with her huge, brown, innocent eyes. Amaran felt his hand squeezed like never before. Elle grabbed it in a grasp so tight that his hand was almost as white as the snow around them.

They entered the thick patch of woods, crossed a partially frozen stream, and then went over a small hill. When they passed around the next bend, they all stopped. There was a huge, ancient-looking tree in front of them. Though it was dead, its white bark and impressive trunk made it an easy tree to admire.

"Wow!" said Rallden. "Look at that tree!"

"It's huge!" said Elle.

"Isn't it something, Amaran?" asked Rallden.

Amaran did not respond. He was desperately trying to figure out where he had seen the tree before.

"It's so weird," Amaran finally said. "That tree looks really familiar."

"Nah," said Rallden. "We've never been out here before. And I would've remembered a tree like that."

Suddenly, Amaran's face became pale. He remembered exactly where he had seen the tree before. It was the same one from his dream. Everything started coming back to him as he looked around. He recognized the other trees, the nearby hills; every detail from his dream was there.

"I don't think we should stay here," Amaran said in a low voice.

"What?" laughed Rallden. "What are you talking about?"

Before he could explain, they all heard a sound. It was deafening, and it came from the sky. Amaran recognized it instantly.

"Run!" he shouted.

None of the three moved at first.

"Rallden!" cried Murken from a distance. "Rallden! Elle! Come now!"

The dragon appeared over the treetops just as Amaran remembered it from his dream.

"Into the thickets there!" Amaran shouted.

Rallden broke into a sprint, moving towards the thick underbrush. Amaran started after him. Both stopped when they realized Elle was still standing in the open clearing, her legs frozen.

"Keep going!" Amaran shouted. "I'll get her!"

Rallden hesitated a moment longer and then continued on. Amaran grabbed Elle by the hand and dragged her. Her legs started moving once his hand grasped hers.

As he raced towards the thick cover, he glanced over his shoulder to see where the dragon was. Unlike in his dream, it did not look down at him or turn towards him. It was flying fast towards the eastern sky, and soon disappeared altogether.

When they reached the horses, they found the guards looking to the skies with arrows tense upon the string of their bows.

"Get on the horses!" Murken shouted. "Get ready to ride as soon as the guards say so!"

Refusing to let go of Amaran's hand, Elle started sobbing. She pulled in close to him, burying her head in his chest. "You saved me, Amaran!" she cried.

He looked down at her and patted her on the back. "You're all right now, Elle. It's gone. Don't worry anymore."

Easing her hold of him slightly, she allowed herself the tiniest smile. "Thank you, Amaran," she said softly.

Amaran tried to release Elle's hand from his. But she would not let go.

Chapter 7—A Pact and a Farewell

News of the dragon spread quickly over the kingdom. For weeks, Amaran and Rallden were pestered by palace staff and visiting nobility to tell the story again. They seldom grew tired of recounting their adventure. Amaran had never felt so popular. The only drawback to the dragon sighting was that they were no longer allowed beyond the city walls to ride in the forest. As such, the three had to find other means of adventure.

One midwinter day, after Elle had been called inside, Rallden led Amaran to the old stone wall in the gardens.

"What are we looking for?" Amaran asked.

"The hidden entrance to the secret tunnel," Rallden said proudly. "I just read about it this week in one of the old books in Murken's private library. It was a book of castle records that goes back centuries!"

"Really? Where is it?"

"Around here somewhere," he said pressing around on the wall. "It was built long ago as a way to save the king in case of a siege. Apparently it leads under the moat and to a small cave just beyond the edge of the woods. Help me find a stone that looks out of place."

Rallden began feeling each of the wall's stones, running his fingers in all of the crevices. Amaran copied Rallden, meticulously examining the bottom half of the wall, while his friend scoured the top.

After a good ten minutes of complete silence, and still no success, Amaran broke the quiet. "Rallden," he started slowly.

"Yeah, Amaran, what?"

"Have you—have you ever thought about how things will be years from now...when we're older?"

"What do you mean, Amaran?" Rallden asked.

"Well, you are Albakranian, I am Kallendrian, you are destined to be a king, and I am not even of noble blood. Do you honestly think we'll always be friends like we are now?"

Rallden studied him hard, temporarily giving up on his secret passage search. "I'm sure things will change some, that is only expected, but I would always expect us to be friends."

"You don't think that the history of our kingdoms and the differences between you and me would make that impossible?"

Rallden again paused, looking carefully at Amaran. "Impossible? I wouldn't say impossible. Tricky maybe or—what brought this on, anyway? Why are you asking?"

"Well...my father brought it up this week. He's mentioned it before and talked about it some, but this week he *really* wanted to talk about it. He overheard one of my friends, Croff, joke with me about going to play in the enemy's castle."

Rallden laughed to himself.

"My father has heard Croff say it before. He knows he was joking," Amaran explained, "but this time he seemed bothered by it more than usual. For the next hour he went on about his concerns for me in the future and how difficult a friendship between us will become in the years ahead. He told me that he didn't disapprove of my being friends with you, but that he wanted me to realize that things will not always stay as they are now. I think he might be right."

Amaran tried his best to deepen his voice as he echoed his father's words: "'You're from very different worlds, and as you grow older you will realize that more and more. As a fourteen-year-old boy, it may be difficult to see that someday things will change, but they will...and it will not be easy.'"

Rallden cracked a smile, but grew serious again when he asked, "You really agree with him? If things continue to improve between Albakran and Kallendria like they have been, who is to say that we will even still be enemies years from now?"

"I said that to him," Amaran replied. "It doesn't make sense to me. My father's always been pessimistic, logical he calls it, but he assured me that even if things do get better, our friendship will still change. I'll understand this better, too, when I'm older, so he said."

"I don't know, Amaran," Rallden said, shaking his head. "I think Kallendria's and Albakran's relations will only get better. If they do, we'll remain friends, even if things do change some between us. Don't you think?"

Amaran knew it went against everything his father had said, but still he wished it could be true.

"Amaran, we are best of friends now, wouldn't you agree?"

"Yes."

"And we want to always be good friends."

"Yes, of course."

"Then we are going to make a pact."

"A pact," Amaran repeated, thinking deeply about it.

"Yes, a pact," said Rallden. "We can make sure we'll always be friends, like brothers. A pact to remain true friends no matter what. Haven't you Kallendrians ever heard the tale of Airostarchus and Lekoren?"

"Yes, of course—many times."

"Well, there you go then," said Rallden. "They remained friends until the end of their days and each one was able to save his own people in the end, simply because of their promise, their pact to one another."

"So what is our pact going to be?"

"We give our word that we shall be good friends until the end, no matter what."

"Very well then, friend," Amaran said proudly, placing his right hand on Rallden's shoulder. "A pact it is."

After Rallden did the same, they shook hands. Soon after Rallden found the rock he had been looking for. Pointing to one large, jutting stone behind a clump of thick vines, he exclaimed, "I think this is it, Amaran!"

Both boys looked at each other before simultaneously pushing on the stone. At first it did not move, but then, with some persistence, it budged slightly.

"Push harder!" said Amaran. "If it's as old as you say, it may need some muscle."

They both planted their feet and pushed using all of their strength. As the stone moved, an entire section of wall started moving. A dark stairway suddenly appeared. It led to an underground tunnel.

"Ready?" Rallden asked Amaran excitedly.

"Ready as ever," he replied.

They disappeared into the passageway.

The winter months passed and early signs of spring soon appeared. By the time summer came, it was a common sight around the palace to see the boys and Elle wandering about, exploring the oldest towers, and riding their horses beyond the palace walls.

One day in late summer, while the three were just heading towards the stables, an elaborate carriage rode up through the main gates. Though Amaran and Rallden did not recognize it, they had seen this carriage once before. Curious to see who was arriving, the two boys stopped to look. But Elle rushed past them, running towards the carriage stretching out her arms.

"Father! Mother!" she exclaimed, waving her arms.

"Elle, my dear!" yelled Councilman Haldegran emphatically from inside the carriage.

Lady Aragelle emerged from the carriage a second later. "Oh, Elle, how I've missed you!"

Amaran and Rallden looked at each other solemnly, both knowing what this meant but neither wanting to voice it. They stood back as the family reunited.

Putting his hand around Elle, Haldegran said, "Well, tomorrow it'll be time to go home, my dear. Come, let's find the king."

Elle looked at the boys with tear-filled eyes as her father offered her his arm. Haldegran then escorted his daughter and wife into the palace, leaving Rallden and Amaran on the walkway. The boys walked up the palace steps without a word to each other.

When it came time for Amaran to leave that day, Elle wished him farewell. "Well, this is it," Elle said with a sigh and a sad smile. "We'll be leaving tomorrow morning, and so I will have to say goodbye to you now, Amaran."

"We are going to miss you, Elle," said Amaran.

"Yeah, you're like our little sister!" said Rallden. "It won't be the same without you."

"Thank you," she replied. "It has been fun. At first I hated it here, but not now!" A tear broke free from her moist, shining eyes.

Amaran smiled. "Although we didn't think we would at first, we enjoyed having you around…after a while." He winked at this. "We'll meet, again, Elle, I'm sure of it." He then leaned down and gave her a quick peck of a kiss on her forehead.

She looked up at him, a look of joyous surprise upon her face. Her lips curved into a smile as her cheeks turned a deep, rosy red.

Rallden went inside once Amaran had left the palace. Elle, however, waited until Amaran had completely disappeared from her view before turning around.

Chapter 8—Five Years Later

Amaran and Rallden fenced in the castle training grounds on one sultry spring day. The sound of clashing swords filled the yard as the two young men dashed about, eyeing each other with fierce determination. A sudden strike from one of them threw the other off balance only slightly. A second swing, even harder than the first, sent the loser's sword out of his hand and into the air.

"Ach! You've done it again. Rallden, you are by far the better swordsman of the two of us…," Amaran gasped for air before continuing, "You have gotten the better of me nine times out of the last ten."

"I may have won this contest and the last few, but I still stand by my claim that if it came down to it, my friend, you might have the better of me in a less carefree match."

"No, I don't think so. You definitely are the better swordsman. I admit it. But I do have the better brains between the two of us."

"Ha!" Rallden laughed aloud, rolling his eyes.

Rallden was tall, a few inches over six feet, and had a strong, lean frame with broad shoulders. His dark brown hair was cut short, his face slender and handsome, and his eyes bright and regal. "Come on," he continued, nudging Amaran. "Let's quench our thirst."

Amaran followed. Amaran, who was a few inches shorter than his royal companion, bore a slightly more thick and muscular look. Like the prince, he was very handsome, but in a rugged way. Though far from polished, he often drew the gaze of many lady guests in the palace.

Once inside the hall, Rallden said, "The Spring Festival begins tomorrow. My uncle and I would love it if you could attend again this year. There should be a pretty good hunt. One especially huge stag has been spotted in the forest in recent weeks. From what I hear, he is as impressive as they come."

"I would love to come to the festival, but I can't escape my morning drills. Things don't come to a halt this week for us Kallendrians like they do for you. I might be able to attend the hunt, though. Maybe this year you and I might at least see a stag."

They both laughed at their memory of the last few hunts, trying in vain to find their trophy deer.

When the morning of the much-anticipated hunt arrived, Amaran moved through the busy city streets after his morning drills. On his way to the eastern gate, he passed dozens of vendor booths. New this year was a merchant who had giant tortoise eggs about to hatch. The wood gnomes had also returned. Wearing their earth-tone, pointed hats and curious outfits made from leaves, the little men from the ancient Larenian Forest sold everything from herbal medicines to cooking seasonings inimitable in taste.

Once Amaran left through the gates and rode into the fields beyond the eastern wall of the city, he saw the growing crowd by the edge of the forest. Passing many arriving spectators, he searched for Rallden among the pod of hunters. He spotted Jareck, Rallden's squire, first. Next to him was Rallden.

"Ready, Amaran?" Rallden asked excitedly. "I think this is the year when we will finally find ourselves a stag worthy of the trophy!"

"I sure hope so," Amaran answered with a wide grin.

"Will you need me to come along, Sire?" asked the squire, a man not much younger than Rallden.

"No, I don't think so, Jareck," replied Rallden. "I will be fine with Amaran by my side. Right, friend?"

Amaran looked at Rallden with one raised eyebrow and a crooked smile. "I'm not coming along to be your squire if that's what you meant!"

"No, of course not! I meant exactly what I said: we'll be fine just the two of us. Besides, the smaller the hunting party, the better chance of spotting a stag."

They led their horses into position, facing the woods alongside dozens of other hunters. A short while later, the blaring horn sounded with three short calls. The hunt was about to begin.

"Gentlemen!" cried the royal announcer. "The day of the great hunt has arrived! You already know the rules, and you know what is at stake—pride, honor, and a grand trophy!—so I will delay the start no longer! When the trumpet sounds again, you will ride, each man in pursuit of the famed Great Stag!"

When the horn blew, the eager hunters took off at a furious gallop, the stampede shaking the ground. Chunks of mud flew up into the air behind the departing horses. Amaran and Rallden rode for nearly half an hour before they saw the first signs of the great Larenian Forest in the distance. Massive trees reached up from just beyond the nearest hills, growing toward the sky. A few miles farther and they could see up close the enormous trees, most of which were a thousand years or older. Many were well over two hundred feet in height, and some even taller still.

Once inside the dense forest, they led their horses over a log of tremendous proportions—a fallen Larenian tree that was now entirely covered in moss, lichens, and emerging mushrooms. A carpet of lush, green moss and clumps of chest-high, emerald ferns covered the forest floor. As they passed one especially thick patch of ferns, a wood gnome dashed in front of them, heading for a hole in the base of a large tree. Turning around to give them a nasty glare, the cantankerous gnome disappeared into the perfectly-sized hole that acted as a doorway.

Rallden chortled as he shook his head. "What ruined his day?"

"I think he woke up on the wrong side of a tree today," Amaran replied.

They laughed quite heartily.

The two hunters passed a gently flowing brook that cascaded down large, smooth-faced boulders. Just beyond the small waterfall they saw large arboreal mice clambering up a tree. Like the trees, many of the animals that inhabited this forest were of abnormally large sizes; not just the large tree-dwelling mice, but also giant tortoises and dog-sized rabbits. They also passed some fiery-orange and vibrant-yellow mushrooms that were almost as tall as a man.

They continued on at a slow, even pace, searching for the perfect location for a hunting post. After an hour of riding, they caught sight of something that captured their interest: freshly scraped bark about ten feet up the thick trunk of a tree.

"Look!" whispered Rallden. "A stag has been here...and very recently."

Amaran nodded.

Careful to make as little noise as possible, they finally stopped at a clump of smaller trees adjacent to a little clearing. They got off their horses and stealthily crept along the forest floor until they came to an open space. The clearing seemed the perfect place to find a stag, so they decided to wait there for a while. They hid behind a cluster of thick trunks, desperately hoping that luck would find them this year.

After crouching in absolute quiet for some time, their legs became stiff as boards. Rallden slowly turned his head to Amaran. He motioned with his eyes towards something in the distance. Careful to remain inaudible and invisible, he pointed with only his index finger.

Amaran looked where he pointed. He spotted the largest deer he had ever seen. Its body was much larger than a horse and its rack of antlers was so expansive he wondered how it could possibly move through the forest. But there it was, grazing upwind of them, oblivious to the potential danger several dozen feet away. Only an awful twist of fate could have ruined the opportunity for them now.

Rallden reached stealthily for his bow so as not to make a sound. Bending his elbow and reaching behind his shoulder, he felt for the nock of an arrow, his eyes remaining fixed upon the prize. But even as he did this as carefully as he intended, the stag threw its head up, stared over its right shoulder with its ears raised, and snorted. To their horror, the stag took off, completely disappearing into the woods within seconds.

"That stupid animal! I didn't even make a sound!" exclaimed Rallden.

"It wasn't you that it heard," Amaran said in a serious voice. "It looked toward its right, so it heard something from that direction. It wasn't us."

"I should have shot while I had the—"

"Shhh!" Amaran whispered as he threw out his hand.

Rallden stopped immediately and looked at his friend.

"Do you notice how quiet it is right now?" Amaran whispered. "Where are the birds and the crickets? Something's out there."

The two hunters cautiously made their way back to their horses, but before they even reached them the horses began to whinny and fidget.

"Shhh. Easy, girl," Rallden said, patting his mare.

His effort was futile. The neighing grew louder as both horses began nervously dancing around, making it difficult to mount them. Rallden and Amaran eventually made it onto their horses and looked at each other nervously. Suddenly, Amaran's horse reared back with such force that it knocked him off. He landed on his rear with a thud. But Amaran never felt the pain because of what happened next.

Out of the dense forest, from behind Rallden, came something— a black, huge something. It sprung at Rallden's mare. It was so quick that Amaran could not tell at first exactly what happened. All he could tell for sure was that Rallden's horse was now lying on its side with a gash across its hind right leg, and that Rallden was on his back leaning away from a large, black beast. It moved like a cat, but it was far thicker and stronger looking. Its muscles rippled under its shiny coat.

Amaran thought he heard Rallden cry out. He was not sure if he had or not. He himself wanted to shout but he could not find his voice.

The animal's enormous, muscular body crept slowly towards Rallden. Rallden in turn matched each of its steps forward with an elbow crawl backward. Its head was somewhat catlike, and it bared its fangs as it snarled. Its long tail stuck straight out behind its body.

Amaran shook his head as if waking from a trance. He did the only thing that he could think of: he reached for his sword. Next, he scrambled to his feet and called for the animal. "Hey! Over here!"

It turned to look at him, let out a low growl—one that seemed to shake the ground and everything inside of Amaran's trembling body—and then turned its head back toward Rallden.

Why was it so focused on Rallden? Amaran wondered. *Did it think he was hurt?*

Rallden had since moved a few feet back during the brief distraction, and was up against the base of a very large tree. He could retreat no further.

Amaran charged the animal, hurtling a large rock straight at its head. It let out a higher-pitched growl, shook its head, and turned towards its new challenger. Amaran raised his sword.

The creature advanced toward Amaran, ready to spring at him. When it was close enough, it took a swipe at him with its front paw. Amaran dove for the ground, rolling under the gigantic paw. He sprung up to his knees once he was underneath the beast's body. Before the beast even realized it had missed, Amaran sliced the inside of the monster's leg with a powerful swing. The blade cut through flesh, causing the animal to roar in pain.

It picked up its wounded leg and hobbled two steps forward. Even injured, it did not look like it would retreat. It locked eyes with Amaran—he didn't dare look away to check on Rallden.

Rallden made a noise. The beast whirled round, throwing its head side to side, looking for him.

Amaran decided to go on the offensive before the beast was ready for another pounce. Since it had its back to him, he slashed at one of its hind legs. This time its growl was not the same; it was fiercer. Enraged, it whipped around despite the substantial wounds on two legs.

Flashing its golden eyes wide before honing in on Amaran, the animal crouched low to the ground and stalked him as it had Rallden moments before. Its immense power was unmistakable as its neck and shoulder muscles rippled with each step forward.

Amaran contemplated his next move. As he did so, he found himself stepping backwards—against his better judgment. The beast was about to spring on him, and he was stumbling backward, feebly retreating with no means of escape. He was about to meet his doom when he noticed Rallden out of the corner of his eye, who had managed to silently climb up onto an overhanging limb.

The beast was eyeing Amaran hungrily when Rallden leapt onto it from the branch. A second later Rallden's sword plunged into its side, through the animal's rib cage. It howled in pain. As it attempted to throw Rallden from its back by rearing upwards on its hind legs, it lost its balance and stumbled onto its left side—the very side on which it had already been wounded twice.

Giving no chance for the beast to regain its footing, Amaran charged it and stabbed its shoulder. Quickly yanking the sword free, he lifted it again for another blow. Grasping the sword by the hilt with both hands, he swung with speed and precision, slicing through the animal's neck.

Thick, red blood spurted forth. The animal exhaled once more before its eyes faded. Blood pooled on the beast's fur and the forest floor.

Amaran stared for a moment at the massive heap of fur in front of him as if to make sure it was really dead. Then he turned to Rallden. "Are you all right?"

"Yes. I think so, anyways...thanks to you." Rallden, like Amaran, sounded winded. The exertion and excitement had left them both shaking. "You've saved my life. I owe you, Amaran."

Amaran smiled, shaking his head as he replied to his friend, "No, no. You owe me nothing. What would you expect: me to run and leave you to die? That was a malken! It would have certainly killed you. Besides, you helped me fight it."

"Only because you jumped in first to fend it off of me, Amaran. Any man would be lucky to have you as a friend. Know that my uncle will hear of your bravery."

"That malken just came out of nowhere."

"It did," agreed Rallden. "It's surprising it was this far south. They rarely come this far down into the Larenian Forest."

"You know, I just had an idea. We have a magnificent tale to tell everyone, but once again no trophy stag to boast. Wouldn't it be quite a sight to see us not return with the stag, but instead with the—"

"The malken," Rallden finished for him. "It would, but how would we ever drag it back?"

"I have an idea. First, let's find my horse. It went this way," said Amaran, disappearing behind the trunk of a huge tree.

Rallden followed, anxious to hear Amaran's plan.

Chapter 9—Return of an Old Friend

A crowd gathered on the lawn around Rallden and Amaran. As more and more squeezed in to see the commotion, the rest stared with curiosity at something covered on the sling behind Amaran's horse. The two young hunters smiled proudly at the growing crowd.

"The stag evaded us again this year!" Rallden announced. "Though I must tell you that it was through no fault of our own. It was not because we are poorly skilled hunters that we have no trophy stag. No indeed!" Looking out into the crowd of men, he paused dramatically before resuming, "We were ambushed by another hunter."

The men looked at them with bemusement. "Well? Tell us!" shouted one.

"We were attacked by a malken deep in the forest!"

"A malken you say?" asked another man from the crowd. "And you're still here to tell about it?!"

"Yes! It attacked me, but Amaran here was brave as I have never seen before!"

Amid the cheers, one of the voices rose above the din. "And what of the beast? Is *that* it?" he asked mockingly, pointing to what was covered on the sling behind Amaran's horse. "Was it a baby malken you killed? What proof do we have of this great tale?"

Many laughed as they waited for Rallden's answer.

Rallden smiled smugly. "Let it be known that anyone or anything that costs me my trophy stag on a hunt will surely pay the penalty! Behold, the formidable beast, the malken!"

With that, Rallden and Amaran simultaneously yanked the cover back to reveal the malken's massive head, severed from its body.

Some of the men took a step back, but almost all commended the warriors on their trophy. "Better than a stag!" "An unbelievable prize!" "A hunting story I'll never forget!"

Amaran and Rallden stood with broad smiles, knowing their adventure had made them into heroes despite getting no stag.

The day after the hunt was the last day of the Spring Festival. A celebration dinner was held to honor Rallden's terrific escape from danger. At the request of many, both Amaran and Rallden told the story at least ten times. Shortly before the meal began, they caught sight of a familiar face entering the banquet hall. It was Councilman Haldegran. His wife stepped through the door behind him.

The two friends stopped short when they saw who followed them in. Walking gracefully through the entrance was a girl so beautiful they could not have looked away if they had wanted. Their eyes were fixed on this beautiful creature as if bewitched by a powerful spell. Her long, flowing hair fell past her shoulders, her skin was soft and fresh, and her alluring deep brown eyes shimmered as she entered.

Elle moved closer, at first not noticing them. When she was only feet from them, she turned her head slightly. As her gaze rested directly on them, her full, pink lips curved to form a perfect, glowing smile.

Neither Amaran nor Rallden could do anything but stare helplessly back.

"Hello, boys. It is so nice to see you," she said brightly.

Amaran felt his heart first flutter, and then melt inside of him. Suddenly remembering who she was, he scolded himself. Elle would be Rallden's wife and queen someday. He dropped his gaze in guilt.

Rallden was the first to regain his composure, at least to some degree. "Elle, I—I did not even recognize you at first," he said. "I didn't know you would be here. When I saw your father and you with him—well, I figured that it must be you." He stopped for a brief second before continuing. "You look so different."

She looked only at him, but still captivated both with her piercing smile. "I look different? Different how?" Smiling, she watched the blushing Rallden squirm as he tried to answer.

Amaran jumped in at that moment. "Oh, definitely different in a good way. I am sure Rallden meant that you are a great deal different than the little girl we remember. You look like a young lady."

"Well, I *am* a young lady," she said, laughing again. "And I am pleased to hear that you think it is a change for the better, Amaran," she added, looking directly into his eyes.

Amaran noticed a tinge of pink color her cheeks as she spoke to him.

"It is really good to see you, Elle," Rallden said. "How long will you be here at the palace?"

"I don't know for certain, but it will be for at least several weeks, perhaps longer."

If it was possible, the young men's smiles grew even wider. "That is good to hear," Amaran interjected happily. "We will have to go riding again and catch up on all that has happened with you since you left."

"Yes, that would be nice," she answered. "I would love that. Riding in the meadows or walking about the palace grounds would be delightful. Now, however, I should meet whoever it is my father wishes to introduce me to. He's waving to me now. It was nice to see you again, gentlemen."

As she walked towards her father, their heads followed her, watching every step of her graceful exit.

After the last of the courses had been served and the guests had started to make their way to their rooms or to their carriages, Rallden leaned over to Amaran. "I think I am going to invite Elle out for a walk through the garden, now that she's less occupied with her father's friends. What do you think?"

Nodding, Amaran replied, "It sounds like a good idea. I need some fresh air myself."

"Oh," Rallden said, surprised. "Yes, of course. You can come, too."

Amaran pretended to ignore the surprise in his friend's voice. He followed Rallden to Elle's table despite the lukewarm invitation. He could decline and remain behind, but something made him decide even more to go.

On their way, Rallden said, "It really is almost impossible to look at her now and think of her as the same little Elle we met only six years ago. I cannot stop thinking about how much she's changed."

"Yes, she's beautiful," added Amaran. "I've got to admit, Rallden, I can't take my eyes off her."

Rallden looked over at Amaran with amusement, raising one eyebrow as he grinned. Amaran felt as if he had just been insulted, even though he knew he had not. He tried to ignore the feeling, but it lingered.

Elle noticed them walking to her and waved to them.

Rallden approached her and said, "My lady, it would be my pleasure—our pleasure—if you would walk with us about the gardens for a while. Would you like to join us?"

She gave an approving smile as she slowly drew herself back from the table. "I would love to."

"I will escort you out if you do not mind," Rallden answered, offering her his arm.

"I would love it," she replied, sliding her hand through the inside of Rallden's arm, and locking elbows with him.

Amaran's stomach turned sour at seeing the smile Elle gave Rallden. He had to look down to conceal his face. Feeling an emotion that was just short of jealousy, Amaran watched the proximity of Rallden's and Elle's arms. He secretly wished he had been as bold as to have offered his own, to have the pleasure of such a perfectly delicate arm touching his. But he knew he was foolish for thinking this. Rallden had the right to do so; he did not. Amaran stood along the other side of Elle, so that she walked between both of them.

"Amaran, how is your father?" she asked.

"He's well," he answered. "He is always busy, of course, with this being our last year in Balankor."

"It's hard to believe it's been eight years," she replied. "At times, it seems like only yesterday when I saw the first Kallendrian troops arrive in our own city at home."

Amaran had a sudden thought come to him. *Was that what she thought of him now? Simply a Kallendrian in Balankor? Would she remember their friendship years ago?*

Rallden interrupted, "It's been a quick eight years, I agree—well, seven and a half at this point. The peace process has been moving along steadily. Despite a few problems out at sea, I'd say the treaty has worked splendidly."

"Oh, look at the moonflowers!" exclaimed Elle, ignoring Rallden. "Even in the darkness, the gardens are spectacular, aren't they?"

"They are spectacular. Beautiful beyond compare." Rallden was looking directly at Elle as he said this.

They first strolled through the gardens before meandering along the walkways in the courtyard. When passing the stables, Elle said with a broad smile, "Do you remember the first time we went riding beyond the city walls together? I had been riding for only a few months, and you took off at a full gallop without me! I thought at first you were trying to leave me behind, but then Amaran came back to get me."

Leaning against the door to the stables, Rallden said loudly, "Yes, I remember that! Always the gentleman he is. Ha!"

Grinning contentedly, she looked over at Amaran. Amaran had been gazing upon her the whole while, admiring the way in which her lips moved to form each word she spoke. When she looked over at him, he quickly shifted his eyes from her gaze, nervous that she would find his watching her unsettling. He felt his face become flushed.

He could not, however, help himself from turning his eyes back in her direction again. When he did, he saw that she was now staring at him. Now she was the one to turn quickly away, pink rising to her cheeks.

Amaran's forehead wrinkled considerably with a thought, fleeting but pertinent, that flashed through his mind. He immediately brushed it aside and followed Rallden and Elle down the path.

Soon after this walk they bid each other goodnight. Once Amaran was alone in the dark and empty streets, he suddenly realized something was bothering him. At first somewhat unclear as to what it was, it soon came to him: he was quite reluctant to leave Rallden and Elle in the palace while he continued home alone.

Even though Elle had paid equal attention to each of them that night, Amaran could not help but feel somehow left out. Rallden and

Elle were members of Albakranian royalty, a commonality that he would never share with either. The purpose of her return was unclear, but he was aware of one possibility: the engagement between the influential councilman's daughter and the future king might be announced soon. Such a marriage would not affect him, for he would already have moved back to Kallendria by the time they were husband and wife. Yet, it still affected him—and he could not stop thinking about it.

Chapter 10—Questions to Face

Several weeks later, Amaran came to the palace to watch an archery contest with his Kallendrian friend, Croff. They met Rallden and Elle there.

While waiting for the next round to begin, Rallden announced, "I am going to give Elle a complete tour of the palace tomorrow before I leave with my uncle for Faralshia."

Amaran shot him a quick glance. "Oh? There can't be that much to show her, can there? She must know her way around pretty well by now. After all, she lived here for several years."

Rallden looked at Amaran, about to respond, but Elle spoke before he could.

"What about the faragrin hunt later this week, Rallden?" asked Elle. "Will you be back in time to join us? My cousin will be visiting the palace this week and I had wanted to introduce her."

"I doubt I will, Elle. It's unlikely I'll be back before next week."

"Who will take your place at the hunt? You and Amaran were to join my cousin and me, don't you remember?"

"Elle," laughed Rallden, as if responding to a child who had just said something foolish, "a faragrin hunt is hardly what I spend my time thinking about."

Elle turned from him and sighed. "Well, Amaran will still get to meet Ganella, and perhaps you can take Rallden's place on the hunt, Croff." She smiled, looking over at Amaran's friend.

"I don't know," said Croff hesitantly. With a short laughed, he added, "Isn't one Kallendrian enough on an Albakranian hunt?"

Elle laughed at his joke and Amaran cracked a smile. But Rallden did not seem amused. "I've already arranged for my squire Jareck to take my place."

A brief awkward silence followed before Elle spoke. "We shall miss you—but we will not miss out on the fun. I've been looking forward to this event for so long!"

Amaran had noticed how serious Rallden had become lately. As expected, the prince had started taking a more prominent role in affairs of the kingdom several years ago. Very recently, however, Rallden had become even more preoccupied with politics and learning to rule like his uncle. Amaran recognized a drastic change in him, one he was not altogether fond of. It had become most noticeable since Elle's return.

Elle on the other hand seemed to have become even more delightful recently. She was the most carefree, high-spirited, happy girl he had ever met, royal or not. Perhaps Amaran noticed it so much in Elle recently because, in so many ways, she was the complete opposite of Rallden. She barely spoke of her almost certain future as queen. She was not haughty or unkind like so many of the other ladies of the palace. Many girls lived every waking moment with the dream of marrying the future king and ruling beside him. Elle did not.

It was for these reasons Amaran was convinced she was not right for Rallden. Of course he knew it did not matter what he thought. It was an arranged marriage, so love and compatibility had little to do with the king's and councilman's decision to join them together. But it did not stop him from thinking about their differences often—even when he was nowhere around Elle and her prince.

Later on that same week, the Kallendrian soldiers performed their usual training exercises within the barracks. On the way back from the training yard, Amaran was talking with his friend Croff.

"So you're participating in the faragrin hunt, eh?" asked Croff. "That isn't until the end of the week. How do you manage to stay apart from your Albakranian friends for so long?"

"Don't start that again," said Amaran, shaking his head. "It's no more than once a week that I visit the palace. Just because my father is the commander doesn't mean I'm granted more leave than you or anyone else."

"Yeah, Amaran, I know," Croff said, rolling his eyes. Changing his tone, he continued, "What good is having your father as your superior officer if there aren't any perks?"

"He wasn't going to have it any other way, Croff. Either I stayed here under his command when I turned seventeen, or he wouldn't let me join the army. His superiors were more than happy to—"

Amaran stopped when he heard someone shout his name. He turned to find Tralov, a large-framed, dark-haired Kallendrian.

"I heard about your act of valor the other day, Amaran," Tralov said, smirking. "That takes true bravery, but I am curious about whose side you will fight on if we ever have to go to war with Albakran again."

The soldiers next to Tralov snickered at the jab.

Amaran knew that they were laughing at his expense, but he kept calm for the moment. Taking one step towards Tralov as he took a deep breath, he replied, "He is my friend. I did only what any man would do for a good friend."

"Right." Here Tralov turned away from Amaran and instead faced the small gathering of men around them. "If you are willing to risk your life for his so readily, what will you do if you see him in battle?"

These last words silenced Amaran for a moment. He could feel the other men staring intensely at him, awaiting his response. "I am a Kallendrian just like all of you," he finally said. "I would fight to the death to protect our kingdom."

"Unless your Albakranian boyfriend appears on the battlefield," quipped Tralov. "Then what would you do?"

"Shut up, Tralov," growled Amaran.

"Would you run to him?" taunted Tralov. "Would you hold out your hand to help him up if he fell?"

Amaran had been trying hard to control his temper but felt his blood start to simmer. He clenched his fists, glared at Tralov, and turned his back to him.

Tralov shoved him. "You just gonna walk away without saying anything to defend yourself?"

Nostrils flared, Amaran whipped around and shoved him back.

Tralov lunged for Amaran, but his friends held him back. Croff and another soldier pulled Amaran back.

67

"It's not worth it, Tralov!" said one of his friends. "We'll all get blasted by the captain if he finds out you and Amaran brawled here. Just let the traitor be."

"That's right!" Tralov shouted to Amaran. "You're a traitor and a coward. You know it, we all know it!"

There was no more said to Amaran about the incident, nor were there any more confrontations between him and any of the other soldiers, but there was still talk. Every time Amaran walked into a room full of soldiers, the conversation suddenly diminished to mere whispers. The looks he received from fellow soldiers did nothing to ease his mind.

Often during that week, and for months afterward, Amaran obsessed about the question Tralov had asked him: "If you are willing to risk your life for his, for an Albakranian, then what will you do if you see him in battle?"

Amaran, when asking himself the same question over and over again, did not know his answer.

Chapter 11—The Faragrin Hunt

A faragrin hunt took place at the end of the week. The rules were simple: a team of four, two ladies and two gentlemen, took off at the sound of the horn, and had to find, tackle, and bind a faragrin by its legs. Intended for fun rather than for fierce competition, these hunts offered an afternoon full of entertainment for everyone involved. Although perfectly harmless to people, the faragrin were difficult to trap, and even more challenging to tie up. As such, the hunts were just as much fun to watch as they were to join.

Amaran found Elle in the courtyard. She was followed by another young lady about her age. This girl had hair that was darker and much curlier than Elle's, and her eyes were a dazzling green.

"Amaran!" Elle shouted.

"Hello, Elle," he answered, bowing his head and glancing at the girl behind her. "And is this your cousin you spoke of a few days ago?"

"This is Ganella, yes. She'll be on our hunting team today along with Jareck."

"It is nice to meet you, Ganella," he said with a bow.

Ganella smiled back at him. "It is wonderful to meet you, Amaran," she replied.

When Amaran left to fetch the horses from the stables, Ganella leaned over to Elle, and said with a scheming smile, "He is gorgeous, Elle. I can see why you enjoy his company so much."

"Ganella!" Elle said reprovingly as her cheeks reddened. "You think every man is gorgeous, including Rallden's squire."

"Oh! Is Jareck the squire I met? He *is* adorable! Do you not think so?"

"He is not unattractive," Elle mused.

"But just not an Amaran," quipped Ganella.

Elle shot her a disapproving glare, her cheeks turning an even deeper shade of red. "Oh, Ganella, you do only ever think of one thing, don't you?"

Elle shook her head and started down the path. When the two ladies entered the stables, they found Amaran gathering the riding gear from the overhang above the first of the stalls. He saddled Elle's horse first.

Ganella went to her horse and gently stroked its nose, while Elle stepped forward to help Amaran ready her horse. When Amaran reached over to buckle the last strap on her horse's saddle, she also reached for the same strap. His hand accidentally clasped hers. Feeling her skin, smooth and cool to the touch, he held her hand for a second.

They could not see each other, but she didn't pull away. Then, against every inner wish, he released her from his hold, knowing how inappropriate it was. He reached for the saddle strap, this time forcefully and deliberately, and finished fastening the strap buckle.

Ganella had since looked over, watching with intense interest. Her eyes sparkled with silent amusement at the scene.

Suddenly, Elle turned away. Quickly and rather abrasively, she said, "Thank you for preparing my horse, Amaran."

Minutes later, Jareck found them. Rallden's squire was a tall, lean man with light brown hair. "Hello, ladies," he said from his horse. "Amaran," he added, nodding to him. "I've brought the ropes and the bait."

"Bait?" said Elle, surprised.

"Bait," repeated Jareck. "Tomatoes. They can't resist them."

"And Elle said you'd be of no help to us...," said Ganella jokingly, eyeing Elle with a feigned look of disapproval. Turning to Jareck, she said, tugging on his sleeve, "You are going to help us win, aren't you, Jareck? I do so love to win."

"I hope so," Jareck answered. "I'll do my best to get us that prize."

"Good," Ganella said, catching his gaze with her own seductive stare. "I always hate to be denied anything that I really want...."

She motioned her horse past him as she smiled teasingly at him. Jareck smiled nervously, glanced back at Amaran and Elle, and steered his horse around to follow her.

Once the hunt was underway, all the other hunting parties took off for the nearby meadows beyond the starting line. Amaran led his group in the opposite direction, moving northward.

"Amaran, why this way?" Jareck shouted behind him. "We won't find any faragrin out here!"

"Trust me," replied Amaran. "I've ridden up here many times before and have seen plenty of faragrin!"

Jareck shot him a dubious glance, but followed just the same.

Elle and Ganella rode several yards behind them. "Honestly, cousin, what do you think of Jareck?" asked Ganella.

Elle paused to think for a second before giving her answer. "He is a good squire to Rallden, and he comes from a very influential family, which is how he was able to secure himself as Rallden's squire—"

"I am not talking about *that*, Elle," Ganella interrupted.

Elle hesitated.

"You know," Ganella said with a crooked smile.

"But he is Rallden's squire, Ganella!" Elle protested.

"With love, it matters not who provides the best match or which family has the best standing. Everyone knows that ladies like us rarely marry a man that we love—we marry who we are told to marry and take on as a lover the one that we truly love. You know about Queen Hanell who married King Narakon when she was a young girl. They say she had many lovers before she was twenty."

Elle shifted nervously in her saddle, looking down at her hands before turning her face away from Ganella altogether.

"Don't you think Jareck is handsome?" Ganella asked. "And charming, even if he isn't yet a knight?"

"Ganella, I don't know. I haven't thought of him like that! He's Rallden's squire and that is all I've—"

"Squires aren't only good for assisting their master knights, you know," Ganella said with a laugh. "Especially ones as attractive as Jareck."

"Ganella!" Elle scolded. "Are you saying what I think you're—?"

"You have him around and it's never crossed your mind to think how exciting it might be to tease him a bit, and perhaps even—"

"Ganella, I can't believe you!" Elle exclaimed. "You are serious, aren't you?"

"Yes, I am!" Ganella replied indignantly. "Are you really that innocent that you've never considered it? Just for some added excitement? To feel his strong arms about you and—?"

"Not until I have found the perfect man," Elle interrupted. "One that I love with all my heart—and not until I have married him!"

"Oh please, Elle, you are a silly girl, aren't you? You don't know what you are missing. Besides, are you really going to wait until you are married to Rallden, assuming your father's plans work out?"

Elle did not reply.

"No man of high standing wants to marry a girl who is completely clueless as to what to do...lacking experience...if you know what I mean."

Elle was bright red at this point, and her tongue was uncooperative as she stammered her rebuttal: "Well, I still—I just don't know what you would expect me to—I am not going to change my mind just because you think I should."

"You are funny to listen to, cousin. You are six months older than I am, but you act six years younger sometimes. You can't stay innocent forever you know."

Elle shrugged her shoulders and said nothing. Refusing to look at her cousin, she watched Amaran and Jareck with undivided attention.

"Well, if you're not interested in him, then he is fair game," said Ganella. "*I* certainly am not going to miss out on having fun because you are so dull, or good, or whatever it is you are!" Ganella laughed heartily as she fixed her eyes on Jareck. Then she dug her heels into her horse's side and crouched lower in the saddle. "Jareck! Amaran!"

Jareck turned around immediately. "What is it, my lady?"

"I've got an idea!" Ganella shouted, her horse closing in on them. "Let's split up to better our chances. Jareck, let's you and I go to the right, and Amaran and Elle can go to the left. We might find one yet!"

"Splitting up won't help if we find one," Amaran said, furrowing his brow.

"Maybe she's right," Jareck said. "We could at least try it and see."

Amaran sighed. "I really don't think so, but—"

"Good!" said Ganella excitedly. "Come on Jareck, let's go! This way!" She urged her horse onward, coaxing him into a gallop, and leaving Jareck racing to catch up.

Amaran turned his horse around to wait for Elle. "Your cousin is something else," he said, once she had caught up to him.

"You don't know the half of it," she replied, rolling her eyes.

"Let's go and see if we can find some faragrin over there."

"Amaran," Elle said slowly, "You know that they're not really finding faragrin. Ganella just wanted to get Jareck alone. I imagine they'll be gone for quite some time."

Amaran raised his eyebrows.

"We can still look if you want," she continued, "but I won't be much help if you actually find one."

"What else would we do, just ride around?"

"Why not?" Elle said, shrugging her shoulders. "It's a beautiful day and we certainly can't return just the two of us."

They cantered off towards the wooded hill beyond.

"You know," Amaran said quietly to himself after a minute, "I think we are close to that spot...."

"What spot, Amaran?" she asked curiously.

"There is this place I found out here when I was riding alone one day. I'll show you."

With a look of blissful anticipation, she said, "Okay, I love surprises! Lead the way!"

Amaran kept just a half-stride ahead of her as they rode up a hill. He steered his horse over the hilltop, skipped over a brook, and moved across another meadow before continuing on through the tree line of a small copse. A minute later they emerged from the trees to find a high hill before them.

Riding up this steep slope, Amaran shouted from over his shoulder, "You'll see it at the top of this hill!"

"Okay! I'm ready!" she shouted.

As the slope began to level out, Amaran slowed his horse. Stopping when they reached the top, he smiled at Elle as she took in the sight. Below them, the hill led gently down to a meadow of soft, plush grass sprinkled with vivid wildflowers. A stream of crystal clear water meandered through the middle of the meadow. In the center of this landscape was a large tree with a thick, sturdy trunk. Its branches were laden with small, circular leaves.

"Oh, Amaran, this is gorgeous...like something from a book," she said in amazement of the picture before her. "So peaceful, so quiet...and so perfect."

Amaran was proud at his success in pleasing her. "We can tie up the horses down there and walk along the stream."

He motioned his horse onward, but this time she did not follow. Instead she raced past him, her hair flying wildly in the breeze. He rode behind her. At the bottom Amaran slid off his horse and helped her down from hers. They tied the horses to a log before heading towards the brook. They walked along the streambed, listening to a songbird nearby.

"It is hard to believe it's been almost five years since I left the palace, isn't it?" asked Elle.

"It is," agreed Amaran.

"What a dreadful day that was...the day I had to leave Balankor. I was glad to see my parents return, of course, but I did not want to say goodbye."

"It was a sad day. We both missed having you around," said Amaran.

"I don't think you understand," said Elle with a twinkle in her eye. "I did not want to say goodbye to *you*. I was smitten with you, you know. Amaran, the handsome Kallendrian...."

Amaran felt his face grow warm.

"Did I embarrass you?" Elle asked, looking over at him. "I was so young then. You know how little girls can be about older boys."

Amaran cleared his throat. "Of course. We were just children. I understand."

"I remember the moment I first laid eyes on you. Your charming smile, and your eyes...your eyes were so kind. Saving me that day we saw the dragon was all I needed to think of you as my knight in shining armor. You remember when you told Rallden that you would stay behind to get me? Oh, it is funny to look back on that all now, isn't it?"

"Yes," answered Amaran. "Strange to think how much has changed, my lady."

"My lady?" repeated Elle. "Why do you address me so formally, Amaran?"

Amaran furrowed his brow. "Do you really need to ask why? When you are the daughter of a powerful nobleman who is a member of the royal council, and I am but the son of a Kallendrian officer?"

Elle looked over at him with the sweetest smile he thought he had ever seen. "Oh, Amaran, we were friends as children, and that has not changed. Call me Elle again, please!"

"I can do that if you wish, but...the time will soon come when calling you that will no longer be proper," he said.

She hesitated before nodding her head slowly. "Yes, I suppose it will."

They continued along the streambed in silence. Amaran thought he sensed her stealing glances at him. Curious to see whether she actually was gazing at him or not, he looked over at her. Their eyes met for a brief second before they both looked down at the ground.

What was that? Amaran asked himself. *She was staring at me, but why? I am not nearly good enough for her! And soon, she and Rallden will be betrothed. Could it even be possible that she still has feelings for me? That she still sees that same kindness in my eyes that she saw when she was a little girl? Oh, Amaran, you silly fool...it couldn't be!*

Amaran considered the thought so ridiculous he cracked a smile.

A short while later, a horn sounded in the distance. "Well, it sounds like someone has won the hunt," said Amaran. "We better head back now."

76

"We have been out here for a long time, haven't we?" Elle said. She gathered her dress quickly and untied her horse. With a little more urgency in her voice she added, "I didn't realize how much time had passed. I hope we can find Ganella and Jareck. If we can't, we'll make a return to the palace that will get everyone talking."

Sensing her panic, Amaran held out his hands to help her up onto her horse.

"If you knew how much the ladies at court love to gossip, Amaran, even if it's about nothing...."

Just as she pulled herself up, her foot slipped in the stirrup and she lost her balance. She fell sideways, but she did not fall far. Amaran caught her in his arms.

"Oh!" she exclaimed, surprised. "How clumsy I can be sometimes. You wouldn't think I've been riding horses since I was a little girl, would y—?"

She stopped herself as she looked up at Amaran. He said absolutely nothing as he gazed down upon her. She looked both flustered and thrilled all at once.

Amaran thought only of the sweet, pretty girl in his arms, her face so close to his. He remembered the touch of her soft, cool hand earlier, and it made his heart pound with excitement. He broke eye contact as he started to let her down, but stopped himself—why, he could not understand. Elle did not protest. Her brown doe eyes moved down to his lips.

He wanted nothing else in the world but to kiss her perfect lips. At that second he could think of no reason not to, so he slowly moved his mouth to hers. They closed their eyes in anticipation. But just as their lips were about to meet, they heard Ganella.

"Hello, you two!" she shouted from atop the hill. "We've been looking for you!"

Amaran immediately pulled away. They exchanged glances, each uncertain as to whether or not Ganella had seen them.

"I'm sorry, Elle," he said softly. "I didn't mean to—"

Elle looked petrified. She did not respond, but instead clumsily mounted her horse and steered it towards the hill.

Seeing the expression on her face, and dying to know what she was thinking, Amaran became angry. "What is wrong with me?" he growled under his breath. "Stupid! Of all the things...!"

He mounted his mare and raced up the hill behind Elle. Just before they were in earshot of Jareck and Ganella, he heard her say, "Don't worry, Amaran, I really don't think she saw us."

Don't worry? he thought. *I nearly kissed her, Albakranian nobility, and I don't need to worry because her cousin didn't see us?"*

He understood the implications of a gossip like Ganella spotting them, but now it seemed like the least of his worries. What did all this mean? What would have happened had Ganella and Jareck not come when they did? If they had really kissed, what then?

Amaran was desperate to know the truth, but the questions did not haunt him nearly as much as the kiss that almost was.

Chapter 12—A Complicated Matter

Later that same day, just as the sun was disappearing beyond the horizon, Amaran returned to the cabin. Though Amaran could not stop thinking about that afternoon, nor did he think he ever would, he tried with all his being to forget it. Just before he went inside, he shook his head angrily, and murmured to himself, "Don't be stupid. She is charming and perfect in every other way, but you know who she is...."

Once he entered, Amaran found his father at the table, intensely scanning a paper in his hand. The commander looked up at his son with a very serious look. "How was the faragrin hunt, son?" Lanellon asked gruffly.

"It was good, even though Rallden wasn't able to join us—"

His father cut him off. "Amaran, I need to speak to you about something."

A wave of trepidation rippled through Amaran as he felt his father's stare strengthen its hold on him. "Yes? About what?"

"I overheard some talk about an altercation between you and another soldier. I had not heard anything about it, so I asked them to tell me the whole story. They told me that he confronted you about saving Rallden's life."

"Yes," Amaran said slowly.

"And about your loyalty to your countrymen." His father paused, his eyes dark as he watched Amaran.

"That's right."

"Son, it is very important that you hear what I have to say. You already know what I think about your friendship with Rallden. I have cautioned you, and still you associate with the king's nephew. Why?"

"We have been friends for so long now. I have always preferred his company to anyone else's here in the barracks."

"What about Croff? Is he not a good friend?"

"He is a good friend, but that is all. Rallden and I are like brothers. In fact, he is closer to me than a brother could ever be!"

"You are no longer a boy, but a young man, a Kallendrian soldier who will soon become an officer. Despite this, you are spending as much time with the Albakranians as you spend with fellow Kallendrians. It seems like you might rather be one of them." Lanellon stared across the table at his son, refusing to look away.

Amaran felt compelled to tell his father at least something to satisfy him. "I haven't gone only to see Rallden. Elle has returned. She is the girl that lived in the palace some time ago. I hadn't seen her in years. Since it had been so long, we had much to talk about."

"The councilman's daughter?"

"Yes."

"And is she who you spent the day with today since Rallden was not in the hunt?"

Amaran hesitated, but eventually answered, "Yes, she and two others."

Lanellon paused for a moment and looked down at the table with a look of intense concentration, as if he were contemplating his next move in a battle. "Amaran, my son, I love you dearly. I want you to be happy, but you are traveling down a road that will lead only to trouble. You have a deep, long-lasting friendship with Rallden, I understand, but you also have a responsibility to your country. The time has come where these loyalties can no longer coexist. They simply cannot. Tensions have been growing over the last few weeks in the southern seas. Although it's far from us here in Balankor, the situation is still not good. Albakran and Kallendria have made great strides over the last few years, but all the diplomatic efforts will be for naught if the situation to the south worsens."

"Is it really that serious?"

Lanellon looked sternly at Amaran before replying. "You need to consider the possibility that we may someday go to war. In that case, Rallden will be your enemy. The men you train with, your fellow Kallendrians, they will rely on you, and you on them. You have great potential both as a soldier and as a leader. The latter is in jeopardy because of your well-intentioned, but unfortunate, friendship with an enemy. Unlike your friends, you don't choose your enemies."

"Yes, I understand," Amaran said.

"Soldiers must be able to trust each other. Seeing how you are willing to spend more time with Rallden, the heir to the Albakranian throne, and risk your life to save his…." He paused and bit his lip before resuming. "Simply put, I would not blame a fellow soldier for having misgivings about where your allegiances may lie."

His father stood and abruptly left the room.

Amaran sat at the table alone. He thought about what his father had just said and knew he was mostly right. He himself was now questioning his own loyalty. Rallden was truly like a brother to him. And Elle—he had grown so attached to her so quickly—too attached, he knew—it would be difficult to forget her. Yet he also respected his father and would never imagine doing something to disappoint him. What would it take to satisfy his father? "Stop visiting the palace," he murmured. "And never see Rallden or Elle again."

When the thought of having to face Rallden in battle passed into his mind, he felt a wave of sheer horror run through him. He forced the image out of his head. When he did this, however, he focused instead on the next thing that came to mind: Elle. He felt the touch of her hand against his again—and then pictured the kiss that had almost been theirs to share.

What am I doing? he suddenly thought. *She will never be mine to love!*

It was a dangerous path upon which he was about to tread, and he knew it. Despite the urgings of his conscience to forget Elle, he continued to think of her. So Amaran listened not to reason and instead allowed himself to think about her. He was happier when he did, so why should he deny himself that joy? It was only natural to think of her smile, her kindness, and everything that made her different than every other girl he had ever met. What harm could come from just thinking of her?

Amaran was greatly troubled, haunted by an unnerving fear that hid itself deep inside him. Thinking of her was a temporary fix, a drug that cured his symptoms for a short while, but the nagging, pulsing warnings of his conscience persisted.

Chapter 13—The Jousting Tournament

The next week, Amaran kept his distance and did not visit the palace. His father assumed he was finally listening to him. However, he had to attend a jousting tournament as Rallden was competing and had invited him. He sat next to Elle and Ganella. When Amaran took his place beside Elle, there was an awkward silence as they exchanged glances. Ganella noticed this and looked at Elle with an inquisitive smile, but she knew that Elle would tell her nothing about it. After all, each time Ganella had broached the subject of the faragrin hunt, Elle had quickly changed the topic.

"Rallden is a spectacular jouster," Elle explained to Ganella, once the tournament was about to begin.

"Of course he is," Ganella replied, leaning closer to Elle. "He has a spectacular squire to assist him."

"Yes, Ganella, I'm sure that's the reason," Elle laughed, shaking her head.

As the squires helped the first pair of competing knights prepare for their match, two young men took the empty seats next to Ganella. Both were tall and handsome and wore lavish capes over their silk blouses and trousers.

"My ladies," the first said, nodding to Elle and Ganella.

"Lord Hargon, Lord Gertran, it is good to see you both," Elle replied.

The one who sat immediately next to Ganella spoke first. "Lady Elle, who is this beauty you've brought with you? I saw her once briefly at the faragrin hunt, but I did not have the pleasure of being introduced."

"She is my cousin, Lord Hargon," she replied. "Ganella of Halkaran. And this is Amaran, a friend of—"

"I see that beauty runs in your family, Lady Elle," the second nobleman interrupted, paying no attention to Amaran.

Elle was about to respond, but Ganella beat her to the punch. "And charm must run in yours, Lord Gertran, for you know exactly what to say to make a lady's heart melt."

"It requires no charm to speak only what is the truth, Ganella," added Hargon. "If you knew Gertran like I do, you would agree: he has no charm."

"Words that only a gentleman unable to recognize true charm could speak," quipped Gertran.

Ganella, who was quite enjoying the competition between the two men beside her, missed the first jousting charge. Despite not caring at all about the outcome, she cried, "Oh, look, now I've missed the first joust. You gentlemen have distracted me! Charm indeed!"

A false look of disappointment swept across her face.

"Ganella," Elle said, pointing to her far right. "Over there, there's Rallden."

Ganella glanced over at him.

"And you can see Jareck from here, too," Elle added.

"Who?" Ganella said quickly. "Oh, yes, Rallden's squire. I see them. Is Rallden up next?"

Before Elle could answer her, Ganella turned back to the noblemen beside her. She pressed her bosom against Hargon's arm after adjusting her bodice to ensure he could see her cleavage. "Would either of you like to walk with me to the fence over there? It is a thrill to watch the jousting from so close, only…," she paused as she glanced playfully at each gentleman in turn, "I am afraid to go by myself. I'll need protection to pass through all the riff-raff. They're like a pack of filthy rats muddled together."

"Lady Ganella," started Lord Hargon, "that is hardly a place I would expect a lady of your standing to want to watch from, but I will take you there if it would make you happy."

"Oh, it would!" she exclaimed, gazing upon him as she brushed her leg against his.

Seeing this, Gertran stood first, saying, "Ganella, I will take you. Hargon here wouldn't know what to do with the peasants should they start to bother you."

Without a second's hesitation, Hargon shot back, "Yes, they're your sort of people, are they? You'd handle them just fine I take it."

Both rose and offered an arm to the elated Ganella.

A short while later, Amaran shifted nervously in his seat and cleared his throat. "Elle, I know you heard me last week, but I have to say it again."

She looked straight ahead, becoming rigid and noticeably uncomfortable.

"I am sorry for what happened the other day, Elle. I never meant to—to…. What I'm trying to say is that I never intended to—"

Refusing to look at him, Elle interrupted softly, "Amaran, you can't bring it up ever again…please. We must go on as if it never happened."

"You must forgive me. I've realized that I placed my friendship with you, and with Rallden, in jeopardy, and I can't bear to think of such a thing. While I know our friendship won't last forever, I still want—"

"I do forgive you. But please, don't mention it again."

The way she said this made Amaran turn and look at her. She seemed pained to think it and sad once she had spoken it. Confused, he blurted out, "I won't, I promise…but know I'll never forget it."

He had crossed a line in saying this, but he had said it nonetheless. He watched her, wanting some signal that she felt the same way.

She glanced over at him briefly before turning abruptly away. She lowered her head and stared intensely at her hands on her lap, intertwining her fingers rapidly before releasing them again. She continued to do this without looking back at him for quite some time.

What did I say?! he thought with sudden horror. *I've offended her now. She thinks I'm an imbecile—a foolish boy who can't mind his own tongue.*

Furious at himself, he wished he could sink through the seat and fall into the pit of peasants below them. *Or, better yet*, he thought angrily, *why not throw myself into the arena as the knights charged one another?* He was glad he did neither, for he would have missed her response.

"I know," she said in a whisper. "I know I'll never forget it either, which is why we must never speak of it again. You know it as well as I do."

Chapter 14—Tension at the Border

In the Kallendrian sector of Balankor, an hour before noon in the middle of the following week, the soldiers had just finished their morning drills. They filed out of the training yard toward the dining hall. Amaran and his friend Croff were among them.

"Amaran, I know the look, and I know you've been distracted this whole week, so tell me…who is it? Corporal Gannet's sister who came to visit last week, perhaps? She's pretty. Or perhaps another? There aren't too many to choose from, you know, so I'll eventually guess." Croff's eyes were open wide and his eyebrows arched high, as if he expected an immediate response.

Amaran stopped walking. He opened his mouth as he started to speak, but closed it again.

"Oh, Amaran, it can't be that bad, can it? It isn't the big farmer lady who brings in the weekly supply of vegetables, is it?" Croff guffawed.

Amaran smiled at his friend with one eyebrow raised. "Nice guess. No, it's not."

Croff grew suddenly serious. "Amaran, don't tell me it's her."

Amaran seemed to know exactly who Croff meant. He hesitated before giving a slight nod. "She is so different than the little girl I remember meeting all those years ago. Ever since I saw her again, well, I can't stop thinking about her. The way she looks at me with those big brown eyes…and the way I feel when I am with her…she is not like the rest of them. Ladies of the palace are concerned only with their status, their beauty, and winning favor with the king. Elle is nothing of the sort. She cares for those she should not cast a second glance at, she has such a kind heart. It's hard to describe, but...."

"The Goddess Amiora has struck you in the heart, hasn't she?" Croff said, trying to suppress his smile.

"Croff, I assure you it is nothing more than—"

Croff interrupted him. "She's beautiful and charming," Croff said, "and...she's Albakranian."

Amaran looked up to study his friend's face before going on. "Right. And now that she's staying at the palace again, I've become...reacquainted with her."

"I see," Croff said, his eyes drifting away from Amaran and fixing on one of the drifting clouds above. Putting a hand on his friend's shoulder, he cleared his throat. "Amaran, you are in love with her, whether you admit it to yourself or not."

Amaran stared back at him. "No," he replied with a nervous laugh. "I am not in love with her. Besides, she will marry Rallden. I know this already. I would not fall in love with a girl I know can never be mine to love."

Croff raised his eyebrows. "Do you get to pick who you fall in love with? Does a man choose not to fall in love with a woman simply because she is promised to another? I think not! How many wars have been started because two men lay claim to the same woman? I'm telling you, you are in love with this girl and you'd better be careful. The business with you and Rallden I understand. You have been friends for a long time. If I were in that situation, I'm sure I would have done what you did—save his life, that is. Tralov and the others are ridiculous to discredit you for that. But when you love a girl, and especially one as utterly irresistible as she is, then she holds over you a certain power that jades your perception of everything."

"Croff, I don't think—" Amaran started.

"You should!" Croff shot back. "Who are you that you are immune? You're going to fall deeper in love with her if you keep on seeing her. Your relationship with Rallden may someday have to end, and you will handle that when the time comes—I trust you in that. But you will not, mark my words, *will not*, be able to forget her."

Amaran stared hard at the ground, saying nothing.

"Sooner or later," Croff continued, "you'll realize I was right. By then it'll be too late. You can't forget who she is. She's one of them!"

Staring back at Croff, Amaran said tersely, "I figured you'd respond like this. That's why I didn't want to tell you. I knew I shouldn't."

"Amaran—" Croff stopped short as Amaran turned on his heel and walked away. Shaking his head, he sighed as Amaran disappeared around the corner.

Amaran continued to walk along the path that led to his cabin. His eyes were glossed over, his head turned to the ground. He walked inside to find his father reading over some papers. Trying to pass through unnoticed to avoid a lengthy conversation, he moved quickly through the kitchen.

"Amaran, hold on. There is something you should hear." Lanellon paused, stared hard at the papers one more time, and then continued. "There is tension at the border."

Amaran looked up at his father.

"Apparently, Albakranian troops in the Southwest Province accidentally killed a Kallendrian woman right near the border."

"What do you mean, 'accidentally'?" interrupted Amaran.

"All I know is that the lady was of noble status and traveling in the countryside close to where Albakranian archers were taking long-range target practice. A stray arrow hit her. As for whether or not the arrow hit her in Kallendrian territory or Albakranian, I still don't know."

"What does this mean?" Amaran asked hesitantly.

"Neither side is admitting wrongdoing or backing down. King Lerendril is out for blood. He demands a formal apology from King

Bardane, and the right to try the archer who struck her in Kallendrian court. If Bardane complies, the Albakranians admit that they were in strict violation of the treaty terms...a significant implication. If Bardane concedes nothing, there is no telling what King Lerendril will do. Fear is contagious, and I believe that both sides will experience it to the fullest soon enough. This was ill timing, considering the current peace treaty is about to expire."

"But war isn't inevitable," Amaran said, tensely awaiting his father's response.

"No, not yet." He stopped for a brief moment and looked very seriously at Amaran. "Nothing is for certain, but there is a good possibility. Because of that, we all need to be on our guard in the city—" here he made a point to look Amaran in the eyes, "and be ready for any orders that may come our way. Be prepared, Amaran."

Chapter 15—The Announcement

After the Kallendrian noblewoman was killed, the number of Kallendrian troops at the border tripled. This, in turn, led to an increase in Albakranian soldiers on watch. Over the next few weeks tensions between Albakran and Kallendria remained high. War was looking all the more likely.

The political strain did not interfere with Amaran's visiting the palace, however. Though he did not go on a weekly basis, he still joined Rallden and Elle and several others on a falcon hunt, and then he attended a formal luncheon during the last month of spring. The following weekend, when his father was busy with military affairs, Amaran left the barracks to eat lunch with Rallden, responding to the invitation he had received the day before. When he arrived, he found Elle just returning from the stables with two servants and one of her ladies-in-waiting, a red-haired, rosy-cheeked girl.

"Amaran!" Elle exclaimed. "What good timing! Now I can walk with you inside." She looked at him then with such an enchanting gaze he forgot what he was about to say. "I am glad all the problems at the border are not keeping you away. It is frightening, though, isn't it?"

"It is," he said dismally.

Forgetting her worry, she said excitedly, "Come to the dining hall with me, Amaran! We are about to eat."

As he followed her to the door, he heard Elle's young lady, still several steps behind him, say, "She is always in brighter spirits on the days that you come. A different bounce in her step, that's for certain."

Unsure of how to respond, Amaran pretended not to hear her, but he smiled to himself.

"Amaran!" Rallden shouted from the nearest doorway once Amaran had entered the palace.

Amaran noticed his unusually jubilant greeting.

"I have to tell you something," Rallden added in a hushed voice, leaning towards Amaran.

Amaran eyed him even more inquisitively as Rallden placed his arm about Amaran's shoulder and guided him down the hall away from Elle.

"My uncle and Councilman Haldegran talked this week. Though it was decided some time ago, they say it's now time to announce the date to the rest of the kingdom. Elle and I are going to…"

Amaran did not hear Rallden's announcement. He knew already what he intended to say. Feeling suddenly dizzy, he put out his hand to brace himself against the wall. He then heard the echo of Rallden's voice proclaiming the news that he and Elle would be married.

It was something Amaran had known about for a long time, but he had always believed it would be years into the future. The announcement should not have surprised him, he knew, but he was stunned, nonetheless. He was not ready to hear it—not yet.

"Elle knows only of the decision made some time ago," Rallden continued. "She knows nothing of the final word of the king or her father. She has no idea that I will be offering a formal proposal to her tonight. She will be thrilled, I know. I can't wait to see the look of surprise on her face."

"Yes, I'm sure," Amaran said quickly.

His friend glanced at him twice, his own face uncertain, but he seemed to let it go. Chills came over Amaran. Had his closest friend noticed something amiss? Could Rallden possibly know about that near kiss, or Amaran's feelings for Elle?

Once Amaran and Rallden entered the dining hall, Amaran saw Elle again. She smiled at him when he approached the table, and he forced a smile back. Her questioning eyes seemed to say, "What is it? What's wrong?"

"Are you all right?" Rallden asked, looking over at Amaran as he put his hand on his shoulder. There was a new edge to his eyes, a cold gleam as he took Amaran in. "You look pale."

"I am fine. I just had a passing queasy feeling," Amaran said feebly. "With so much tension...and my father... Well, that is another matter altogether."

Rallden eyed him dubiously before turning to Elle. "Elle, you are looking exquisite as always."

She thanked him before stealing another quick glance at Amaran. But Amaran did not notice; he was staring blankly at the floor.

They soon took their seats. Two long tables were filled with talkative guests. Murken, one of King Bardane's advisors, sat beside Rallden. Councilman Haldegran sat next to Bardane, laughing heartily at everything the king said. Amaran clenched his fists under the table. He found the merriment quite annoying and was in no mood to hear the councilman's raucous expressions of amusement.

Sitting quietly in his seat, Amaran could concentrate on nothing but his thoughts. *Why am I so surprised? I knew it was coming. Did I ever think anything different would happen...?*

He felt a terrible pain eating through him—a pain that had started in his stomach, but had made quick work of his insides as it spread to nearly every inch of his body. He spent much of the meal biting painfully into his tongue and trying to avoid eye contact with anyone—surely his eyes were dark with anger, his face hard.

An hour after the last course was served, the room was mostly empty. When Rallden asked Elle to walk with him, Amaran was left alone at the table. He sat in his seat only a few moments longer before abruptly standing and murmuring angrily to himself, "I am such a fool!"

Murken saw Amaran leaving and walked briskly towards the door to intercept him. Amaran saw him, but pretended not to notice. He quickened his step, but was too late.

"Amaran, young man, you seem distraught," said Murken from behind him. A tight-lipped smile that was intended to seem sympathetic spread across the royal advisor's face.

"It's nothing."

"It is obvious that you are...," Murken continued carefully, "concerned about something."

"I'm just a bit out of sorts today, that is all," Amaran said unconvincingly.

"Out of sorts," repeated Murken thoughtfully. "I wonder why you might seem...out of sorts, as you say."

Amaran glared back at him and said, "You don't need to worry about it, Murken. It is nothing that concerns you."

"Perhaps not. Oh, but there is one matter I must discuss with you before you leave today."

"Some other time? Like I said, I am feeling—" but Murken did not let him finish.

"No, I am afraid this cannot wait. It is of utmost importance. I would guess you know the news that will become public later this week."

Murken looked expectantly at Amaran. Amaran gave him no satisfaction, staring blankly back at him.

"Rallden mentioned he was going to tell you. You do realize that things are about to change, and change considerably. As one of His Majesty's royal advisors, and an advisor to Rallden as well, I feel it is my obligation to remind you of this. Your visiting Rallden here, and Elle, will be quite different from this moment on. The frequency of your visits and so forth...you understand."

Amaran replied boldly, "Oh, I understand quite well, thank you, Murken. I understand, but I'll leave those decisions to Rallden and Elle." And with that, Amaran left the room.

As Amaran moved down the corridor, he felt his face grow warm and his heart thump wildly against his chest. He had always disliked Murken, but now he hated him—it was without question. He was also annoyed by Rallden's obnoxious happiness. And, of course, he was angry at himself, too. His pace quickened the closer he got to the door.

Just as he neared the door to escape this wretched place, he heard something that stopped him. It was so overpowering and so compelling all at once that he wished he had not heard it. Amaran fought against the urge to turn around, but lost. Elle was walking towards him, and looking more magnificent than ever before.

"Amaran, I was hoping I would find you. Murken said you had just left. Are you all right? You looked so upset earlier."

"I am fine," he replied curtly.

"Nothing is wrong? Nothing at all?" she asked.

"Nothing is wrong. Why do you ask?"

"Because you look upset!" she said impatiently. "Tell me what's wrong, Amaran."

"Why should I be upset?" he said coldly, starting towards the door again.

Elle marched after him. "I don't know. That's what I wanted you to tell me."

"Elle," Amaran said so forcefully it startled her. "I won't be visiting the palace as often as I used to."

"Oh," she said, surprised. "Why do you say that?"

"I have decided, that is all. I have many other affairs I need to attend to in the barracks, and there is little reason for me coming here with Rallden being so busy nowadays."

"You have decided..." she repeated.

"Yes, that's right."

"I don't understand. Why would you stop—?"

"You'll understand why soon enough. If you will excuse me, I have to go now."

"Amaran, what is the matter with you?"

Ignoring her, he stormed through the door, marching for the stables.

"Amaran!" she shouted.

He did not respond.

Amaran rode through the streets, hearing Rallden's announcement again and again in his head. He pictured Elle looking up into his eyes, pleading with him to tell her his troubles. Shaking his head to clear his mind, he said angrily, "I have to get her out of my head!"

He let his anger grow inside, and for a minute it made him feel better. Soon enough, however, he began to hear her voice again in his mind. Then, no matter how hard he tried, he could not forget her.

Croff and my father were right. I should have stopped seeing her long ago. It's made me want only to see her more. I am stupid to have ever thought that I could....

All of the previous thoughts that had been rattling about in his mind evaporated instantaneously. Only one remained. He had never realized it before, not until this day—not until after he had heard for himself that she would marry Rallden. But now that he had heard the news, now that it was final, now that it was too late, he realized the truth. He was in love with her.

Chapter 16—The Engagement Banquet

Amaran rode through the meadow towards the road. Still several miles from the city, he kept his eager young stallion from breaking into a full gallop. Suddenly, the sky started to change. Clouds rolled in at an alarming rate, darkening the sky. Lightning flashed in the distance.

A deafening clap of thunder followed, but Amaran paid it no attention. He had heard something else. It was something more terrifying than the violent storm that seemed to have come from nowhere. The cry of a dragon drowned out the howling wind and sent a wave of fear through Amaran's whole body. The winged giant flew across the stormy sky, right over Amaran's head. It was flying towards Balankor.

"Go!" Amaran said to his horse, steering it onto the dirt road.

What he intended to do, he did not know, but he had to do something. The dragon could destroy the city. He had to try to warn them, or try to stop it himself.

The horse tore down the road, racing after the flying beast. As soon as the dragon realized it was being followed, it changed course. It tilted its body, circling around in the sky before lowering itself to the ground. It landed in front of them, blocking the road.

Amaran brought his horse to a stop. Quickly dismounting, he drew his sword and faced the giant reptile. It eyed him fearlessly, bearing its treacherous teeth as it let out a terrifying growl.

Trembling, Amaran stepped forward with his sword held high. What was he thinking? What was he going to do? Kill it himself?

Without warning, the dragon lunged towards Amaran. It had tried to snatch him in its saber-like teeth, but Amaran darted out of the way just in time.

Amaran did not miss his chance. With the dragon's head only feet from him, its neck outstretched, he thrust his hands down fast and hard. His sword sliced through the olive leathery skin, leaving a gash where its neck met its head. The dragon roared as it pulled its head away.

But Amaran attacked again. He slashed twice at its leg, breaking through the coat of scales the second time he struck it. The dragon stumbled when it pulled its injured leg out of Amaran's reach. Seeing the dragon off-balance and distracted, Amaran charged forward and came underneath it. Up close, he saw a small hole in its chest where several scales were missing. Wasting not a second, he plunged his sword deep into the opening.

The dragon shrieked in pain, pulling away from the fearless warrior. The sword was still in its chest as it reared back. It began clawing at the blade, trying in vain to remove it. It had already lost blood from its neck and leg wounds, but now blood also seeped from its chest. It grew weaker and weaker until it fell onto its side.

Amaran pulled the blade from its chest and raised it above the gash on its neck. With a powerful swing he cut deeper into the open wound. He struck it again in the same spot, this time cutting through flesh and bone. The dragon's eyes dimmed as it groaned and gurgled. Then it breathed its last.

Suddenly, the skies cleared. The clouds vanished as quickly as they had appeared, and the sun shone brightly. Amaran could scarcely believe his eyes when the dragon itself disappeared. He was even more confused when he realized he was standing just outside the walls of Balankor. The city gates opened and King Bardane rode out with his royal guards to meet him. Noblemen surrounded him, praising him for his victory over the dragon. Amaran saw Elle in the distance, looking proudly at him.

Then Amaran awoke.

This had seemed more real than any dream he had ever had—even the dragon dream he had had as a boy. And this time he had not just seen a dragon, he had slain it. What did it mean? Why had it seemed so real? After dwelling on it for days, and recalling the events—still as clear in his mind as the moment he dreamed it—he became more and more convinced that it was more than just a dream. What that meant he did not know, but the more he thought about it, the more convinced he became that he was right.

Four days after the dream, Amaran walked up the steps of the cabin. He found a message waiting for him inside. As he opened the envelope, he muttered, "An invitation no doubt. It's time to celebrate the news of their wedding...."

He found a hand-written note scribbled at the bottom of the page.

Amaran,

For eight years we have remained friends against all odds—you a Kallendrian, I an Albakranian. An impossible friendship, yet, we still are devoted friends. I ask that you oblige my request to attend this banquet to share in our joy. As my dearest friend, I could not imagine the banquet without you—nor could Elle, I am certain. I hope to see you there.

Rallden

He took the letter to his table and read it again. He knew his friend had no idea about anything between Elle and himself. Surely Rallden would not invite him if he did.

Amaran folded up the envelope as he rose from the table. He stuffed the envelope in a small pocket as if the letter meant nothing to him, though nothing could have been further from the truth. It would have been best for Amaran to simply toss the invitation aside, stay home on the night of the banquet, and see neither Elle nor Rallden again. Then, in time, he would get used to the idea of seeing them no more. Amaran knew this would be the best choice for the future—the most painless one in the end.

However, ending his ties with Rallden and Elle would be difficult—easier said than done. His father and Croff had both warned him, and now would be as good a day as any to break ties with his Albakranian friends. The sooner he did it, the better, and easier, it would be for him. But deep down, Amaran knew he would not be able to pass on the invitation.

"I can't refuse him. Rallden invited me, and I have to go. It would be wrong of me not to go."
He said this with resolve, holding his head high, trying to convince himself that this was the only reason he had just decided to attend.

On the evening of the banquet, just as the setting sun disappeared beyond the distant hills, Amaran arrived at the palace. As he entered with the other guests, he distracted himself from what he had feared to dwell upon for the last few days. Tonight Elle would be by Rallden's side, in front of hundreds of guests, acknowledging her intention to marry him.

Shortly before the food was served, King Bardane stood to welcome everyone. He then beckoned Rallden and Elle to stand. Elle rose beside Rallden, her flawless beauty shining for all there to see. The elated guests applauded. Amaran slowly, callously, joined in the clapping. It mattered not how much he had repeated in his head that he was attending because he owed it to Rallden as a friend—his closest friend. He knew well the real reason he could not stay away: he had to see her again.

After dinner, Rallden led Elle onto the dance floor. Amaran could not stand to watch. As the other guests escorted their partners onto the dance floor, Amaran walked outside to the much quieter balcony. Feeling the light breeze, he looked down upon the gardens below. He remained undisturbed for some time until a hand touched him gently on the shoulder. He knew immediately who it was.

"Hello, Amaran," she said. Her pink cheeks rounded as she smiled sadly at him. Her usually bright eyes did not sparkle.

"My lady Elle," he said, bowing.

Looking out over the balcony beside him she said, "I am glad you came, Amaran. I was unsure if I would see you tonight or not, or if I would have the opportunity to speak with you if you did."

"I had to come," he replied with a strikingly serious tone as he looked into her melancholy eyes.

She glanced hesitantly up at him when he said this, but immediately looked down again over the balcony railing. "I am sure you were surprised by the news. Even I wasn't expecting it to come so soon," she said.

"Yes, surprised. I was very surprised," Amaran said in a distant voice.

"Is that all you felt?"

Furrowing his brow, Amaran stared straight at her. "What else would I feel?"

She glanced nervously down at the floor, her eyes shifting. "Nothing else, I suppose."

They stood for several moments, saying nothing to each other.

"Queen Elle," he said, looking down at the gardens again. "That's what you'll be called some day."

"Yes," she said flatly, forcing a smile. She sounded so sad, and Amaran wondered about that. He remembered her bright smile as she stood next to Rallden not two hours earlier....

"Amaran!" Rallden said loudly from behind, startling them both. "Good to see you, friend!"

"Rallden," Amaran replied, forcing emotion into his voice. "I was just offering my congratulations to Elle. Quite a celebration tonight!"

"Yes, yes, it was," said Rallden proudly. "Nothing but the best for my bride-to-be, the future Queen of Albakran."

Before turning back to Rallden, Amaran looked quickly at Elle. He saw the same half smile as before, but then she turned to face her future husband.

"It was a splendid banquet, Rallden," she said. "Thank you."

Beaming, Rallden looked back into her eyes. "Elle, would you walk with me back into the hall? Lord Fellarum and his wife have not yet been able to congratulate us."

She followed him obediently, sliding her arm through Rallden's as he led her away.

Amaran turned as they left him, missing the glance that Elle stole towards him over her shoulder.

Chapter 17—Amaran and Elle

Even after reading it four times, Amaran still clung tightly to the folded note in his hand. Elle's lady-in-waiting had given it to him in the hall as he left the palace that night. She had said only, "It's from my lady, for you."

The secrecy with which she had delivered the message left no doubt in his mind as to the dire need for discretion, and so he had not opened it until he had hidden himself inside the stables. Now, as he was riding down the street, he could scarcely contain his racing heart as he heard her voice speak the words she had written:

"Amaran, please do not think ill of me for my boldness, and I hope you do not think me improper or foolish for writing this request to you. There are things I want to tell you, but they can be told only in person, and in private. If you are willing to hear what I must say, which I pray desperately you are, then meet me in the valley in the woods where you and I rode the day of the faragrin hunt. I will be there the day after tomorrow, two hours before sunset."

There were a multitude of reasons why he should never see Elle again. He knew this. Yet, something inside him compelled him to ignore his conscience. *You will never forgive yourself if you don't,* a voice in his head said. *What harm could possibly come of it?*

Even though he knew deep down that there was something dreadfully wrong with the logic of this persuasive thinking, he continued listening eagerly to the voice. He would go to the spot Elle had told him the day after tomorrow. There was nothing sinful about a conversation, especially between two friends like them. After all, why should he deny himself happiness that he so much deserved?

Amaran slept poorly that night and the next despite having made the decision to meet her with such a clear mind. When his commanding officer finally released him from drills on the afternoon of the second day, he quickly left the grounds, avoiding eye contact with Croff and pretending not to hear him calling his name. He led his horse out of the barracks and towards the west gate of the city before racing into the hills. When he arrived, he looked down from atop the ridge and saw her. With a wide grin, he coaxed his horse down the slope towards her.

"You came," she said when he neared her. "I hoped you would come, but feared you might not," she added as he helped her off her horse.

The hopeful and innocent look in her eyes held him captive. His heart pounded in anxious longing for her as he released her small hand from his. "Why did you want to see me? Why here?" he asked.

She shifted her gaze down to the ground, and her cheeks reddened. "I wanted to tell you...I wanted to say that I...." With tears welling in her eyes, she blurted out, "Oh, Amaran, don't you know? Can't you guess why I wanted you here?"

He stared at her for the several seconds of silence that followed, trying to decide what he should say. His heart wished him to admit defeat and cry out to her, 'Yes, I know! That is why I came!' Yet there was still a part of his mind governed by reason, weak though it may have been. He heard again the advice of his father and the counsel from Croff. With his last ounce of resistance, he offered his answer. "Elle, how can we? You are engaged to Rallden. He is my friend, and you...you will be his wife! I can't see you anymore, Elle. I am sorry."

Just before she looked down at the ground, he saw an expression of utter devastation on her sweet face. He knew he had shattered her. Pain tore through him as well—pain he knew would stick in his heart for years to come, if not forever.

"Amaran, you can't simply walk away and never—"

104

"I can and I must!" he shot back. "Don't you understand? When I am with you, *every* time I am with you, and even when I am not, all I want to do is—"

He stopped himself short.

"What, Amaran? Say it!" she cried out. "Say it, Amaran!"

Looking back at her silently for a moment, he said, "No, I can't. It's the same reason why I can never see you again. It has to be that way. This must be goodbye."

He turned abruptly away from her and reached for his horse's reins.

"How can you be so cruel?" she cried, as her tears broke free and ran down her cheeks. She grabbed onto his arm.

"Elle, you know this is how it must be. We should both go," he said as convincingly as he could, though secretly he wished she would disobey him.

"Amaran, I must tell you something," Elle said softly.

He did not lift himself into the saddle, for her next words stopped him.

"I don't want to marry him. I don't love him! I want to marry someone whom I love, not someone my father has chosen for me!"

He hesitated, trying to look away from her, but her sad yet beautiful gaze held him with crushing force.

"Please, don't leave," she pleaded. "Walk with me here and let's talk, only if for a short while."

Amaran knew that he must refuse. But his legs did not move. As he looked into her eager, expectant eyes, he could not find the strength to resist her. Blood rushed to his face. His knees grew weak.

He was going to say something else, but could not manage, for the urge to kiss her became too overpowering. Standing closer, he put both arms about her shoulders, looked deep into her eyes, and moved his lips towards hers. Elle leaned to meet him, grabbing onto his shirt. The soft warmth of her mouth against his sent a surge of electricity through him. They kissed passionately as they stood beneath the tree, him holding her in his arms. She pressed close to his body, her breasts against his chest and her arms wrapped tightly around him.

"What do we do now, Amaran?" Elle asked a short while later. He was helping her onto her horse. "What does all of this mean?"

"I don't know. We cannot go on like this, I know. Yet, the thought of life without you is...it's unbearable."

"Oh, Amaran, I must see you again."

"Elle, I don't think—"

"No, we cannot leave things as they are now. Meet me here again next week, the same time."

She kissed him quickly and prodded her horse forward before he could protest. He watched her leave, feeling as if the world were a completely different place now.

That night, Amaran could not stop thinking about what had happened that day. Elle was Rallden's to love. Despite this he could not simply cast aside his feelings for her. He had tried to forget her, but this day had proven it was impossible. If it was so, why fight it any longer? Her face was with him always, in front of him around every corner, and smiling at him when he closed his eyes. He was in love with her, and that was all that seemed to matter. He could never give her up, and so he would not.

Chapter 18—Conflict—Growing Suspicions

The next morning, Lanellon found Amaran sitting at the table. With deep lines across his forehead, he sternly approached his son. "Amaran, something terrible has happened."

Amaran stared gravely at his father, waiting for him to continue.

"A Kallendrian warship was transporting cargo to the island of Rhaenalia in the South Sea. They wandered into Albakranian waters. An Albakranian ship on patrol spotted the Kallendrian ship. The Albakranians defended their waters against what they thought was a dangerously bold intruder. They took the matter seriously and warned the ship to turn around."

"Why would our ship do that? Didn't the captain realize the risk?"

"I don't know, son. Perhaps they miscalculated their route."

"Our ship then turned around?"

"No. The captain failed to realize how far into Albakranian waters he had gone. He refused to back down. The Albakranians attacked, but they didn't stand a chance against a Kallendrian warship. We fought back and sank the Albakranian ship."

Amaran jumped to his feet, his heart hammering. "What?"

"Nearby Albakranian ships sought out the Kallendrian warship, following it into Kallendrian waters. The skirmish escalated as each side called more ships to the battlefront. When news reached my ears this morning, a large-scale naval battle was about to unfold."

"What does this mean for us here?" Amaran asked gravely.

"Matters will escalate. War will almost certainly break out on land soon."

"But how can this have happened?" Amaran asked angrily. "With all the efforts to maintain peace, how can something like this just happen? How could any Kallendrian captain be so careless as to let his ship wander that far into Albakranian waters?"

Lanellon put his hand to his face and rubbed his brow, even though there was no sweat to wipe. "All I know is that we should expect orders anytime now, so be ready. The access of all Kallendrian troops stationed in Balankor has been restricted to only the southern sector of the city. There will be no reason for you to go to the Balankor palace. If you did, you understand that you would be punished like any other soldier. You would be charged with—"

"I understand," Amaran interrupted, looking sternly at his father. "I've already decided I'll be going there no more."

"Good," Lanellon replied. "It would be unfortunate for the commander's own son to be tried for insubordination, especially during a time of war."

"War?" Amaran said with disgust. "We are not at war *yet*."

With a grim look in his eyes, Lanellon said solemnly, "We will be, Amaran. Mark my words: war will soon be upon us."

That week, Commander Lanellon halted all military exercises within the barracks. The Kallendrian soldiers waited to hear the inevitable orders: that they would move out and leave Albakran altogether. No orders had come yet, but it would not be much longer.

Despite his father's orders, Amaran still sneaked away on the afternoon he and Elle had agreed to meet. It was bold, it was dangerous, but he had to see her. When she arrived beneath the large tree by the stream, Amaran extended his hand to lower her off her horse. His anxious eyes looked deep into her troubled gaze.

"I have missed you so," she said. "Things are so complicated now, so difficult and—" She did not let herself finish.

"I know," he said with a sigh.

"Oh, Amaran, Murken suspects something. I don't know exactly what or how much he knows, but...."

"What do you mean? What makes you think that?"

"He must have seen me return the last time we met here. He said something about my riding alone with Helanor and questioned my whereabouts. He insinuated he knew something—and that whatever I had done might have bearing on Rallden's bid for the crown. I probably shouldn't have come here today, but I had no way of getting a message to you in time."

"It is terribly foolish of both of us to be here. If anyone found out I left the city, Elle, I'd...." He trailed off.

"And then there's Rallden," Elle continued. "What am I to say to him? When I am in his presence I can scarcely live with myself. He has done nothing to deserve this. I am promised to be his, yet all I can ever do when I am with him is think of you. When I am with you, all I can ever think of is my guilt over what I've done to him...and my fear of what may happen."

"This can never become what we both want," he said sternly. "Especially now that things have turned for the worse between our kingdoms and—"

"Amaran, don't say it," she pleaded. "I can't stand to think of it."

"My father says that war is almost certain at this point. When that happens—"

"What have we done, Amaran?" she asked, cutting him off. "Oh, why did it have to be this way? Why did I ever have to fall in love with you? Why can't it be you that I am to wed?"

When she began to cry, he pulled her close, holding her while sobs racked her body. It was a blatant reminder of what they had done—what he had allowed to happen. Why had he been so weak? He should have never allowed things to go this far.

"I love you so much, Amaran, but I don't know how much longer I can survive like this."

"I am sorry," he replied. "I should have run from you the moment I saw you."

"It isn't your fault. Do you really think that you are the only one to blame in this?"

Amaran had started to reply, but he stopped short. Looking away from her, he craned his neck. With squinted eyes, he looked up to the top of the hill.

"What is it?" she whispered.

"I don't know. I guess nothing. I thought I heard a horse in the distance, but I think I was hearing things. I don't see anyone."

"Are you sure there's no one there?" she asked apprehensively.

"I'm certain."

Elle looked at Amaran. "So you don't think...."

"That you were followed?" Amaran said. "I doubt it."

"I suppose you're right. I am very nervous about all of this...after talking with Murken. He really acted as if he knew something about us. And if he did, how would he know unless he followed me out here?"

Amaran thought for a moment. "Elle, we shouldn't see other again. It is too dangerous for both of us. And things are only going to get worse."

Elle's eyes became moist. Her lip quivered. She wanted to refuse. But she knew he was right.

***

Not too long after this, in one of the council rooms of the palace, Rallden was reading some documents when Murken entered brusquely. "Rallden, there is something I must speak with you about."

Not moving his head one inch, Rallden allowed only his eyes to look up at him.

Murken took a deep breath as he continued, "It is about Elle...and your Kallendrian friend."

Now Rallden raised his head fully towards the advisor and stared at him intently. "Amaran?" Rallden asked with surprise. "What about them?"

"They have been meeting together...alone."

The news clearly surprised Rallden. At first, he started to smile as if he planned to brush it off and remind Murken that Elle and Amaran were friends. But the smile faded. His brows drew together. Events ran through his mind.

"What are you talking about?" Rallden demanded.

"I had my suspicions that she was seeing someone in secret, but I never dreamed it would have been with *him*, the Kallendrian of all people. I wouldn't have believed it had I not seen it with my own eyes."

"What did you see?"

"I saw them together in the woods beyond the city. They met secretly and talked for a while before I—"

"They talked? And what else?"

"What else would you need to see to be disturbed by this, Rallden? It matters not that I didn't see anything more—they talked like lovers talk. The circumstances under which they met were evidence enough to suggest they—"

"But there was nothing else? You saw them do nothing but talk?" Rallden pressed.

Murken hesitated before proceeding. "Rallden, I must speak freely, and without fear of offending you." Not waiting for Rallden to respond, he continued, "If this news became public, imagine the—"

"Yes, I'm aware, Murken."

"What reason would they have for meeting in the woods alone? She is your betrothed and, since we are nearly in a state of war with Kallendria, Amaran is your enemy. Yet, he is taking the future queen into the woods to do who knows what!"

"That is enough!" Rallden hissed. "I'll hear no more about it. There must be some reason, some logical explanation for it."

The rebuke silenced Murken for a moment.

"I think not," Murken eventually said softly. "I think there is only one reason for it."

"Murken, I refuse to believe that he would—or that she would—do something as dishonorable as what you have suggested. He is my friend! I will ask Elle about it, she will explain, and that will be the end of it."

"Forgive me, but whether you trust him or not, you should associate with him no more. He is a lowly soldier, a commoner of Kallendria. He is the enemy! I do believe that even if nothing has happened between Amaran and Elle yet, it will one day...I would bet my life on it. I've seen that look of desire in many a young man before."

"My friendship with Amaran will not be ruined because of war or because of an affair that has not yet—and never will—come to be."

Both of them turned toward the window in response to the whinny of a horse.

Murken glanced over his shoulder to catch a glimpse of the rider. Raising his eyebrows as he turned partially around, he said, "You could ask Elle about it yourself, for it is she who returns now to the stables. I do wonder where she has been this afternoon." With that he turned and slinked away.

Now alone, Rallden approached the window and looked down at the entrance to the stables. Emerging from the doorway was Elle and her lady-in-waiting, Helanor. They were dressed in their riding cloaks. Staring down, he followed Elle with his eyes until she disappeared from view. Gripping the window ledge so hard his fingernails scraped the stone, he swore under his breath. Then he turned abruptly and left the room.

Chapter 19—A Pact Broken

"The final estimates are in following the battle at sea," Lanellon told Amaran when he entered the cabin. "The damage to both sides was severe. Irreparable harm has been done...peace is nearly impossible now. Tensions are high everywhere."

"Things aren't good in the city either," Amaran said grimly. "Croff and several others went down with me to the market. People started throwing rotten fruit on us and shouting all sorts of insults. Most of the onlookers laughed, some joined in. Things have changed. A few weeks ago, I wouldn't have thought this possible."

"It's the same elsewhere. In Gredania, civilians severely injured two Kallendrian soldiers. There have been several small-scale riots in several other cities. It's bad, but it'll only get worse."

Amaran looked at Lanellon apprehensively.

"We may not be here in Balankor much longer," added his father. "A few weeks at most, but probably much less...unless something changes, or some miracle comes."

"So the treaty will be worthless?"

"Treaty?" His father's face became like stone. "There will be no need for a treaty between warring nations."

***

He should have ignored the note. There was nothing safe or right about their riding to the meadow beyond the city—they had both agreed about that. But could he risk allowing Elle to ride out there alone and wait for him without knowing that he had refused to meet her this time?

Amaran reread the message that Elle's servant had just brought. Yes, the other soldiers had seen who dropped off the note, but he would slip away when they were not watching. Shaking his head to try to clear his mind, he pushed aside the nagging warnings of his conscience and his direct disobedience to his father.

"Amaran, I am sorry, but I had to see you again," Elle said to him that afternoon. "I know we agreed, but I cannot think clearly, I cannot sleep, I—"

Amaran's face was like stone. "I came only because I feared what might happen if you came and waited by yourself. It is dangerous for you, and it is insane that I left again. If they found out where I went...!"

"Yes, well, I just had to talk to you. Rallden is furious with me. He suspects I have been unfaithful. He's suspicious of us."

"All the more reason to not come here anymore!" said Amaran irritably.

"Murken has been talking to him," Elle continued. She told Amaran all that Rallden had told her about his conversation with Murken.

Amaran bit his lower lip hard. With sudden agitation, he spurted, "Soon enough, we won't have to worry about our seeing each other! War will break out within the week. Then I'll be gone forever from Balankor...off to battle...."

"Amaran, please," she pleaded. "Please don't talk like that. It's all so frightening and upsetting."

He pulled her closer, caressing her hair as she leaned against him. She held him just as tightly as he held her. She leaned back and looked at him.

"Amaran, I—" Elle stopped suddenly.

"Elle, what's the matter?" Amaran saw soon enough what she had seen.

A rider had come from behind the clump of trees nearby. They released each other, Elle springing back a step.

"Rallden, you scared me! I did not expect to see you here!" Elle shouted with a high, shaky voice that ended with forced laughter.

Rallden looked first at Elle and then at Amaran. He held them with a piercing stare as he said blandly, "I am sorry. That was not my intent. I simply wanted to see for myself what Murken suspected."

Rallden paused and looked at them with dead eyes. He watched one and then the other, as his horse pawed nervously.

"I at first thought he was crazy for saying what he did, Murken that is. Now I'm not so sure." Rallden's eyes harbored anger, but his tone was devoid of nearly all emotion. "At first I didn't believe Murken. I figured there must be some logical explanation, but it did stir my curiosity the more I thought about it. That was what prompted my questions the other day, Elle. After all, what harm is there in asking if there is nothing to find out? But when you gave me your answer, it did not put my mind at ease. It did quite the opposite."

Amaran and Elle remained silent. Elle's eyes had shifted as Rallden spoke, and she forced a smile upon her face that did not convince Rallden.

Rallden's face reddened and his jaw tightened as he said slowly, "Murken claimed he has seen you leave the palace several times to ride out of the city, Elle. He told me what he suspected, and I told him he was a fool for expressing such concerns, that there was no way either of you would betray me."

They both shifted their eyes towards his, but neither spoke.

"I want to know if I was the fool." His stare became even fiercer, uncompromising in its hold upon them. "Tell me, my future queen and my trusted friend, am I the fool?"

Elle desperately fought to steady her trembling hands.

"Can you assure me that there is no reason for me to worry?" Rallden pressed. He flared his nostrils and scoffed. "No, I thought not."

When his eyes rested solely on Elle, his anger quickly faded. "Elle, why?" he asked, sounding more wounded than enraged.

She answered him in a feeble voice as a tear fell down her cheek, "Oh, Rallden, what would you want me to say?"

"Speak the truth, Elle."

"Rallden, I—"

Amaran could not stand to see her struggle. "Rallden," he said as he glanced at Elle.

Elle gave him a look to say, "No, don't say anything!"

"I am afraid it is true," Amaran continued, ignoring her silent plea. "We care for each other. We—"

Rallden cut him off. "You, my friend, my very best friend for all these years, look what you have done to me!" He took a deep breath, huffing as he exhaled.

Elle interrupted. "Rallden, I am sorry! We did not mean for this to happen...not at all, not like this! We were just drawn to each other. It wasn't planned. We couldn't help it."

"Couldn't help it?" he snarled. "Certainly you could! Was there someone holding a sword to you to force you?"

"Rallden, that's not—that isn't what I meant," stammered Elle.

"No, of course it wasn't," Rallden sneered. "And do you think that your telling me that it was inevitable makes it any better? It fixes nothing! You are to be my bride, yet this is the devotion you shall give me as my wife? A queen who goes behind her king's back...with his own friend? You've both betrayed me!"

Rallden's face was scarlet and the veins bulged in his temples as he spoke these last words. Controlling his anger for the moment, he turned slowly towards Amaran. In a much lower tone, he growled, "I don't know how you could have done this to me, *friend*, but rest assured it will not happen again. She is not yours to sneak around with, or to talk to. Now I see that I should never have trusted you. This is how a friendship is repaid."

"Rallden," Amaran started slowly, "you know I didn't mean to betray you. It was just how it happened. You have everything. You will be a king and can have any woman in the kingdom you want. All I wanted was her. I knew it was wrong, but I couldn't help it. Elle was all I needed to be happy, and—"

"I don't want to hear any more," Rallden snapped. "You will never be welcome in the palace again, even after this war is over. I forbid you to return. You shall never lay eyes on Elle again as long as I can help it. She will remain with me and fulfill her destiny as queen. I will make sure she stays far from you, out of sight of your lustful eyes, you backstabbing traitor!"

Elle spoke with a trembling voice as desperation filled her moist eyes. "Rallden, please! It was not his fault. I was the one who pressed it. He even spoke of you and how he could not betray your trust. It was just something that happened. We did not mean for it to hurt you!"

"Is that supposed to console me? To know that it was you who pursued him and sought him out? You are both guilty, you because you are supposed to be faithful to me, and he because he betrayed my trust."

"Rallden, please!" she yelled. "He is still your friend! He saved your life!"

"Is he my friend?" spat Rallden, seething with wild anger.

"Rallden," Elle said gently, "I was not entirely unfaithful to you. It was just—"

"Just what? Just a kiss? Just one night?"

Amaran spoke. "We did not spend any night together, not one. She did not give herself to me."

"Enough!" Rallden snapped.

118

Elle looked up at him with her soft brown eyes. "Rallden, I—I don't know what to say."

"I don't want you to say anything," he growled. "Nothing will make this all right."

Rallden suddenly swung down from his horse. He marched towards Amaran, his hand upon the hilt of his sword. "You have dishonored me."

"No!" Elle said, stepping between them. "It wasn't his fault. It was mine."

Rallden looked at Elle. His eyes softened only slightly. He sighed and pulled his hand from his sword. Looking over her head, he stared back at Amaran. "To pay back the debt I owe you—when you saved my life in the forest that day—I am going to allow you to leave here. Know that I could have had you arrested for this—and that I should draw my sword against you."

Amaran said nothing as he stared back at Rallden.

"Mark my words, Amaran, if I ever see you again, I will kill you." Rallden motioned for Elle. "You are returning with me."

Elle went to her horse and mounted. Right behind her, Rallden slapped the mare on the rump, sending it off at such a speed Elle could do nothing but hold on. Rallden swung himself upon his horse's saddle and glared at Amaran. He galloped off, leaving Amaran alone in the grass.

Amaran could scarcely breathe. What would become of them now? What would happen to Elle? He jumped onto his horse, seized the reins, and raced toward the city.

Chapter 20—War

The rays of the setting sun chased Amaran back to the city. He returned to find the training yard boiling with excitement. With men running everywhere in full gear, no one noticed him enter. Commander Lanellon and his chief officers marched up to the front of the yard.

The soldiers went completely silent. Their eyes were glued to their commander, waiting to hear his news. Croff glanced over at Amaran with a face that said, 'Do you know what's going on?'

Knowing nothing, Amaran shrugged his shoulders and shook his head.

"My fellow Kallendrians!" Lanellon boomed. "News has just reached us! Following the incident at sea, the Albakranians have decided against returning the Plurian Territory to us. Now we have declared war against them. We must leave the city at once!"

Amaran felt his stomach twist violently before knotting somewhere in his lower gut. Some men were as shocked as he was, but others were enthralled with the news. To Amaran's disgust, he heard dozens of men around him holler their approval and shout with fists raised in triumph.

"Silence! There is more!" Lanellon paused a moment before continuing. "We have been given safe passage out of the city only if we leave by dawn, so we must quickly prepare our exit. Any who remain after dawn tomorrow must surrender as a prisoner of war. We leave tonight and make for the military stronghold in the Ecklandrian Hills, just south of the Albakranian border."

Just before the sun set, the soldiers started filing out of the barracks. Someone stopped Amaran and pointed behind him. "A special visitor for you."

He stepped aside and motioned the visitor inside. It was a woman wearing a hooded cloak. Her slender nose was barely visible from under the shadow of her hood, and a lock of reddish brown hair was curled by her cheek.

Her hair fell past her shoulders as she removed her hood. With a low-cut dress revealing much of her buxom cleavage and layers of dark makeup and eye shadow, Amaran barely recognized her at first. Soon he realized she was not, in fact, a harlot as he had first thought. She was Helanor, one of Elle's ladies.

"Sir," she said, once they were out of earshot of the other soldiers. "My lady Elle asked me to come to you. Something has happened, but she can only tell you in person. It is urgent, and she must see you tonight."

Amaran's heart pounded against his chest. Was she in danger? What else could be so urgent? He tried to calm himself, to think rationally about this decision. It was obvious to him that there was no decision to make. If she needed him—if she were in danger—he had to go.

Amaran used the mass exit of soldiers to hide as he fled the barracks. Instead of moving for the southern gate with the rest of them, he left through the eastern gate. Once across the drawbridge, he guided his horse away from the main road.

He took off for the woods beyond the eastern wall of the city, heading toward a stream bank. He followed the stream for a half mile until he found an entrance to a tunnel in the thick underbrush beside a mess of tangled roots. It was the very same tunnel he had discovered with Rallden when they were boys. He tied his horse to a tree and disappeared into the dark opening.

When he came to the palace end of the tunnel, he pressed his ear to the door, listening closely before opening it. He opened the door slowly and proceeded stealthily through the gardens towards the palace.

Moving behind a low building, Amaran climbed onto a wagon to help him reach the edge of the roof. He pulled himself up onto it. The guards atop the nearest tower did not notice because they were not watching the palace grounds, but rather the city streets beyond the walls. Crawling along the roof, Amaran stayed as low as possible to draw no attention. He finally ended up directly underneath the balcony outside Elle's chambers. Amaran leapt up as far as he could, just barely grabbing onto one of the stony outcrops protruding from the wall. He scaled this section of wall up to the base of Elle's balcony railing before pulling himself up and over the stone railing.

Once on the balcony, he walked up to the large glass doors, which were covered on the inside with curtains that fell to the floor. He rapped softly on the glass, hoping that she was inside—and alone. He waited a moment before knocking again. Anxious, but forcing himself to be patient, he stood in the shadows a short while longer until he heard the faint sound of footsteps growing louder. Amaran waited with suspense, hoping it was Elle. A face peered through the curtains.

"What are you doing here? Have you gone mad?" Elle demanded as she opened the door.

"Your message..." Amaran said, trailing off.

"What message?" Elle blurted out.

"Helanor came to..." Amaran trailed off.

"Helanor?" Elle asked, confused. "I didn't send her. I haven't even seen her today, come to think of it...."

Looking straight into Elle's eyes, he muttered, "It's a trap. It must be if you didn't send her to find me."

"I am happy to see you again, Amaran, but you must leave at once."

He nodded. "We are leaving the city. All the troops are being forced out tonight." A pause, and then, "This is goodbye."

"Oh, Amaran," Elle said suddenly, clinging to him.

"Elle, you were always meant to marry him and become Queen, not to love a Kallendrian soldier like me! I could never give you what he can offer you."

"I don't want to be Queen," she sobbed, "I don't want any of it. I want only to be with you. If only it could be...."

"Elle, Rallden will make you happy. He does love you, and you will learn to love him in time. I am sure of it."

"*Learn* to love him? Oh, Amaran! How can I marry someone I must *learn* to love? I love *you*, Amaran, not him. I will always love you."

Suddenly from the doorway came an awful noise, a startling crash. Elle instinctively lunged for Amaran. He in turn put his arms around her and pulled her to him. When she saw who had just burst through the door, however, she slowly backed away from him. She released her hold of him as she stared with ghastly paleness at Rallden standing in the doorway.

The veins bulged from Rallden's reddened face. Stepping towards Amaran, he snarled, "I told you, I warned you to stay away. Yet here you are, in her bedchambers of all places!"

Amaran stared fearlessly at him as Rallden continued. "We are at war, and you are my enemy! Do you understand, Amaran? I must have you seized and thrown into the dungeons. You will be killed!"

Trembling, Elle shouted desperately, "Rallden! How can you say such a thing? You are friends! You are like brothers!"

"How can *I*? How could *he*?" Rallden roared. "How could he betray *me*? You are mine, not his!"

With his jaw clenched, Amaran pulled his shoulders back. Slowly, he raised his head to meet Rallden's unyielding stare. "I told you already that we did not mean for any of this to happen. I was just telling her goodbye once and for all."

Rallden replied in an icy voice, "She was never yours to give up, Amaran."

"Guards!" shouted Murken, who had appeared behind Rallden moments earlier.

"Amaran, go!" shouted Elle.

The brazen look in Amaran's eye remained as he stared at Rallden. He did not take one step, however—even when the guards appeared.

The two guards grabbed him on either side and dragged him from the room. Murken looked satisfied. Rallden stared at the floor, fists clenched. Elle cried as Amaran disappeared from sight.

Chapter 21—A Desperate Escape

Amaran waited in the cell of the dark dungeon. He began to pace back and forth with his hand on his head, lightly tracing the outline of the bruised bump that protruded from his skin. The uncertainty of his fate gnawed away at him, fueling the growing sense of hopelessness. How would he escape? Would he ever see her again? Would he even be allowed to live?

His concentration was broken when he noticed a cloaked figure approaching. The figure was too small to be a soldier. It moved quickly down the passageway, looking from side to side the whole time. Amaran watched closely, trying to figure out who was approaching his cell. All of a sudden, he recognized her. It was one of Elle's ladies-in-waiting.

"What are you doing here?" he whispered.

"Shhh! Elle is in danger, but there's no time to explain. Let me see which one it is," she whispered, fumbling frantically through the keys that she pulled from her pouch. She tried one, then another, and found the third to be the correct key.

"How did you get those?" Amaran asked her, his head cocked to watch for approaching guards.

"I know the Captain of the Guard well. He thought I had come to—"

"Hurry! The guard is making his way back around again. He'll be rounding the corner any second." Amaran grabbed the bars of the door in anticipation. The second he heard the click of the key, he pushed the door open and slipped out.

They rushed down the corridor, watching everywhere for other guards. Just before they reached the end of the hallway, a guard walked around the corner, turning into their path. All three froze for a moment.

The guard hesitated for only a moment before crying out, "The Kallendrian prisoner has escaped!" He looked from Amaran to the young lady, and then back at Amaran before reaching for his sword.

But Amaran was quicker. He threw himself at the guard, grabbing the arm that reached for the weapon. The guard pulled back and away from Amaran and reached again, but Amaran's fist flew at him. The blow landed firmly on the guard's jaw, sending him stumbling into the wall. Before the guard could regain his balance, Amaran slammed his body against the guard and elbowed him sharply in the ribs. When the guard's knees buckled, Amaran's boot flew straight into the side of the guard's face, knocking him to the ground unconscious. Amaran grabbed the sword, snatched the guard's tunic, and threw it over himself.

"Come on!" he shouted.

Amaran pulled her around the corner and led her up a stairwell to their right. They flew up the steps so fast they were barely able to feel their legs moving underneath them. A guard appeared at the top of the stairway, blocking their path.

Amaran braced himself. Already one step ahead of Helanor, he grasped his stolen sword tightly and swung hard at the guard. The guard deflected the blow with his own sword. The rancorous clanking of swords then filled the stairwell, causing Elle's lady to cover her ears and cower in fear.

Having the advantage, the guard at top seemed confident, and came down on Amaran with forceful blows. But Amaran stood his ground, and waited for his moment—an opportunity to demonstrate the sword skills he had gained during both his training as a Kallendrian soldier and with Rallden in the palace. With one quick strike, the surprised guard's sword flew from his hands. Amaran plunged his sword into the guard's stomach.

Before pulling the sword back out, he yelled, "Watch out! Get against the wall!"

Amaran then pulled his sword out of the guard as he pushed him with his foot. The guard tumbled down the stairs, landing with a thud on the floor.

Only vaguely recognizing where they were, Amaran asked hurriedly, "Where do we go from here?"

"This way," she said.

Amaran followed her as she raced into a nearby room. Between breaths she gasped, "I rescued you not just to free you...but so that you could—so you could rescue Lady Elle."

Perplexed, Amaran looked at her.

"Once Rallden left the palace, Murken gave orders to execute you. Elle pleaded with Murken for your life, but when that got her nowhere, she fled on her horse...for the Rhalkadan Fortress to find Rallden."

"The Rhalkadan Fortress? She'll be killed! That road is right along the battle front!"

"She went to save you, Amaran. There was no stopping her. This was the only thing I could think to do. If only I had thought of it sooner—" she stopped herself suddenly. "Go down those stairs and through the door at the bottom. You'll end up in the stable yard. Please hurry!"

He flew down the stairs and disappeared through the door.

Spurring the horse on out of the palace courtyard, Amaran adjusted the Albakranian cloak to cover as much of himself as he could. As soon as he passed out of the city's eastern gate, he brought the horse to a full gallop, crouching low to its back. The horse kicked up dust and pebbles as it tore down the path. With his cape flying behind him in the wind, Amaran fixated on the road ahead, looking all about him for any sign of Elle. After four miles of finding nothing—not a sign of her anywhere—he slowed his horse down to save the animal's strength for what might be a long search.

After riding for more than fifteen miles, Amaran's fear was beginning to outweigh his hope. Getting closer to the Kallendrian border, and well into the heart of the war zone, he peeled off his Albakranian soldier's cloak. He tucked it into the saddle for when he would need it later.

After another mile up the road, something caught his eye. Along the roadside were two horses, one of which he recognized all too well. It was Elle's mare. He then noticed a Kallendrian soldier standing over something—someone.

Amaran veered off the road, and made straight for the soldier. He saw Elle lying on the ground underneath the soldier. She was not moving. "What are you doing with her?"

The soldier looked up at him as he started dragging her towards his horse. "You're Kallendrian, what's it to you?"

"You'll not harm her!" Amaran said, sliding off his horse.

"Why do you care what happens to her?" pressed the soldier.

Intending to scare him off, Amaran reached for his sword. "Back away and let me take her! She's hurt and needs care."

The soldier glanced down at Amaran's hand, which was resting upon the hilt of his sword. He hesitated a moment. Then his hand flew to his own weapon. He swung at Amaran.

Amaran pulled out his sword just in time. He deflected the blow as he moved to his side. He blocked a second strike from his right. When the soldier came at him yet again, Amaran meant to swivel out of the way, but instead slipped. The soldier came down on him, his sword outstretched. Amaran threw up his blade. The guard's eyes opened wide as he landed on Amaran. Then he coughed up blood. He had fallen directly onto Amaran's sword.

Amaran threw the soldier off of him and rushed to his feet. Dropping his sword to the ground, his face softened as he fell by Elle's side. He gazed upon her bruised face and limp body. Putting his head to her heart, he closed his eyes with relief when he found a heartbeat.

A tear came to his eye as he whispered to her, "Elle, I'm sorry this has happened. Don't worry...I'll save you."

He looked again over her body and, holding back all emotion, took her in his arms and draped her over his horse. He slung himself up and repositioned her so that she sat over his lap, partially cradled in one of his arms. Amaran grabbed the reins with one hand, and motioned the horse onward. He headed for the closest place he might find help: the Rhalkadan Fortress.

He spent equal time looking at her face as he did the road ahead. Each mile traveled seemed to take years, but on he rode, holding her close the whole way.

"What have I done?" he muttered to himself. "If only I hadn't been such a fool and gone to the palace last night...."

Finally he saw the Albakranian fortress in the distance. When he approached the gates, he heard the shouts of the guards ordering him to slow down. Amaran ignored the commands. He rode boldly forward through the entrance, saying, "I have the lady Elle. Don't shoot!"

The guards did not lower their crossbows until they realized that he had spoken the truth. "Lower your weapons! He does have the lady Elle!"

Another shouted, "She needs help! Call for Lord Rallden!"

Once Amaran slowed his horse, the guards helped Amaran with lowering her off of the horse. Two men emerged from the door of the central building of the compound. It was Rallden and Murken.

When Murken recognized Amaran, his eyes opened wide with surprise.

"How did this happen?" Rallden exclaimed, taking her into his arms. He pulled her closer as if to shield her from Amaran.

"She was on the side of the road. A Kallendrian soldier had found her. I knew this was the only place close enough to save her."

"Take her into the care room immediately. I will be there in a moment," Rallden ordered.

Amaran watched him hand the bruised, though beautiful figure over to the soldiers.

"Amaran," Rallden said through gritted teeth, "Why did you come here?"

"I could never have let her die, Rallden. She was hurt. There was nothing else I could do."

Rallden said nothing for a long moment, but he refused to look at his friend. Amaran could tell the wound was too recent. Finally, Rallden replied with only a nod to show his thanks.

Then Rallden said to his guards, "This Kallendrian leaves here today unharmed, untouched. See to it my orders are followed."

The one officer standing at his side nodded and then moved to the gate to relay the message.

Before he left, Amaran said, "She loves you, Rallden, and she will realize it in time. She will become a good queen."

Rallden closed his eyes, nodding ever so slightly. "Take care, my friend," he replied gravely.

Amaran turned and swung back on his horse, slowly this time and with a distant look in his eyes. Rallden turned also, heading for the room where they had taken Elle. At first watching Amaran with a thoughtful glare, Murken quickly followed Rallden inside the building.

By the time Amaran reached the front gate, Murken rushed back outside and yelled to the guards, "Stop him! He cannot pass through those gates! Apprehend the Kallendrian!"

"Sir," said the guard next to Murken. "Lord Rallden gave—"

"It is on his orders that I now act! Bring him to me!"

Amaran froze. Bewildered, he saw the guards close in on him. They yanked him off of his horse. He did not resist. His face was void of emotion. After his feet hit the ground, one of the guards shoved him towards Murken, who stared haughtily at Amaran.

"Bind his hands," Murken said to the guards who held Amaran.

Amaran looked Murken straight in the eye. "What is the meaning of this, Murken? Rallden ordered that I be let go!"

"You can't really think that he would let you, a Kallendrian, leave this fortress so freely." He let out a short sniveling laugh. "Rallden agrees with me that this is for the good of the kingdom. Since I gave him my word you would not be killed or thrown in the dungeons, he conceded. And I shall keep my word. You will not be killed. No, indeed. I have found something much worse than death for you...a living hell far, far away from this place."

"I don't believe it," snarled Amaran. "He would not have given such an order, I know."

"It matters not what you believe. Guards, put the prisoner in one of the holding cells until morning."

One Albakranian on either side, they dragged Amaran towards the prison building while he struggled to break free. Wriggling with all of his strength, he managed to get only one arm loose. He turned and faced the captain nearby.

"Tell Lord Rallden what's happened!" Amaran shouted to the captain. "Tell him that Murken has defied his orders!"

Two more soldiers approached Amaran to subdue him. One grabbed his free arm and the other punched him hard in his gut. Amaran bent over in pain. Once they chained his hands together, he was jerked forward and dragged across the yard. They threw him inside a small prison cell and slammed the door shut.

Hardly believing what had just happened, Amaran did not know whether Rallden had ordered his capture or not. And he had no idea what lay in store for him come morning.

He saw Murken's smile once more, sending chills down his spine, as he heard the advisor's last words to him: "I have found something much worse than death for you...a living hell far, far away from this place."

Part III

Chapter 22—Amaran's Destiny

Amaran worked hard as a slave nearly every waking hour for three months. His story came out during breaks and late at night. Harron was glad the story stretched out and eagerly asked to hear more. For Amaran, however, reliving the details made him dwell all the more on the injustice that had brought him to this hell.

Fostered in part by his hatred for the slave driver Bellok, he was obsessed with thinking about Murken and Rallden. The more he thought about them, the further he was able to escape from the horrors of his ruthless daily routine—but the more angry and bitter he became.

"It will continue to eat away at me for as long as I live, I think," Amaran said to Harron several days after he had finished his story.

"Hmm?" Harron mumbled, while swallowing a mouthful of cold stew.

"Murken ordered the arrest, but did Rallden know? Or was it Rallden's orders like Murken said? If it was Murken, how would he have gotten away with it? There wouldn't have been any hiding it from Rallden."

"You're probably right," Harron said. "It'll eat away at you for as long as you live. You think you'll ever find an answer? Might as well forget about it. Dwelling on it isn't going to do anything but make it worse. And if Rallden did do it, do you blame him? If you were in his place, would you have been forgiving?"

Amaran looked at him with surprise. After he paused in thought, he said, "Perhaps not. But if he did order it, he was a coward. He couldn't give the order while facing me?"

"If it was Rallden who ordered it."

Amaran nodded. "If only I hadn't been such a fool, I would never have ended up here. I betrayed my best friend, my country, my father...and I've paid dearly for it. I'm a slave for all eternity."

Harron shook his head in sympathy. "Life is unfair, that we all must learn, but perhaps your life isn't over. What if there is more? Perhaps it will take a turn for the better."

Amaran laughed. "Are you serious? You have always been optimistic, but perhaps the sun has started to affect your mind!"

A smile appeared on Harron's face, but disappeared just as quickly when he heard Bellok shout, "All right! Back to work!"

With a crack of his whip, the slaves scampered back to moving beams and hammering nails.

The next morning, Harron found Amaran sitting alone at the breakfast table. Amaran said nothing to him, and did not even look at him.

"What are you thinking about?" asked Harron, seeing the glassy stare in Amaran's eyes.

"Harron," said Amaran, still not looking at him, "you remember the dream I told you about...from when I was a boy."

"The one with the dragon," confirmed Harron.

Amaran nodded slowly.

"Of course. Why?"

Amaran waited a moment to respond. "I had the same dream again last night—or at least one quite similar to it."

"Oh?" said Harron. "What happened?"

"I was back in Albakran. I saw the dragon fly overhead, only this time I could see a desert city to the west, Kelishran I think, and an army of great warriors to the east. My father was beside me, along with Rallden, Elle, you, and others."

"All that thinking about your past has stirred up some old memories...and dreams," said Harron.

"Yes," replied Amaran, sounding unconvinced. "It was so strange—just like the first dream. It was so real, everything around me so clear, as if I were actually there."

At the end of the day, the slaves were corralled. But something rather unusual happened on this particular evening. A rider passing the slaves stopped his horse abruptly. Amaran thought the man was looking directly at him, but he knew he must be mistaken.

Tall with fair skin, bold eyes, and confidence etched upon every line of his face, the man approached on a handsome, snow-white horse. It was one of the finest stallions Amaran had ever laid eyes upon. The man wore a robe of tetrelia fabric, worn only by the wealthiest of lords. But it was none of the obvious signs of wealth and power that kept Amaran staring; it was the way the man looked at him.

Do I know him? Amaran asked himself. *He is certainly looking upon me as if he knows me.*

Finally, the man took his eyes off of Amaran and turned to Bellok. Amaran strained to hear what he said to the slave driver, but the din of the city around him drowned out the man's voice.

The man was still talking to Bellok even after every last slave had gotten into his wagon. It seemed as if the stranger were trying to convince Bellok of something. By now, Amaran had maneuvered closer to the front of the wagon, close enough to overhear their conversation.

"I've already told you no," growled Bellok. "I don't sell 'em, I just keep 'em in order. Now we've got to get mov—"

Bellok stopped short when he saw the man reach deep into his pocket and pull out a large pouch.

"You can count it, but there's more than enough there. It's probably three times what he's worth. Buy several like him to please your masters and pocket the rest."

Bellok's eyes opened wide. "There's gotta be almost four hundred hural in here! Why would anyone want a slave like him so bad?"

The man felt no need to answer Bellok. He simply turned and motioned Amaran over. "Come, young man. Come with me."

Confused, Amaran did not move at first. A shove from behind got him moving. "Go on," said Harron. "This might be your chance—a twist of fate."

Amaran turned to look at Harron.

"You know now I might've been right," said Harron. He added with a smirk, "Perhaps the sun's not affected my mind as much as you thought."

Amaran climbed slowly out of the wagon and approached his new master. He looked hesitantly up at him on his horse.

The wagon started up and rolled around the corner. He took one last look at Harron peering out from the rest of the slaves. Now alone, Amaran faced this stranger, unsure of what to do or say.

Looking down augustly at Amaran from atop his horse, he said, "I am sure you are wondering why I bought you, but in time. For now, you will accompany me to the inn where I'm staying tonight. We'll leave tomorrow morning for my home in Geldar. I will tell you more when we arrive. What is your name?"

"Amaran."

"Amaran," the traveler repeated, looking at Amaran as if he were a long-lost son. "My name is Leandros. Come up," the man added, holding his hand out to help Amaran up onto the saddle behind him. "He'll carry us both across the city. Tomorrow, though, we'll get you your own horse for the journey."

Though this man, Leandros, had told him nothing about himself or his reasons for buying him, Amaran did not complain or worry. It had been months since he had a good meal and a soft bed to sleep in, and tomorrow would be the first time in months he did not have to wake before dawn to begin his work.

The next morning, both men rode out of the city. Amaran rode the horse Leandros had bought after breakfast.

"Where in Geldar are we heading?" asked Amaran.

"I live just outside the city of Heliim. It is at least five days' ride from here."

As they followed one of the main roads away from Kelishran's western gates, Amaran stared out into the barren desert terrain. He saw a small ridge of bluish-gray mountains far in the distance. He guessed these were the mountains they would cross to get to Leandros' home in Geldar.

Amaran looked over at Leandros, studying him closely. Leandros had specks of gray in his hair, but youthful skin and a strong, lean frame. It made his age difficult to discern. He was obviously wealthy and undoubtedly confident, yet he also seemed quite humble. As Amaran stared at Leandros, he tried to figure out what exactly it was about him that seemed so unusual.

Who is he? Amaran thought. *What reason could anyone have to buy a slave like me as he did? And what of the way he looked at me so strangely...as if he knew me?*

"So tell me, Amaran, where are you from?" Leandros said, turning to look at Amaran. "You're not Valencian."

"I am Kallendrian by birth, but I lived in Albakran for almost eight years."

Leandros' eyes brightened with interest. "A Kallendrian raised in Albakran? An interesting circumstance considering the history between those nations, wouldn't you say?"

"My father was a Kallendrian commander. He took a post in the Albakranian capital, Balankor, because of the peace treaty. I moved there with him, and lived in the city up until only a few months ago."

Leandros asked Amaran questions about his past and listened with interest during the entire account. "Thinking of all that has happened to you, all the circumstances, the outbreak of war and your capture, it is a wonder things worked out as they did, is it not?"

"Exactly how do you mean?" Amaran asked.

"It is obvious you have experienced much hardship in your life. You lost your mother as a child, you fell in love with a girl who could never be yours, you sacrificed everything to be with her, and then you were arrested and sold into slavery. All of these things happened and yet here you are, alive and healthy, free from that horrid slave life, with a chance for a fresh start."

"I suppose," Amaran said, trying to sound convincing. "I am grateful I am riding on this horse rather than breaking my back under the whip of a slave driver in Kelishran."

"It is easy to focus upon the ill fortunes we find in life, but then forget those that strengthen us."

Amaran raised his eyebrows at him.

Leandros continued. "You were fortunate enough to be freed from the dungeons to save Elle. She could have died before you found her. When you were seized at the fortress, you were not killed. Instead you were taken as a slave—what I am certain seemed unbearable at first, but it eventually led you here. It was surely a better fate when considering what could have happened under Murken's orders at the fortress that day."

"It's true that my being freed from slavery is a far better providence than I could have wished for," Amaran conceded. "And for that I must thank you. But even so, I wonder why fate has dealt me all of these hardships. I have nothing now. Anything that I did have once is gone. I just don't understand why."

There was a slight pause before Leandros replied, "*Why* is not the question to ask. It doesn't matter why these things have happened to you. They have happened and there is no use in trying to understand why. Instead focus on how you deal with it, and what good might come of it in the end."

Amaran's tone became sharp. "I cannot see how any of it could possibly lead to good. How could all of this have happened to one man—to me? All I ever wanted was to live a simple, happy life like anyone else. Don't I deserve that?"

Leandros' face became stern and his voice deepened, though he did not sound angry in any way. "Tell me, do you know for sure that your life is more difficult, more tragic than any other man's? Can you say with complete certainty that these things you say you wanted would have brought you happiness?"

Amaran looked at him, slightly taken aback.

Leandros continued. "Do we exist for the sole purpose of making ourselves contented, focusing on only those things that we see as important? Or is there something else—something greater for which we exist? Something that, although intangible, is far grander than any we can comprehend?"

Leandros looked Amaran straight in the eye as he continued. Amaran wished to look away, but found it impossible to do so. "You can never know what lies in store for you—no one can. You do not know what will happen in the years to come or what good will come of what you have yet to offer the world. Some good *will* come from all of your suffering, I know."

When Leandros said this, Amaran was perplexed. What did he mean by, "some good will come from your suffering", and how could this man possibly know such a thing?

"You will understand what I mean soon enough, Amaran. As I have already said, there is a very important reason why I purchased you."

"The reason you chose me to come with you...," said Amaran slowly.

"Not exactly. You were chosen, but not by me."

"What do you mean by that?" Amaran asked, starting to wonder about his companion's sanity.

"You shall soon find out, my young friend," was all Leandros said in reply.

Chapter 23—Leandros' Home

After several days, the road eventually took them up onto a plateau, leaving the desert valley behind them. A day later they reached the foothills of the nearby mountains.

"There is the Baldrian Forest," Leandros said. A thick, emerald forest filled a nearby valley. Meandering through its center was a sapphire river that stretched westward to the great blue sea in the distant horizon.

By late afternoon of the fifth day, they reached the mountains that had only several days before been far in the distance. "The city of Heliim," Leandros said, looking down into a valley to their right. Speckled with lights, the city became more luminescent the darker the sky above it grew.

"Only several miles more. I live up there."

Leandros pointed to the top of a ridge that overlooked the valley. They wound up a steep pebbled road that cut back and forth up the side of the hill. Finally, at the top, Amaran saw the large manor house. Two sentries stood on guard. They bowed to Leandros before opening the gates. Once Amaran dismounted, he followed Leandros down a cobblestone path that curved up to the rear of the manor. Small torches lined both sides of the pathway.

The manor house wrapped partway around the landscaped grounds of the estate. There was a verandah that ran the length of the rear of the house, overlooking the gardens, which were impressive even in the darkness. A sculpted stone statue of a winged horse stood in the center of the gardens. Its body reared back on its powerful hind legs, its majestic wings stretched outward, and its head looked skyward.

They entered the house through a set of glass doors. "Well, Amaran, this is my home. I hope you will feel welcome. Frilo will show you where you will stay tonight."

A young, well-dressed man appeared. Nodding politely toward Amaran, he led him down the nearest corridor. He stopped at a door and said, "Dinner will be ready shortly. I will be back in a quarter-hour to escort you to the dining hall."

That night, as soon as Amaran had finished his meal, he returned to his room. He fell down on the bed without bothering to undress and fell asleep within seconds. He woke the next day an hour after sunrise, bathed, ate his breakfast, and followed Frilo outside.

"Leandros wants to see you. He is in the courtyard," Frilo said.

Amaran saw the gardens in their full glory as the morning sun shone down upon them. Perfectly pruned shrubs lined meandering pathways. Splendid flowering trees grew near a cascading waterfall. Crystal clear water fell into a small pool filled with neon green, fiery orange, and vivid blue fish.

"There you are," Leandros said from behind him. "What do you think of my gardens?"

"Impressive," he answered. "These put the Balankor Palace's gardens to shame."

Leandros smiled briefly before folding his arms behind his back. Drawing in a deep breath, he said, "Amaran, I told you that once we arrived here I would tell you why I wanted you to come with me."

Amaran nodded.

"The entire continent of Albantria is in danger, though most of its people are unaware. It is threatened by an evil power that was foretold many centuries ago."

"Evil?" Amaran asked, wrinkling his forehead.

"Come, walk with me," said Leandros. Following the garden path, he began. "Many centuries ago, when times were different, magic was more than a tale read about in books. It was quite common. Beyond magic, men had other powers, too—powers that people now would not believe. Among these was the power of prophecy, a gift bestowed upon only a small number of men in those days, those whom we now call the Ancient Prophets."

"The same who wrote the Ancient Texts?" asked Amaran.

"The very same. These prophets foretold a number of things, one of which was a great and evil power that would one day spread across the entire world."

"That sounds vaguely familiar," Amaran said. "I remember something about the Prophecies from my school studies. I don't remember much, though."

"Yes, I am sure that they would have been only mentioned...glossed over. The majority of scholars today regard them not as the factually-based accounts that they are, but merely as some interesting writings of ancient cultures."

"You believe they are true?"

"Absolutely," answered Leandros.

"Why would you believe that these accounts aren't merely legends like they say? Wouldn't the history scholars know what they're talking about? In fact, you are the first person I think I've ever met who believes they are true."

Leandros stopped at the edge of a fountain pool and turned towards Amaran. "Why should I *not* believe in something just because few do? Does that mean it cannot be true? And should it be dismissed solely for that reason?"

Leandros started walking on the path again, beckoning Amaran to follow. "If I knew of some grave danger of which few others knew, then no matter how unbelievable it may be do I not have a duty, a responsibility, to protect others from the danger? Or do I simply ignore my responsibility and let them suffer...merely because I doubt they will believe my warnings?"

Amaran could not argue against this.

"This is the dilemma we are faced with today."

"You mean protecting Albantria from the danger that it itself does not realize to be a threat?"

"Yes. There are signs given in the Ancient Prophecies that suggest the time of darkness is coming soon. There is much work to be done before the evil forces advance."

"What is this evil? How would other nations not recognize it if it is as grave a threat as you say?"

"You know of the Malakronian Empire."

"Of course. It is the strongest power in eastern Albantria. You think the Malakronians are evil?"

"There is a reason why they have become such a powerful empire in such a relatively short time. Many nations do not see the Malakronians as anything other than a very fast-growing empire. They attribute this young empire's success to their military strength and limitless resources in the Maldavian Mountains. If they had studied the Ancient Prophecies and taken the prophets' warnings seriously, they might recognize the signs. The kingdoms of today have all but forsaken the Prophecies, though."

Amaran looked at Leandros with uncertainty. "You mean...."

"Malakron is a powerful force lurking in the shadows, waiting for its chance to consume all of Albantria in a war like no one has ever before seen. The Emperor has untold powers, and soon he will begin calling the dragons to him. He will eventually use them as weapons to conquer the world. Kingdoms will continue to underestimate the Malakronian armies until they read and believe the words of the ancient prophets. Only then will they know what we know."

Amaran stopped short. "We? Who is 'we'?"

"Centuries ago, the world started changing. Men began to abandon the Prophecies. Soon, most had forgotten them entirely. Recognizing the importance of the Prophecies for the future, a group of knights joined together to form an order. This order's mission was to protect the Ancient Texts, to study them, and to pass the knowledge on to each new generation of knights. They hid the original scrolls in a secret, well-protected place. Studying the accounts extensively, they prepared for the day when the great evil would cover the world in darkness. They did this so that the texts would never be completely forgotten. For if none believe the prophecies or study them, how would they recognize the very evil that preys upon them?"

"Do these knights still exist today?"

"Yes," Leandros said with a smile. "I am one of them."

"You?" said Amaran with surprise.

"We call ourselves the Knights of the High Order. We are a secret society of scholars and warriors, committed to protecting the truth of the prophecies." Staring down at Amaran, he added even more solemnly, "And my hope is that you might join us."

Amaran looked at Leandros, uncertain of how to reply.

Leandros followed the path around a tall brick wall, and Amaran went behind him. Standing on a smooth-stoned patio with the brick wall to his back, Amaran approached a sparkling white railing in front of him. There he saw a stunning view beyond it: the majestic peaks of the mountains across the valley. With a few steps closer he saw that he was atop a high, steep cliff. In between this cliff and the mountains, far below him, were tiny buildings and streets.

"The city of Heliim," Leandros said, standing next to him. "Amaran, there is something else you must know now that you have learned about the Knights of the High Order. I told you on our journey here that I did not choose you, but that you were chosen — and that there was a very important reason for my freeing you."

"Yes," said Amaran.

"I've already told you that many centuries ago there were prophets. They could see the future in their visions. Though I can't believe it myself at times, I had a vision."

"You?" Amaran asked, raising both his eyebrows.

"Yes. I saw something very similar to what one of the ancient prophets described from his vision long ago. I saw you in this vision."

Amaran's jaw dropped. "What do you mean, you saw me?"

"I saw you," repeated Leandros.

"How long ago was this?"

"Months ago."

"But that's impossible, Leandros. You didn't even know me—"

"It was you. I told the elders of the High Order about it. They agreed that if it was truly a vision, I would not even need to look for you—you would find me. They were right. I could scarcely believe it when I saw you in the street the other evening. I knew it was time to bring you here."

"I would think anyone hearing this might think you were insane, but...."

"But you don't," finished Leandros.

"I have had several dreams myself—and they seemed so lifelike. When the first dream I had came true some time later, I could scarcely believe it."

Leandros listened with interest as Amaran described the dream and then seeing the dragon in the forest months later.

"What is perhaps even stranger is that the night before you found me," continued Amaran, "I had the dream again. It was similar, yet different. I saw the desert city where I was enslaved on one horizon, and a vast army on the other. Now that I have heard what you've told me, I wonder if it was the Malakronian army."

"It certainly sounds as if you have had several visions. It only confirms what I believe about you."

"Right," said Amaran dubiously. "Let's just say for a moment that I do believe all of this about me being the one you've been looking for. What does it mean?"

"In my vision, you stood up to the dragon who led the armies of Malakron. The dragon symbolized Malakron's emperor, Emperor Nalldron, and you were there to save the people from the Dragon-Emperor."

"Me?" laughed Amaran. "Leandros, this is absurd. I know nothing about all of this. I am no one important!"

"The Prophecies tell us that three Dragon Slayers will come along. I believe you are one of them."

"This is—it's preposterous. What dragons am I supposed to slay?" Amaran asked, shaking his head.

"You know as well as I do that they are waking, Amaran. You saw one yourself—and that was years ago. They are beginning to wake all across the continent. When the last of them awake, it will usher in a very dark time."

"What of these Dragon Slayers you spoke of?"

"The Dragon Slayers are said to possess the rare courage and skill to defeat the terrible fire-breathing dragons. I believe you have this gift."

"Because of your vision? Leandros, you can't really expect me to—"

"Choose not to believe, but you will be able to run from the truth for only so long."

Amaran looked at him with disbelief.

"The first Dragon Slayer fought dragons from the mountains which had been awakened by the Malakronian Empire more than a century ago. It is said that the second Dragon Slayer will come when the dragons wake again. When all of them have woken, the Emperor will begin his war. It will take years for his army to spread across the land and reach us here, but it may start soon."

"How can you be certain of all of this, Leandros?" Amaran interrupted. "You know this all from the Ancient Prophecies, but what if you're wrong?"

"The Prophecies are vague, and much seems to be symbolic. We can assume the Dragon Slayer will not only slay dragons, but also challenge the Emperor and his army. After all, dragons are the symbol of the Malakronian Empire. The Emperor's soldiers bear red dragons on their flags, tunics, and shields. It is even said that one day the Emperor will command the dragons and use them to achieve victory."

"So I am the second Dragon Slayer," Amaran said, looking at Leandros carefully.

Leandros nodded. "The signs are very clear."

"What of the third Dragon Slayer? You've spoken only of two."

"The last Dragon Slayer will appear during the dark reign of the Emperor—many years from now. When he comes, he will defeat the Great Dragon, Emperor Nalldron, once and for all."

After thinking a moment longer, Amaran threw up his hands and said, "What do I know about any of this? I know nothing about slaying dragons or fighting the emperor of a powerful—and evil—empire."

"You will learn. I cannot tell you what your exact role will be, but I assure you that it is your destiny to fight with us. If you join us, you will have a chance to make something great of your life. However, I must warn you that the path to becoming a knight is very difficult. What you must sacrifice to become one of us, a Knight of the High Order, is more than you can imagine. You will devote your entire life to our cause. Once you join us, there is no turning back. But I also see no way for you to escape your destiny. You must do this."

"Even if I choose not to," said Amaran.

"You have no choice. It has already been decided. This is who you are."

148

Amaran swallowed.

"There will be a meeting here with the other knights next week. I've just sent notice to them that I have found you. You will be confirmed as a Knight of the High Order in front of all of them."

"Then what?" asked Amaran.

"Then you will begin your training."

Chapter 24—Bitterness and Hope

"The Malakronians established their empire that long ago?" Amaran asked once he had finished reading about the history of the Malakronian Empire's rise.

"More than a century, yes," answered Leandros.

"Emperor Nalldron was alive then, and is still alive now...and from what I understand he is not an old, frail man."

"He is almost one hundred and forty, but he hardly seems old," said Leandros grimly.

"I have heard strange tales about him, legends of him being immortal, but I assumed most of it wasn't true."

"Nalldron learned much about the dark arts from a sorcerer— and it seems that he learned the secret of unnatural long life. He has become a man who does not age, a man with untold powers, and a man who commands one of the most powerful armies in all of Albantria."

While Amaran was busy reading the Ancient Prophecies over the next few days, there was also still much weighing on his mind. He thought of his father and his guilt over having left him. He asked Leandros about the status of the war, wondering about his father's welfare. He also thought of Rallden and Murken's condemning words. He was haunted by the echoes of the sounds of whips cracking behind him as he heard his former slave masters beat him. Amaran also thought of Elle; it was she whom he thought most about.

"Surely they brought her back to full health," he said often to himself. But there was always still a lingering doubt—small though it was—in his mind.

Two nights before the day of the knights' meeting, Amaran awoke with a start. He had heard a noise. Or at least he thought he had. It sounded as if it came from the hallway, but he was not certain. Then he heard it again: a sound—a voice—a familiar voice calling to him. The voice was soft, sweet, and compelling. It was Elle's voice. Without thinking it strange one bit, he got out of bed and made his way for the distant echo.

"Amaran...Amaran," came the voice.

As he followed it down the hallway he could not catch up to it. Even when he increased his pace, the voice was always just as distant as when he had first heard it. He followed the sound out into the gardens, but when he made his way around the corner of the house, he stopped short. He was no longer at Leandros' estate. It was not even nighttime. Instead, he was in a field of golden grass, looking at Elle.

Standing in the middle of the field with her hair blowing in the wind, she started walking towards him. He saw her delicate fingers outstretched toward him. There was desperation in her eyes—the eyes that had entranced him so many times before. Behind her, two boys played in the meadow. One was a Kallendrian boy and the other an Albakranian. He recognized them: it was Rallden and himself as young boys.

When Elle called to him, Amaran tried to go to her, but he could not. His legs would not move.

"Amaran, what is wrong? Why won't you come for me?" Her face was troubled; her smile faded. "Amaran! Come here!"

Amaran tried to shout to her, but no words came. He watched as her eyes welled with tears.

"Amaran! Please! I love you!"

He tried again to shout, but still there was nothing. He couldn't cry out or tell her how he felt.

Suddenly, two soldiers on horseback appeared. Swords outstretched, they galloped towards her. She screamed. Then he noticed that one of the men changed course and headed for another person in the fields: it was his father. His father also called for him.

Amaran cried out and was relieved to hear his own voice once more. "Father! Elle!"

He moved forward, finally realizing that his legs were no longer paralyzed. But as he ran to save his father and Elle, the distance between them increased drastically: first ten yards, then twenty, and then one hundred yards stood between them. Not knowing whom to save, he stopped running.

Then his father disappeared and the horsemen stopped charging. Elle now lay on the ground, pale, lifeless, but even more beautiful than he had remembered her to be. He watched as another Amaran, with a sword in his hand, stabbed the soldier nearest her. This Amaran seemed cold and heartless. He repeatedly slashed at the soldier's body, unaffected by the gruesome sight as he diced the soldier to pieces.

Amaran then took a step closer to where Elle lay on the ground, but he could not move more than a step. A pair of strong arms held him back. Amaran turned to find both Murken and Rallden beside him, laughing.

"You fool! You thought you could save her...and then have her for yourself, didn't you?" scoffed Murken.

Then Rallden said to him arrogantly, "You, a commoner? A Kallendrian? Did you think she would love you enough to run to you? No, my friend, she is mine! Elle is *my* beautiful wife! I will be happy with her, while you...you will have nothing!"

With eyes wide and nostrils flaring, Amaran screamed aloud, "Why? Why have you done this to me? I love her, and she loves me! Me!"

And then Amaran woke up. It was morning. It had all been a dream, yet still his heart was racing, his fists were clenched, and his mind was greatly troubled.

"I don't know if I will ever be able to forget it all," he moaned to himself. He walked over to the window, rubbing his temples. "Why did I allow myself to fall in love with her?"

Later that morning, while Amaran was looking down at Heliim from the balcony, Leandros approached him with a grave expression upon his face.

"Amaran, I have news to tell you." His eyes were sad and his voice severe.

"What is it, Leandros?"

Leandros hesitated briefly before saying, "Your father. He is dead."

Amaran's face lost all expression. "How?" was all he could muster.

"I heard it through a friend of a friend. I made a number of inquiries and just received word this morning. He died in battle. A massive Albakranian charge on the northern Kallendrian battlefront wiped out many of the Kallendrian troops. Few Kallendrians survived the battle."

Amaran looked into Leandros' eyes, seeing that Leandros quietly lamented with him in his loss. Then Amaran turned away from him and leaned on the balcony railing, looking out once more over the city far below.

"I am sorry, Amaran."

"You know, I never said goodbye to him, Leandros. I never spoke with him again. He died never having been able to say goodbye to his son...and perhaps he never understood why I did what I did. He died thinking his son was a traitor—and a coward. I deserve to die myself for being so selfish. I should have gone back to find him and tell him." At last, Amaran's face softened, and his eyes moistened.

"Amaran, you could not have returned. You know that. You think now that it would have eased your guilt, but it wouldn't have. Returning would have accomplished nothing. Your father already knew why you left. Nothing can be done now to change what has happened. Mourn your father's loss, but don't dwell on what you should have done differently."

When Leandros left him, Amaran remained alone, staring blankly out over the valley. Amaran lamented the loss of his father, but without tears or sobs. With sadness visible only in his distant stare, he gazed on the horizon as he said to himself, "So he is also gone. I now have nothing there...no reason to go back. My life is here now, and so here I shall stay. I will devote myself to the High Order and their cause. When they ask me, I shall have my answer."

Then he disappeared into the gardens behind the large stone wall.

Chapter 25—The High Order of Knights

The day of the meeting arrived. Two hours after breakfast Amaran heard the whinny of a horse near the front gates. A nobleman wearing a colorful tunic dismounted and made his way down the pathway. Another rider arrived soon afterward. Older and taller than the first knight, he rode a sleek black steed that marched triumphantly into the courtyard. The majestic creature wore a black riding cloak and its reins were a deep, vibrant yellow. The man was dressed in a black tunic with broad diagonal stripes that were the same vivid yellow as the horse's reins. He talked with the younger knight behind him as they moved inside.

Guests arrived over the course of the day, some alone, some in pairs. Amaran stopped counting once he got to around fifty.

An hour after the last knight arrived, everyone but Amaran moved into a large meeting room. The massive doors shut behind them, while Amaran anxiously waited in the foyer for when they would call upon him. An hour later, the door opened. Leandros appeared and nodded to him.

"We are ready to speak with you, Amaran."

Amaran felt a sudden surge of adrenaline as his heart raced and his breathing quickened. He followed Leandros into the room. The knights sat in chairs arranged in concentric circles, so that each of the guests was easily able to see whoever stood in the center. The oldest men sat in the innermost ring of seats, while the youngest sat in the outer rings.

All eyes rested upon Amaran as he entered. He followed Leandros to the center of the room, feeling the knights gazing upon him the whole while.

"Amaran, my name is Celdron," said the striking man wearing the black and yellow tunic whom Amaran had noticed earlier. The man's deep, rich voice continued, "Leandros told you about the history of the High Order of Knights."

"Yes, he did," Amaran answered.

"Very good. He said you have also read the Ancient Texts, and learned who we believe the evil power is."

Amaran nodded. "Malakron."

"Yes," said Celdron. "Their emperor is a powerful man. Evil surrounds him...it consumes him...and it has given him great strength. Using his dark magic, he is now calling the dragons to wake from their century-long slumber. Soon they will be everywhere across the Albantrian continent. This is a sign that the Great War is coming...and we need you to join us. Fight to protect the people of Albantria as Malakron sets its sights on the lands beyond its borders."

"What Leandros did not tell me yet was how we will fight Malakron. There are not enough of you to wage war against such a huge empire."

"We use any means we can. Though all of us are accomplished warriors, we do not fight unless it is necessary. Many of us are influential in our governments or have connections to those who are. We use our positions to guide kings as they make decisions, foil plots, and help in any other way we are able. This is our way."

"There is something I have been wondering..." Amaran said hesitantly. "If it is prophesied that the Evil Empire will consume all of Albantria as you have said, why do you try to stop them? If it has already been foretold that they would conquer the world and you wholeheartedly believe this, then why enter a war you can't win?"

"Should we admit defeat before war even comes our way, knowing the Malakronian Empire will find victory one day? Would it be better to give up and do nothing?"

"No, I suppose not...."

"There is another reason," continued Celdron. "If you remember from reading the Prophecies, Albantria will be conquered by the great army...but the Emperor's reign will not last. The prophets also tell us of his demise. Eventually one will rise up and deliver the people from the dark reign."

"And then there will be a time of great peace," said Amaran, remembering what he had read.

"Yes," nodded Celdron. "So we must continue to study the texts and teach those who will listen. We must be prepared for the days ahead, to recognize the signs as they come. We cannot abandon the prophecies for any reason, especially during the reign of tyranny. That is what you would help us do."

Celdron looked to another knight sitting in front of him. The elderly knight rose. His hair was white as snow, his face quite wrinkled, but his eyes were still bright and alive.

"Amaran," the old knight started, "all of us here have made a strict commitment to abide by the ways of the order. It is a lifelong commitment that is both highly rewarding and demanding beyond all scope of the imagination. We live every day of our lives to preserve the Truths and are willing to give our lives if necessary. Can you make such a commitment, to dedicate your entire life to becoming a warrior for the truth?"

Amaran felt his face grow warm when the eyes of all in the room fell on him. He was all too aware of the weight resting with such a decision. Yet, he did not hesitate further, knowing that joining the High Order was his chance to start anew.

"Yes," he answered.

The old knight continued, "Becoming one of the Knights of the High Order, the protectors of the Truth and guardians of the Ancient Prophecies, is not a calling offered to many. Do you understand the graveness of the decision before you?"

"Yes, I do."

"Do you understand that this will be lifelong servitude—something which can never be forgotten or abandoned?"

"I do."

"And that if you should accept the charge, you will begin your training immediately. You will forever remain in the service of the High Order to fulfill all of your duties as a knight."

"I understand."

"You will learn from your teacher, Leandros, who has been a successful teacher to many knights in years past. You will become a warrior endowed with skills that will make you superior to even the most formidable foes. Although it may sound like a glorious challenge, you will find it grueling at times. It will be no easy task."

"I understand these great responsibilities," Amaran said. "I am ready."

"Very well. I now act on behalf of all of the Knights of the High Order. Kneel, Amaran."

Amaran felt his heart in his throat, but he did not hesitate to obey.

The old man said in a loud, clear voice, "Do you, Amaran, accept the charge of knighthood?"

"I accept."

"Then rise, Amaran. Rise and let your fellow knights greet you."

Every knight stood one by one and walked up to Amaran to offer their congratulations. Leandros finished up the line.

"Thank you, Leandros," Amaran said. "Thank you for all that you have done—not only for freeing me but also for giving me a chance to have something to live for once more."

Leandros smiled briefly, nodding his head. As he started to walk away, he said from over his shoulder, "We shall see how thankful you are once you begin your training, my young friend. You will soon find a new meaning for dedication—and pain."

Chapter 26—The Training Begins

"Your first lesson will be a test," explained Leandros the next morning.

Carrying a jug of water and some food for the day, Amaran followed Leandros out of the gardens and onto a wooded path that eventually led them to the edge of a cliff. Reaching the edge, Amaran saw a steep slope that led down to a small, flat overlook. There he saw a pile of different-sized rocks.

"This will be a test of perseverance," Leandros said. "Physical training requires mental preparedness. This exercise, although physically demanding without a doubt, will be even more so a lesson in mental conditioning. Move each of those rocks up the path to where we are standing. Lay them down here." He pointed to a flat spot near the top of the sloping path as he added, "Do it once every day until you have finished moving every last rock within the allotted time."

Leandros took out a large hourglass filled with white sand. He tipped it over so the sand began to slowly spill downward and said, "Go! Time has already started!"

Amaran began down the sloped path. Trying not to slip on the sliding gravel, he held his arms out to help keep his balance. Scrambling down a natural step at the base of the path, he picked up a melon-sized rock to start. Amaran pulled it to his chest and started up the steep slope. Already sweating profusely by the time he reached the top, he dropped the rock on the ground as he glanced at the hourglass. About a tenth of the sand had already spilled into the bottom chamber.

"There is no way I'll finish in time," he grumbled to himself. "No one can move them all in such a short time. I am going to fail my first task."

Leandros looked him in the eye and said, "Well, then I guess this is over. You have already deemed it impossible and you've moved only one rock. I will tell you this, though: you will be the first of my pupils to fail this first test." With that he disappeared into the trees, leaving Amaran to continue with his task alone.

Amaran repeated this task every day, finishing a little quicker each time. He pushed himself to his limits, even when he felt he had no strength left. He eventually completed the task before the hourglass had finished spilling sand. When he realized he had finished, he could not believe his eyes. He raced back to the manor to tell Leandros.

"Good," was all that Leandros said. He then walked to the nearest wall, grabbed two swords that had been mounted on the wall, and led Amaran out to an area of open lawn. "You are now ready to begin. You have passed your first test, but I warn you: it was also the easiest. New challenges await you each passing day. You will, at times, think some of the things I ask you to do are impossible. I assure you they are not, and you must believe me in this. Remember your commitment to persevere through the training no matter what."

"I won't forget."

Leandros cast a look at Amaran that seemed to say, "We shall see...." Handing Amaran one of the swords he said, "We will begin skill training. First you must unlearn everything you have learned about the sword."

"Unlearn...everything."

"Exactly. You will never reach your full potential as a swordsman unless you learn another way. I shall teach you our way. Watch."

160

With that, Leandros began to move his sword in a series of smooth, yet undoubtedly deadly strokes, repeating each several times before moving on to the next. He did this slowly so Amaran could watch the way in which he moved his sword.

As Amaran studied his moves, he copied the motions with his own sword.

"No. Your elbow needs to be up more," Leandros corrected.

Amaran raised his elbow and continued on, but heard a few strokes later, "No. Higher. Elbow needs to be higher." Amaran modified his swing, but was corrected yet again.

"It must be perfect. Fundamentals are key to the swordsman seeking perfection. You cannot have even the slightest hint of a flaw in your stance or stroke. We will do this for years if that is what it takes to get it correct. We will not stop until you are able to perfect each of the strokes one hundred times consecutively. Now go."

Again Amaran continued. Within a few minutes he had managed eleven consecutive flawless strokes. After his twelfth, he heard Leandros grumble, "No. That last one was sloppy. Start over. There must be not a hint of error."

The lesson continued for over an hour, with Leandros repetitively, yet very patiently, correcting Amaran. Finally Amaran reached his one hundredth flawless stroke.

"There will be other expectations as you begin this next phase of your training. Do you see that small mountain visible just beyond the trees?"

Amaran nodded.

"You will run to that mountain every morning at dawn and climb to the top. It will improve your stamina, strength, and agility, and continue to toughen you mentally for the later stages of your training. Sword drills will follow that, and then at midday you'll study the prophecies and other books I find for you. More sword drills will follow for the afternoon—one thousand swings a day. When I am done with you, you will be a deadly warrior. You'll be able to kill even the largest, strongest man with your bare hands."

Amaran's second phase of training commenced at dawn. Already winded before he even made it halfway up the mountainside, climbing the steeper slopes near the top became excruciating. Completely exhausted after this, and with bruises and scrapes all over his hands and legs, he found the sword swinging practice that followed to be nearly as painful and twice as aggravating.

As Amaran swung his sword, Leandros walked along the paths, watching him from various angles. He yelled out to Amaran in a most unforgiving manner, constantly reminding him to focus more on his form, and ordering him to redo any improper strokes.

"If I ever see a swing as careless as the one you just took, you will restart your count—even if you are only one away from finishing!" Leandros yelled at one point. "You'll learn quickly that I will not tolerate laziness!"

During the course of that afternoon, Amaran grew to hate the voice of his teacher as well as the sight of his sword. By the time the sun set, he was nearing his eight hundredth stroke. He could barely raise his arm, and could almost not even feel it.

"Okay, the day is over," yelled Leandros from the center of the courtyard. "One thousand will have to wait for another day."

But Amaran looked at him and said stubbornly, "No, I am going to finish even if it takes me until morning. I cannot fail so miserably on the first day."

Leandros replied firmly, "No, Amaran, you need rest, or else you will not last the week. It is to be expected that you will not complete everything on the first day. Come inside."

Amaran refused. "Not with this. I have to finish." And so he stayed until long after the sun had set, repeating the strokes over and over, until at last he reached one thousand. He ate the cold leftovers from dinner before collapsing upon his bed.

The next morning, he awoke with a severe pain in his shoulder and intense aching in his legs. He winced in pain when he stood up and hobbled to the door, feeling the effects of yesterday's climb. Only minutes after Amaran set out for the mountain, his legs started burning. He felt a sharp pain shoot through his side. The rest of the trip up the mountain only got worse. He felt as if he would rather die than continue, but he did not stop. When he slipped on a rock, he cursed at his own weakness, but refused to admit defeat. Amaran clenched his teeth as he pressed on through the pain.

He found relief in an unexpected form. His anger for those who had helped destroy his life—Murken, Rallden, the slave drivers, and still others—gave him strength. He pictured the events over and over in his mind, those events that had forever changed him. And it was this that allowed him to persevere through the challenges of his training.

"If I fail with this, then they have won—they all will have won. I will do this, even if it kills me."

And so he continued without stopping until he finally reached the top.

Amaran found the rest of the day no less trying. When he fell asleep during his reading later that afternoon, he was rudely awakened by a book slamming the table just inches from his face.

"This is not a time for sleep," reprimanded Leandros. "It is daylight, Amaran. I told you to stop last night, but you didn't. Now is not the time to make up the lost sleep. Read."

Leandros had become not only stricter, but also a much colder sort of man in recent days. Amaran liked him less and less all the time.

Amaran eventually was able to finish the run and mountain climb without stopping. He made tremendous improvement with his sword drills, and had already grown stronger. Despite his success, he was

163

hard on himself. He became a perfectionist with his sword drills and rarely acknowledged his own improvement.

Seeing praise as a detriment to his student's progress, Leandros never praised Amaran for his success. Yet, he was nonetheless impressed with his accomplishments. One day, as Leandros watched Amaran practice with his sword in the courtyard, Frilo approached.

"I have never had a pupil like him, Frilo," Leandros said.

"He certainly has improved much over the last few months," agreed Frilo. Noticing the scars on Amaran's back from the many floggings he had received as a slave, he said, "He has been through a lot but is determined like no one I've ever seen before."

Leandros turned and looked at his servant. "He is still angry and bitter deep down, but he is healing. There is something inside of him that drives him on, though. He will not let himself be defeated by any challenge I've given him. And he seems to enjoy the pain and suffering he endures each and every day."

Chapter 27—Laila

One spring day, Amaran sat at a table with several books, a pad of paper, and a pen in his hand. He moved aside *The Fakrevian Wars: An In-Depth Study of Military Strategies* and opened *The Demise of the Ancient Relakranian Civilization.* Amaran now looked very different from the young man who had been freed from slavery. His neck was noticeably thicker, his jaw line more defined, and, with broad shoulders and strong arms, he looked like he could tackle a bear.

Leandros entered the room and sat down at the opposite side of the table. "After nearly a year of intense training and studies, we're going to begin a different sort of lesson today."

Amaran raised one eyebrow.

"We have neglected something that is a cornerstone of becoming a knight of the High Order. It is imperative that we develop the skills to build connections in society. Our connections in government and various social circles are incredibly important to carrying out our missions. I have found the perfect teacher for you. You'll begin today."

"Who?" Amaran asked curiously.

Leandros offered a rare, beaming smile. "You have practically been a recluse, training alone every day for nearly a year without any interaction with the outside world. A knight needs to be capable with his sword, but he also needs to be eloquent in his speech and able to command respect from his peers. For the good of the Order, he must achieve status in the highest social circles."

Half an hour later they were on their way.

"Relkaren is a member of the Order," Leandros said on the way down the winding mountain road. "You will begin your lessons at his house."

"He will teach me then?" Amaran asked.

"No, not him...his daughter Laila. She is a young lady close to your age. Not only is she very well-educated and a good teacher, she is also quite lovely. You should very much enjoy your lessons."

"Oh?" Amaran said skeptically, noticing a slight smirk on Leandros' face.

"You will learn about cultural traditions in Heliim and elsewhere in Albantria, and you will also become familiar with various dialects from the southern kingdoms. We will go to his house on the last day of every week from now until you learn all there is to know."

A half-hour after they passed through Heliim's gates, Leandros stopped his horse at a large stone house with white gables and shutters. Amaran followed him through an open black iron gate and into the circular drive that curved around to meet the broad steps of the front entrance. A tall, fair-haired man emerged through the doorway.

"Greetings, Leandros. Welcome, Amaran. Come in," the man said, beckoning them in.

"Good to see you, Relkaren," Leandros said warmly.

"It is good to see you, too, friend," he replied, walking swiftly into one of the rooms at the far end of the foyer.

An attractive woman about the same age as Relkaren sat in the chair nearest the door. Her hair was reddish brown, but looked like it had once been a deeper, fierier red. Her smile was captivating.

As the lovely woman stood and turned to face them, Amaran noticed Leandros' expression suddenly change. Amaran had never seen Leandros become flustered as long as he had known him. He could not describe the look on Leandros' face in any other way, though. Relkaren's wife and Leandros locked eyes for a moment longer before the awkward silence finally broke.

"It is good to see you, Elendra," Leandros said to her, bowing deeply.

She offered a sincere, though slightly uncomfortable smile as she curtsied. "It is good to see you again, Leandros. So good."

"And here is Laila," announced Relkaren.

Amaran thought no more about the strange interaction between Leandros and Elendra, for he was too distracted by the beautiful girl standing in the doorway. The tall, blonde-haired girl walked gracefully into the room. As he gazed upon her striking beauty, many thoughts suddenly flooded his mind. She looked nothing like Elle, yet still, somehow, Elle came to mind.

"Hello again, Leandros. It has been quite some time," she said. Turning towards her other guest, she said, "Hello, Amaran. It is nice to meet you."

"It is nice to meet you as well—Laila." He was so nervous he had almost forgotten her name, but remembered it just as he was about to awkwardly end his sentence.

"Laila will be a fine teacher," boasted Relkaren. "And she is quite eager to make the acquaintance of a handsome young man such as yourself."

As Relkaren said this, Laila shot him a quick look. "Father, please," she said through her teeth.

"Well, there is much to do, so why don't you get started, dear?" Relkaren said, ignoring her reprimand.

"Of course," she replied, glancing once more at her father before turning back to Amaran. "Follow me, Amaran."

He followed her out of the room and onto a long balcony that wrapped around the back of the large house. She walked proudly, her head held high as she looked straight ahead of her. She was undoubtedly a very attractive girl, her eyes an alluring green with locks of golden hair falling about her rosy cheeks. Laila was also self-confident—and this intimidated Amaran.

Once they reached the outdoor patio, Laila broke the silence. "You must forgive my father, for he is very forward and expresses too freely what he is thinking—mostly wishful thinking." She shot Amaran a piercing glare as if to stave off any ideas he may have had about her.

"Oh, well, that is fine. I did not think anything of what he said. Not really."

She looked at him doubtfully, but moved on. "It was certainly not my idea to be a part of this, you must understand. I am doing it only because my father insisted."

"Oh, I see," said Amaran, shifting uncomfortably in his seat. He glanced across the patio where Leandros had just sat.

What had Leandros gotten him into? Why had he picked her of all people?

"If you are ready, we will begin now," she said quickly.

Before he could even answer, Laila had already started.

Whether she disliked him or simply hated having to sacrifice her time to do this, Amaran did not know. Perhaps it was both. He could not blame her. Despite her apparent disgust for the situation, however, she took the matter of teaching him very seriously. She was, as her father had said, quite knowledgeable, and did a good job of explaining every last detail. She even quizzed Amaran after she finished each segment to ensure he was listening.

Admitting she had been coerced into teaching him along with her stern demeanor was unsettling to him at first. But Amaran soon began to change his opinion of her. She was beautiful without question, but there was more to her than beauty. Everything she said that should have annoyed him made him smile, and her brusque manner made him like her all the more—why exactly he could not understand.

"No," she scolded, when Amaran answered one of her questions incorrectly. "That is not what I said. Were you listening to me?"

"I was, but—"

"No, you weren't. If you had, you would have answered correctly."

The angry retort made him smile. He could not help himself.

"Why are you smiling at me like that?" she asked. Her cheeks turned pink. When she realized she was blushing, it only made the color spread and deepen.

"I'm sorry if I made you uncomfortable. I simply—"

"There is no need to apologize," she said primly. "You did not make me feel uncomfortable. I was just curious why you were smiling when I said nothing funny. If you are not going to take these lessons seriously, then I will simply tell Leandros and my father that...."

A sudden thought ran through Amaran. He knew she had no legitimate reason to be angry with him. He had done nothing that awful. The only thing that made sense to him was that she was nervous, and this was her way of masking her fear. He had been intimidated by her at first, so was it not possible she had been also?

Amaran felt his confidence grow considerably at that moment. "I smiled only because I found your reprimanding me quite charming," he explained. "I have never been scolded by any lady as lovely as you."

She blushed more severely this time. Amaran thought he noticed the slightest sign of a smile—but it was difficult to tell because she had looked back down at the book she was holding.

"Are you ready to continue, Amaran?" she said sternly. "Or must you continue with your silly attempts at flattery?"

"I speak only the truth, Laila," he said, looking directly at her.

She looked nervously away for a split second before clearing her throat. "Very well. Let's continue."

169

Their session had lasted for more than three hours when Leandros waved to them from the other end of the patio.

As Amaran rose from his seat, he turned to her. "Thank you for your efforts today, Laila. Even if you don't agree, I think I've learned a lot from you."

"Good day, Amaran," she replied matter-of-factly. "I shall see you next week."

"I am looking forward to it," he said.

"I am sure you are," she replied. Her unyielding seriousness finally broke as a genuine smile appeared.

When Amaran saw that smile, it sent his heart racing—a feeling he had not experienced in quite some time. He had to make extra effort to pull his eyes away from her.

Chapter 28—Leandros' Story

In the days that followed their trip into Heliim, Amaran continued his training. Leandros introduced him to other methods of combat each week, while Amaran also continued his daily readings. On the last day of each week, Amaran had his lessons with Laila. Each time they met, Laila warmed a little more to Amaran, and they both secretly began to look forward to the day of the lesson. The fifth time they met, Relkaren brought Laila to Leandros' home.

"He's in the courtyard," Leandros said to Laila.

She turned around the corner and saw Amaran. He was just pulling his shirt over his head after finishing his sword drills. Laila stared at the long red lines that ran jaggedly across his back. She was unable to pull her eyes away from the hideous scars until he turned and saw her looking at him.

That afternoon they walked about the gardens as Laila instructed Amaran in a new language.

"It is pronounced El-*Arr*-Dea," she corrected. "Stress the second syllable, roll the r, and then finish up the last 'dea' as one quick syllable."

"I'm glad you think my pronunciations are so humorous," Amaran said playfully. "But I insist that last time I did say it just like you did."

"No, Amaran you didn't. You are not stressing the second syllable enough and you are saying the last 'dea' at the end as if they are two syllables, which they are not."

"But they are two syllables—two vowels, Laila. How can I say two different vowels in one syllable?"

He then said it again, this time making a deliberate attempt to stress the second syllable in a much exaggerated fashion. He contorted his face as he blurted out the last part of the word as quickly as possible—all in order to squeeze the letters into just the one syllable as he had been instructed.

"Yes! That was it!" Laila said excitedly. "Although I hope you don't have to make the face you just did to speak every word correctly." She held back a smile as she added, "Or else I think I might prefer your mispronunciations and horrid accent."

Grinning back at her, he said, "I feel like that's what I have to do in order to speak the language correctly."

"I am sorry for making fun, Amaran. I know you are trying, and I suppose you really are progressing quickly. It is just so funny to hear your pronunciations! But I love to hear you speak the language just the same."

Despite knowing the word love was not intended in a romantic way, it stirred something within him. It was how she had said it. He looked over at her to find her looking back at him, now with a different smile.

He looked away, but feeling her stare still on him turned back to her and asked, "Well, what are you going to teach me next?"

Her eyes sparkled but she did not answer immediately. At that moment, he suspected that she saw more in him than simple friendship.

"I suppose we should continue with more Ladrian words." She walked close by his side, almost brushing up against him as they moved down the flat stone path.

As they walked, Laila cleared her throat. "Amaran, I wanted to ask you...but I don't know if I should."

He looked at her. "My scars?"

Seeming ashamed, she nodded.

"As if I needed a reminder of my slave days, I have those to ensure I never forget."

Her mouth popped open in shock. "I—I am sorry, I didn't know. Do they hurt?"

"No, they don't hurt, but they are a painful reminder nonetheless. Back then, I thought I would never again be free. That's where Leandros found me and saved me, you know."

"How did you become a slave?" she asked reticently.

He hesitated before finally saying, "Someday, maybe, I'll tell you my story."

While they continued on with the lesson, Amaran did so without the full focus of his mind. They walked along the paths, and she spoke words as he repeated them over and over. Amaran tried to focus solely on the new words, but he found it impossible to keep from gazing at her. He watched with delight as she spoke each word and her eyes grew brighter whenever she laughed.

It was also then that he realized how lonely he was. He craved companionship, the touch of a beautiful girl's soft hands in his, the exhilaration of a kiss once more....

***

"She is quite lovely, is she not?" Leandros said later that day.

"She is," Amaran admitted, looking down at his boots.

Leandros looked at him questioningly. "You agree, but you sound reluctant to admit it. She is one of the most sought-after ladies in all of Heliim, you know."

"I am not surprised."

"What is it, Amaran? Why are you so hesitant to admit your feelings for her?"

"My feelings?"

"Yes," Leandros answered. "There is no mistaking it. It is quite obvious, especially when you are with her."

Amaran sighed. "I don't know why I am so afraid. I do care for her quite deeply. I suppose I fear what might come of this. She is beautiful and charming. I am drawn to her like I never thought I would be drawn to anyone again. The last time I felt like this about a girl, though...."

Leandros waited a moment before offering his thoughts. "You have put much of your past behind you, but you are still healing, I know. It is time to put Elle behind you, too."

"Maybe it is," Amaran said glumly. "But what if I was to fall in love again and she did not love me in return? I don't know if I could stand to lose another like I did Elle."

"You cannot avoid love because you fear loss. What happened with Elle is in the past. Don't deny Laila the chance that she and you both deserve. Laila can be more than a teacher to you," continued Leandros. "She can be a friend, a comfort, the beginning of a fresh start. I did not choose her only because she would be a good teacher, you know. I told Relkaren my thoughts, and he liked the idea."

"I see," Amaran said, thinking about everything that Leandros had said.

"Let's say that Laila did not love you in return. Confessing your love and desire for her would hurt your pride, but what else? Forget your pride! To have such a proud heart and be so self-absorbed...it can impact your life more than you might think."

"How would—?" Amaran started to say, but quickly thought better of it.

"How would I know? Believe me when I say that I know better than any man how one foolish decision, one rooted in pride, can have significant bearing on the rest of your life. I would hate to see you make the same mistake I did."

"You?"

"When I was a young man about your age, I fell in love with a young lady. Although my father was a nobleman, my family was not as wealthy or powerful as hers. Her father made it very clear that I was not good enough for her and he refused to let me marry her. I planned to do whatever I could to improve my status to win her father's approval. I joined the Geldarian army, earned medals for bravery, and was soon promoted to captain. Her father did not care.

"I left the army and studied under a successful businessman in Heliim. Before long, I was out on my own, making my own investments. I became very rich—and still her father cared nothing for me. I continued my quest for winning my lady's hand in marriage. Yet somewhere along the way I became too blind to see that my obsession with becoming rich and powerful had less to do with love and more to do with impressing her father—and others I met in my new social circle.

"A longtime friend, a girl I had grown up with, tried to help me see this. I hated hearing the truth, and I said some regrettable things to her. I hurt her terribly. She was a good friend to me—and always had been. I was not. Despite how cruel I had been to her, she still insisted on remaining friends. She continued to advise me. She even comforted me when my lady—the one I had pursued fruitlessly for so long—finally married another man."

Amaran interrupted. "This friend of yours, she loved you. It seems obvious."

Leandros sighed, his eyes dark. "Yes, she did. Fool that I was I realized it too late. She was the perfect mate for me—a good friend who truly loved me. When I finally realized the truth, that she loved me, I knew I loved her, too. But it was too late. She had grown tired of waiting for me, and accepted a proposal from another man in Heliim. He also was a good friend of mine."

As Leandros said these last words, Amaran opened his mouth and said slowly, "This girl, I know who she is. I think it must be."

Leandros did not turn to look at him. "Yes, you have met her before."

"It is Elendra, Laila's mother. It was her, wasn't it? It was Relkaren that she was engaged to when you finally realized you…."

"Yes, it was," Leandros whispered. A moment later, he turned and left Amaran on the balcony.

Alone again, Amaran thought about what Leandros had told him. What a sad story! It explained a lot about Leandros—why he had never married. Amaran had always wondered about it but never dared ask.

Hearing the story prompted Amaran to reflect on his own life, knowing that he had pitied himself for far too long. He had allowed himself to dwell on his own misfortunes instead of any good that had found him. He now had a home and he was becoming a part of something truly great, something that would have exceeded any dream. Perhaps there would be even more good to come his way—if he gave her a chance—if he gave himself another chance for love. Maybe there was a possibility of happiness once more.

Chapter 29—The Mountain Path

One day Leandros and Amaran rode down a path Amaran had never traveled before. "Today you begin yet another phase of your training," Leandros said. "You have physical strength and the necessary foundations for becoming a fine swordsman, and you have increased your knowledge on a great many subjects. Still there is much to learn."

They passed through a grassy alpine meadow and then moved up a steeper path. Soon Amaran heard the roaring of river rapids. When the path narrowed to where they could no longer ride two abroad, Leandros pulled his horse off to the side. Tying the horse to a tree, he said, "We walk from here."

Amaran followed him up a sharply climbing footpath. It ended near a cliff ledge. Amaran looked out upon a gorge. Below, the fierce, white rapids of the river crashed into dozens of giant boulders along the base of the chasm.

Behind Amaran, twenty feet from the ledge, Leandros walked over to a thin log propped up across two boulders. "Jump up and balance yourself, then walk across this beam."

Amaran looked at him, perplexed. "Will it hold? It's quite thin."

"It will. It is strong wood. Now go," he said impatiently.

Amaran jumped up, found his footing, and started slowly at first. He picked up speed as he carefully stepped from one end to the next.

"Was that it?" he asked as he hopped off, cocking one eyebrow as he looked back at Leandros.

"Now do it blindfolded." Leandros pulled out a cloth and wrapped it around Amaran's head tightly so he could not see. Again Amaran jumped up, taking a second or two more to steady himself this time, but moved across with similar ease and almost as quickly.

"Very good. No problems with your balance at all. You are ready to begin then. This way."

Amaran followed Leandros to the edge of the gorge. They walked a quarter-mile to where the gorge narrowed considerably. There was a long, thin, fallen tree, stretching across this narrower section of the gorge to the opposite side.

Amaran looked hesitantly at Leandros. Slowly he approached the edge and looked out over the ravine. Below, the water raged.

"With ease you demonstrated your ability to move across such a log, and you shall do so again, only with a distraction."

"Leandros, this is—surely you don't want me to—"

"Surely it is. Do you think I would have brought you all this way for nothing?"

"No, but—"

"Of course not. Now go. It is easy—as you have already proven to both of us. In fact, the tree is slightly wider than the practice beam you just mastered. You just need to focus yourself on the challenge and not be distracted by the potential danger below. That is the purpose of this exercise."

Amaran thought once more about the task and then briefly about the height at which he stood. He mustered up enough courage to stand upon the end of the log. Taking a deep breath, he took one step forward. However, he could not take another step. With his heart racing, his knees trembling, and his stomach queasy, he slowly lowered his eyes down the sheer cliff-side. Far below him, the river roared as its rapids violently crashed against the rocks.

"Perhaps you are not ready for this yet, Amaran?" Leandros said derisively.

Instead of responding, Amaran closed his eyes and swallowed. He desperately tried to quell his fear so he could concentrate—and so his legs would stop shaking. Yet, no matter how hard he tried, how many times he envisioned himself crossing successfully, he was unable to move another step. The ground below him seemed to spin.

"It is no different from what you did on the beam back there." Leandros' tone was reprimanding.

"No different except for what's below the log," Amaran pointed out.

"It does not matter, Amaran. You are walking on the beam itself, therefore it does not *matter* what is below it. Focus on the log and ignore the gorge, for it is of no consequence to you at all, as long as you stay balanced."

"Yes, Leandros, I understand that. But it is the thought of danger that makes it impossible."

"Impossible," Leandros scoffed with a disgusted look upon his face. "Surely you do not believe it is impossible. But if you do, then your training is done. If you want to continue, you must complete the task; there is no choice in the matter."

"I cannot cross it, but I also cannot quit. I have to complete the training."

"There are only two options, Amaran. You either master *this* task or you do not. If you want to complete your training, you must cross the log."

"But how can I?"

"Practice. Practice on the beam over there until you become so at ease you can move across like you would on solid ground."

Amaran shook his head and said nothing as he walked past Leandros and towards the log he had practiced on. He began walking back and forth, first slowly, then quickly, hands outstretched, hands at his sides, repeating it over and over in every way he thought possible. This went on for some time.

"Ready to try now, Amaran?" Leandros asked, while looking towards the log-bridge.

Amaran's silence was his answer.

"Very well, then. Let's return home. We will try again tomorrow. You will practice on the beam every day until you are ready to cross the gorge...even if it takes years. Come, it'll soon be dark."

A quiet Leandros and a disgruntled Amaran left to find their horses.

***

"It is such a lovely day, isn't it Amaran?" Laila asked later that week.

"It is," Amaran replied. "It's too nice a day to waste studying."

"Oh, Amaran, you know you enjoy our lessons. Admit it," she said playfully, nudging him with her elbow.

Laila walked closely beside Amaran. She looked frequently at him as they made their way along the central garden path behind Leandros' manor. Amaran also watched her. He admired the elegance of her steps and the way her golden locks fell by her cheek to frame her perfect face.

"I was thinking of wearing my hair like this tomorrow at the dinner party, only perhaps curling it some here—and here. What do you think?" she asked with hopeful eyes.

Amaran took a long pause before saying, "It is perfect, Laila. I'm sure you will capture the attention of everyone there. You will certainly catch every man's eye...and all the women will be jealous."

"Thank you, Amaran," she replied, smiling. "That is nice of you to say."

Laila turned to her right, making her way to the gazebo in the corner of the gardens. As she walked down the path, she looked over her shoulder, noticing that Amaran had hesitated a moment in following her. Laila reached out for his hand and tugged on him, and then squeezed his hand as she dragged him to the gazebo. "This way, Amaran."

Inside, Laila stopped and turned towards him with a coy smile. She looked up, holding Amaran in her gaze.

"Amaran, I have never told you this before, but I am so glad we were introduced. Aren't you glad that Leandros thought of me to teach you? Now we can be such good friends." Her cheeks rounded with her eager smile.

"I am glad," he replied. "I look forward to these lessons, I really do."

She smiled as she sat. "I couldn't wait to see you this morning." Her voice was full of joy, but she quickly added, "If that's not being too forward."

"No, it isn't," he said, sitting next to her. "I feel the same way."

Her smile widened as she looked up at him again. She slid her arm through his, then gently laid her head down upon his shoulder and rested it there while humming softly to herself.

Amaran placed his free hand over hers, clasping her fingers. He tried desperately to contain the wild beating of his heart, fearing she might feel it pounding against his chest. He felt his face grow warm and his hands become sweaty.

I cannot hide my feelings anymore! I must tell her how I feel, he thought to himself.

She picked up her head and looked directly into his eyes. He leaned in closer to her as she moved towards him. But then they heard Relkaren calling for Laila.

Laila's smile evaporated and her eyes closed. "Oh…" she started with a groan.

"I hoped that they might have quite a lot to talk about this afternoon," admitted Amaran. "But—we shall see each other again tomorrow night—at the party."

Her smile returned immediately, almost as wide as before. "Yes, we will. You are right—and I will be looking forward to seeing you there."

She looked deep into his eyes as she moved towards him. Her face flushed, she leaned in closely so that her breasts brushed against his chest.

To Amaran's great surprise, Laila closed her eyes and brought her mouth to his. Her supple lips pressed against his as she delicately enclosed his lower lip with her mouth. His heart thumping, Amaran kissed her back.

After the second kiss, they stood looking at each other for a moment. Then she turned and ran towards her father. She glanced over her shoulder as she moved down the path.

Amaran smiled broadly, just like the very first time he had fallen in love. Walking back toward the house, he thought, *I will not be able to stop thinking of her until I see her again tomorrow.*

***

Amaran followed the steep trail to the gorge on a late summer day, making his way to the log-bridge. He approached the fallen tree that lay across the huge chasm. As his heart raced and his breathing quickened, he stepped forward.

When he neared the edge and heard the deafening roar of the river below, he doubted his resolve. But he quickly reminded himself that he had decided that today he would conquer this challenge. He would cross the bridge no matter the outcome.

"I have nothing to lose, nothing to fear," he said to himself.

His eyes blazing with determination, he took one step onto the log. He took two more steps, leaving the comfort of solid ground behind him. Far below the narrow bridge, blurry in the background, Amaran could see the river rushing fiercely. Still he continued, boldly taking yet another step away from all assurances of safety. After one more step, Amaran felt his confidence grow. He now moved at a steady though slow pace along the log, making his way to the center. The wind blew about him and the roaring of the current echoed upwards.

Amaran felt almost as if he were not in control of his movements. Nonetheless, he felt better about each step he took. It was not the impossible task it had first seemed; it simply required the initial will to leave the safety of the cliff's edge.

Once he reached the opposite side, he closed his eyes and sighed deeply, silently expressing the sheer joy in his accomplishment. He then clenched his fists in triumph. "I have done it. Finally. I know there is nothing that can hold me back—nothing."

He turned back to stare at the log for a moment before marching to the cliff's edge again. He took one slow step onto the narrow overpass and started his return trip across the gorge. Still cautious, but with considerably more self-assurance and grace, he made his way back again. As soon as he hopped off of the end of the log, he was startled to hear a voice.

"I see you've finally found the courage. It's about time. I was beginning to wonder if it might ever come."

"I've finally made it, yes," he replied to Leandros.

"Now you must work on your sword skills here, over the gorge. Be conscious of your footing. Go slowly at first, and always strive for perfection in every swing you take."

Amaran did as Leandros instructed every day. Standing on the fallen tree bridge, balancing above the raging river hundreds of feet below, Amaran swung his sword skillfully, gracefully, working to perfect each stroke that he had been taught. Flashes of light flickered off the metal of his sword as it sliced through the air and then rose again over his head with blazing speed.

Amaran continued his training with full force. Weeks passed into months. Seasons came and went. There were new challenges each day which required endless focus, but he pressed on. Motivated by his new love for Laila and his commitment to Leandros and the other knights, nothing could stop him. His training became his passion. With eagerness he awaited the time when the world would need the Dragon Slayer. That time was near.

Chapter 30—Pharon's Plan

A large castle sat atop a steep hill in the Albakranian countryside. Its crenellated walls and high watchtowers rose high above the rocky outcrops of the surrounding steep slopes. A winding road led to the front gates of the fortress.

Inside the castle, two men sat inside the central keep. One man was older, about sixty, with mostly grey hair. The other was a tall, robed man with thick eyebrows and dark eyes. His head was bald and his face shaven—though a dark shadow covered his beard line where the stubble began to grow again. He also wore several rings on his fingers indicating he had both wealth and a position of authority. He was lord of this castle.

Just then, there was a knock at the door.

"Come in," said the lord.

"Lord Pharon," replied the man who opened the door.

"Temeran," Lord Pharon said. "Please, sit!"

"Thank you, Lord Pharon," he said, taking a seat across from the older man.

"Temeran, you remember Valken."

Temeran nodded, glancing at Valken. Clearing his throat, he began, "My lords, things are progressing as well as we had hoped in the capital, and perhaps better. Just as we had anticipated, Mildren has officially accepted his seat upon the Royal Council, something that may help our cause immensely. He is well-liked and has much experience in politics, but his moral standing is...shall we say...less than exemplary."

"He should be easy to manipulate you mean," offered Valken.

"It is even better than that." Temeran smiled. "You see, I just discovered that several of his recent investments have turned sour. It is rumored that he will sell several of his manor houses, certainly a sign that he is desperate for money."

"We'll see just how desperate he is," Pharon interjected with a grin. "If he is as much as I think, it will be one more seat on the council for us."

"So there will then be three councilmen who are at your mercy to vote as you would have them," Valken said thoughtfully. "Three in addition to your two longtime allies who already sit on the council. Then Maldock, if another spot on the council opens up, will give us yet another."

"Oh, don't you worry, Valken, there will soon be another council seat open," said Temeran.

"And as soon as it opens, Maldock will win the seat easily," said Pharon. "He could give us the sixth seat we've been long waiting for. He is very young, yes, but he is so charismatic, and after his heroics in the Kallendrian War he is too popular to not win. The nobles should give him his seat and forego the voting."

"Despite the fact that they know nothing about his politics and allegiances?" asked Temeran.

"It's exactly that ambiguity that will help him," said Pharon. "Most of the council won't look past his being a true Albakranian hero. He's pulled the wool over their eyes."

"Not all of them," said Valken gruffly. "Not Haldegran or Lapellium. They seem wary of him."

"And if all goes according to plan, one or both of them won't be around all that much longer, will they?" Pharon smiled.

"Speaking of...," said Valken, looking up.

"Yes, they've agreed to our terms," answered Temeran. "A final word from us and they'll move forward with the deed."

"Good." Pharon said, nodding his head.

"When we choose the exact time, we'll give them confirmation," said Valken.

"Yes, once we have control of at least half the Royal Council," said Pharon. "And when that happens—"

Valken finished his sentence for him. "Then we shall no longer need to call you *Lord* Pharon."

A devilish smirk slowly spread across Pharon's face as he turned to face the window. Gazing upon the landscape that stretched for miles about, he spoke in a deep voice. "Then all of Albakran shall be mine to rule."

Chapter 31—The Final Task

One morning in late fall, when the air was noticeably cooler and the trees had lost their leaves, Leandros approached Amaran in the gardens.

"Today marks the end of your training," he began. "You have learned much and perfected every skill that I've taught you. One thing remains: your final task. When you complete this, you will prove your worth to the council and be a true Knight of the High Order."

"What is my task?"

"Climb Mount Arashellar, in the mountains to our north. At its summit you will find and bring back a fruit from the Lanerra tree. Upon your return you will plant a seed contained within the fruit. Though it will not grow like it does atop Arashellar, and will most likely bear no fruit, it will grow to be a symbol of your commitment to the High Order of Knights."

"How will I find it?"

"Its magnificent splendor makes it unmistakable. Once you see it, you will have no doubt you've found the right tree."

"So that's all? That's my task? To find this tree and bring back one of its fruits?"

Leandros was solemn. "Amaran, this task may sound simple, but do not underestimate any mission. The road to the mountain is long. It is an arduous journey for any man, no matter how strong and prepared he might be. Beautiful though they are, there is danger in those mountains."

He looked at Amaran as he continued. "What danger awaits you, I cannot say, but be cautious, brave—and remember all that you have been taught. You should leave today."

Amaran left at midday down the northern road towards the mountainous wilderness. He traveled into the evening hours, stopping only to give his horse time to rest and drink when they found access to a brook. By sunset, he was no longer on the road, but instead on the grassy, sloping terrain of an alpine meadow. Above his head he saw a giant eagle soaring with its enormous wings outstretched. Herds of white, wooly mountain sheep scampered up the rocky slopes in the distance.

By dusk, he reached the base of Mount Arashellar. Knowing that the terrain would become more treacherous with every step forward from that point on, he decided to stop for the night. Amaran tied up his horse and draped a thick canvas over several boulders to fashion a makeshift tent. He settled in quickly under this shelter, knowing he would have to wake early the next morning to cover plenty of ground.

When the morning light crept over the mountaintops, Amaran had already eaten his breakfast. Soon he was on his way, riding up the lower slopes of Mount Arashellar. After four hours of ascending increasingly steeper slopes, Amaran saw a suitable place to secure his horse. He tied it under an outcrop of rocks to protect it from the weather, gathered some grass, a quickly disappearing commodity the higher they traveled, and placed it within reach of the animal. He left his other belongings with the horse, and began the rest of his climb with only his weapons and a small sack upon his back.

Amaran's climb became more strenuous the further he traveled. Soon he was using all four of his strong limbs to clamber up the cliff. He grasped protruding rocks and pulled himself up with his strong upper body. The higher he went, the colder the air grew, the fiercer the wind blew, and the more barren the landscape looked. Despite how far he had come and how many cliffs he had scaled, there was always another cliff awaiting him around the next bend. He thought he might never reach the top, and daylight was fast disappearing.

Soon, the slope led him to a path. Amaran followed this gradually ascending path for a while, only to find that it narrowed considerably as it curved around the outside of the mountain. With each passing minute he was forced closer and closer to a ledge thousands of feet above the rocky ground below. Amaran moved on a trail so thin there was room for only his two feet and not an inch more.

Finally the path widened again, but his relief was short-lived as he soon found himself immersed in fog. The cloud covering this mountain was so dense he could see nothing. Panicking at his sudden blindness, he stopped short in between steps to allow his eyes time to distinguish what was ahead. He proceeded forward, feeling the ground with his foot before stepping.

Just as he took his third step forward, however, something made him stop. He saw it move ahead of him, something large enough that he could see it even in this dense sea of mist.

As his eyes adjusted, he could make out what looked like a pile of dead tree branches a dozen feet in front of him. He stepped closer to examine the branches, his heart beating rapidly. They were not just small branches, but whole portions of tree stacked lengthwise in what appeared to be a ring. At this point it dawned on him: he was approaching nothing other than a nest—a huge nest.

He saw the movement again, observing what appeared to be a very a large wing flapping inside the nest. *A giant eagle's nest. I'd better get moving before mother returns.*

He walked by the nest slowly to make as little noise as possible, but right before he had passed it, he heard a strange noise. It sounded nothing like a bird. Looking wide-eyed at the nest, he saw a reptilian head. A sickening sense of fear washed over him.

The only reptiles that live this high up in the mountains are—

And with that thought, the nervous feeling in his stomach gave way to that of sheer terror.

Chapter 32—Atop Arashellar

Dragons. Dragons were the only logical possibility. They nested on cliffs like these. A nest of dragons right in front of him, and he had not one idea as to where the mother—or father—was.

He hoped that these nestlings, which were already almost as big as him, would remain calm and quiet. Tip-toeing stealthily past the nest, he cringed at the occasional squawking, guttural noises coming from inside the nest. Then it happened. The baby dragons began to screech loudly all at once.

Amaran thought they had heard or smelled him. But he realized soon enough that they screeched because something was returning to them. He sprinted for the next closest boulder as he heard the growing sound of gigantic wings flapping.

The sound grew closer with each second. Soon he saw a shadow through the mist that covered the cliff ledge, blocking most of the evening's light. Terrified to the point of paralysis, he hoped the beating of his heart was not as loud to the dragon as it seemed to himself. From behind the rock Amaran saw the tops of two massive, outstretched wings.

Suddenly, an awful noise pierced the air. The sound resembled that of the nestlings, but it was lower in pitch and more powerful. He was sure he had been detected.

Amaran felt the pounding of ground-shaking footsteps coming closer. Searching around for a means of escape, he knew his only choice was to leave the safety of the boulder. Just as he had started to move, the dragon's massive head peered over the rock. When

Amaran saw its huge, golden eyeballs looking down at him, he scrambled out from behind the boulder and sprinted down the path.

The gradually darkening sky lit up behind him. He also smelled smoke—a lot of smoke—but Amaran did not dare turn around to see how close behind him the flames came. The lingering light from the dragon's fire helped him in one way: it illuminated the otherwise dark path ahead. Now seeing clearly what was ahead of him, he dashed down the narrow trail. To his horror, he realized that it ended abruptly several yards ahead.

He shot back around to see if the dragon was behind him, and at first saw nothing. Then he heard the roar of the dragon directly above him. It was hovering in the air, eyeing him hungrily. If he was going to survive this, he would have to do some quick thinking.

Amaran looked to either side of him before scrambling between two large rocks jutting out from the cliff. Though this spot hid him from the dragon's view, he was still somewhat vulnerable. Yet, it was exactly what he needed. He had a plan. It was risky—but it was nonetheless a plan.

The dragon swooped down closer to him and hovered above the small crevice. It thrust its head forward while snapping its jaws, trying to extract Amaran with its huge teeth. Amaran was able to pull himself further into the crevice, just out of reach of the monster's snout, only to watch it back up and lunge for a second attack. This time, however, when the dragon moved towards him, again coming extremely close, Amaran thrust his left hand upward forcefully and with lightning speed. Holding onto a dagger he had just grabbed, he plunged it deep into its lower jaw.

It pulled its whole head back violently, clawing at the blade embedded in its flesh. Amaran took advantage of this distraction. He pulled himself up on top of the boulders. He then picked up a large, sharp rock and hurled it at the dragon's head. When it hit the dragon directly in the eye, the dragon shrieked in pain and crashed into the side of the cliff with one of its wings.

The dragon was hurt, but not enough to forget Amaran. The great reptile looked directly at him as it swooped down. As it came closer, Amaran noticed something. It had a small tear in one of its wings. He drew his sword.

Just as the dragon was about to reach for him with its talons, he ducked and rolled to his side. He sprang back up to his feet, and swung at the dragon's leg. The powerful blow sliced open the inside of its thigh, ripping through scales and exposing raw flesh.

The dragon stopped its charge. Anticipating this, Amaran made his move, his hands tightly grasping his sword. Before the dragon even noticed, he thrust his blade through the wound in the wing. Then he used all of his strength to bring the sword across the leathery skin, tearing it like a curtain.

The dragon roared, its cry shaking the entire mountainside. It pulled its wing away, and stumbled backward on its hind feet.

Seeing the dragon was off balance, Amaran charged forward. He pulled his sword back. Using every last drop of strength, he thrust it forward. It punctured the armored belly of the beast. He withdrew the blade quickly, and stabbed the same spot again.

It let out a deafening cry, a piercing wail that echoed off the rocks. The dragon tried to take flight, but instead crashed to the ground, collapsing onto its belly. It was not dead, but it was mortally wounded. The dragon lay motionless on the ground, its eyes following Amaran closely.

Amaran looked into the dragon's eyes and felt sorry for it. It was obviously suffering and he could not bear to look at it any longer. Still hearing the nestlings shrieking, he turned quickly and headed for the cliff before the other parent returned. But he stopped himself there. After closing his eyes, he turned around and saw the fallen beast still looking at him. He drew his sword quickly, stepped towards it, and raised his blade above his head. With a mighty blow, he swung down on its neck. A second swing sliced off its head. It suffered no more.

Waiting not a moment longer, Amaran ran for the nearest boulder and climbed on top of it. From here he scrambled up a steep incline to another outcrop of rocks. His legs feeling like jelly, he scaled the rocky wall of the mountain. At one point gravel beneath his feet began to give way. He slipped, but caught himself on a tree root that stuck out from the cliff's side.

He tugged on the root to test its strength before pulling harder on it. He then pulled himself up and over the lip of the cliff top. The sky was now dark, but he could make out just enough to see what he needed. There were no more cliffs around or above him, only below him. He had reached the summit.

Amaran saw nothing but a few boulders and the lone silhouette of a tree, which he hoped was the Lanerra tree. Being unable to tell for sure in almost complete darkness, he decided that he would wait until dawn. He looked about for a suitable place to rest near the boulders and curled up to sleep. He planned to sleep for only an hour at a time to make sure no dragons stalked him, but once he fell asleep he did not wake until morning.

When daylight appeared on the eastern horizon, Amaran woke with a start. He leapt to his feet and walked towards the tree. It was magnificent—a tree no more than twenty feet in height, but with a thick trunk, twisted at its base. It had uniquely smooth bark and waxy, dark green foliage. Seeing this ancient tree growing atop an otherwise barren mountaintop, he approached it reverently. There were large, round, purplish-red fruits growing on the underside of the leaf clusters. He pulled a sack from the bag on his back, plucked one fruit from the tree, and dropped it in the sack.

Amaran returned in the evening, two days after he had left Arashellar. He and Leandros planted one of the seeds of the Lanerra tree behind the gardens while Amaran told Leandros about his adventure.

When Amaran finished telling him about killing the dragon, Leandros became very serious. "Now there is no doubt in my mind you are him, Amaran. You are the second Dragon Slayer."

Amaran shook his head. "I am no hero. I'm just a Kallendrian who happened upon all of this."

"Just a Kallendrian soldier who I saw in a vision before I ever met you. Amaran, the vision was clear. The Great Dragon wore the Emperor's crown and threatened a large city, just like in the Ancient Prophecies. Also like the Prophecies, a young man courageously stood against the Dragon-Emperor to save the people before the army returned to devour them. That young man was you."

"And now that I have killed a dragon...."

"There is no question. Few have ever killed a dragon, and no one has in the last hundred years. If the dragons are already nesting on Arashellar, they are waking everywhere. It means the Emperor is indeed ready to begin his war. I hope you are ready, Amaran. Things are changing."

Chapter 33—The Dragon Slayer

"I am glad you are back, Amaran," said Laila brightly. They were walking through a meadow on a crisp, clear autumn day, only two days after Amaran had returned. "Had I known about what you actually faced on that mountain...!"

"No need to worry anymore," Amaran said, squeezing her hand.

"No, not now anyways," she said with a sigh, "but you are to leave again soon, aren't you?"

Before either said anything more, an earsplitting cry filled the air. They both looked up to the sky.

"Get down!" Amaran yelled. He shielded her with his outstretched arms as she scrambled behind the log beside them.

It flew across the sky like an arrow, its giant wings flapping. The dragon was coming straight for them. Laila flattened herself along the ground as Amaran drew his sword.

"When I tell you to run, head straight for those trees behind us—as fast as your legs can carry you."

The dragon stretched out its legs and opened its claws. It looked like it was about to snatch Amaran in its talons. Amaran stood his ground, ready to strike the dragon as it came closer. To his surprise, it flew over him and landed behind him. He pivoted round to find it pinning Laila to the ground with its great talons.

"No!" he yelled. "I'm the one you want! Come get me, beast!"

The dragon did not move, instead staring hungrily down at Laila. Amaran charged forward. He pulled his sword back and sliced hard across the dragon's leg. The sword barely penetrated the scaly armor.

The dragon raised its front left leg and swiped at Amaran, but he ducked just in time. Coming up underneath it, Amaran thrust his sword forcefully into its underside. Despite the force of his swing, the blade did not go in deep. It left a shallow gash in the dragon's chest. The wound was just severe enough to make the dragon pull back in pain.

When it moved, Laila was able to break free and scramble to her feet. Before she had run two yards, the dragon swiped at her with its front leg. The talons, as sharp and long as sabers, cut through Laila's side.

The pain would have been excruciating, but she did not cry out. The dragon's blow knocked her unconscious, and she fell hard onto the ground.

She didn't move. Amaran saw the blood on her dress. His heart pounded against his ribcage. With fury, he rushed towards the dragon again. He swung his sword as hard as he could. This time the blade pierced the scales. Blood spurted from the wound.

The dragon raised its front leg to strike back. But Amaran was ready. The beast left its underside exposed for a brief moment. The earlier stab had left a gash in its chest. Both hands on the hilt, Amaran plunged his sword straight into the open wound. The blade went deep.

The dragon pulled back, clawing at its chest. Then it came back down again on all four legs. The ground shook under its weight. It started heaving, its throat glowing. Smoke billowed from its nostrils. The dragon lowered its head as it prepared to release a firestorm upon Amaran.

There was no time to waste. He used his entire upper body to power his next blow. His hands dropped fast, his eyes on his target. The blade sliced through scales and flesh on its neck.

There was a low growl as the dragon stumbled forward. In that pause, Amaran saw Leandros racing down the hill toward them.

Amaran raised his sword high and swung down again. More of its neck had been cut open. Its body wriggled, but it could not move its head or legs. The light in its eyes began to fade. With one more blow from his sword, he severed the head from the body.

Amaran raced for Laila. Leandros was already there by her side, examining her motionless, pale body. His face was grave, his eyes dark. He looked up at Amaran and shook his head slowly.

"Laila! It's all right now! I've killed it!" Amaran cried out to her as he fell beside her. "She was hit hard, Leandros. She's still unconscious and—"

"Amaran," Leandros said in a low voice.

Amaran knew what he was going to say. He could not hear it, though. He did not believe it was true. "No, Leandros," he said. "She is okay. It struck her only once. She's wounded, but she can't be— she will wake."

Leandros' silence angered Amaran. "Why are you saying nothing?"

"Amaran," Leandros said again. "She will not wake. She—she has no heartbeat."

"You're wrong!" Amaran pressed his ear to her chest, listening intently for proof that Leandros was wrong. He heard nothing, yet still he left his ear upon her breast, clinging to the hope that there might be some miracle.

"Laila!" Amaran cried. Cradling her in his arms, he wailed, "Laila! Come back to me!"

He had not noticed until that moment how much blood there was. His hands were covered in it. Her dress was soaked with red. Blood pooled beneath them both, and it stained his own clothes.

"My poor, Laila," he moaned. "Why, why, why?" he repeated over and over. His throat tightened, and his eyes burned. Tears fell as he wailed over her lifeless body.

Leandros placed his hand on Amaran's back, and said with great pathos, "I am sorry, Amaran. I tried to get here fast enough, but it came too quickly. I heard it, and then I saw it in the distance. I came as fast as I could, but...I am sorry."

A week later, Laila's body was laid to rest. Once Amaran had returned to Leandros' manor house that afternoon, he retreated to the balcony overlooking Heliim—where he often went to think. His mind was blank with pain. He could hardly stand it.

After some time, Leandros found Amaran and stood next to him.

"Leandros, how could this have happened? Where did the dragon come from?"

Leandros hesitated, seeming afraid to say what he was thinking.

Amaran noticed. "What?"

"You found a nest, but killed only one of the parents. Dragons are very protective of their young."

Amaran shook his head. "You're not saying...."

"It is unlikely there is more than one nesting pair on one mountain. I am surprised, too, but I can think of no better explanation. That was the mate of the one you killed. It must have tracked you back here."

Amaran became pale. "So if I had not slain the first, this would never have happened. This dragon would not have come to find me and—and done this!"

Leandros sighed. "I don't know, Amaran. What I do know is that the life of the Dragon Slayer will not be an easy one. He must sacrifice much—including those he loves most."

"So this is the price I must pay to fulfill my destiny. I didn't ask for this. I want nothing to do with it. I'll take happiness and a simple life—and Laila back in my arms...." Amaran hung his head and wept silently.

"Losing Laila was tragic, and I am sorry, Amaran. But you are the Dragon Slayer, and your work has already begun."

Chapter 34—A Threat to the Throne of Albakran

Time passed. Amaran mourned but slowly grew used to the idea that he would never see Laila again. He would hear her voice no more. Her kiss, her tender touch, her warm embrace—they were merely things of the past.

Life had been sweetened with Laila's presence. Since her death, he had resigned himself to the fact that happiness was not for him. Bitterness began to harden his heart, allowing him to replace his grief with a desire to focus only on finishing his training. The High Order would call on him soon, and he would be ready. He had endured too much to give up. And he could not let Laila die in vain. He would avenge her death by doing whatever he could to fight the evil that had woken the dragons.

On one bleak winter day, when it was cold and windy and the skies were grey, Leandros came to Amaran. "The news is not good in Albakran."

"What's happened?" asked Amaran.

"One of the Royal Councilmen was found dead, and the circumstances raise many questions. You'll hear more when the other knights arrive. There will be a council meeting here early next week."

The knights arrived on the first day of the following week. They congratulated Amaran on the completion of his training, and marveled at how different he looked from when they had first met him some years before. Now twenty-six, he was no longer a boy but a full-fledged member of the council, a Knight of the High Order.

"My fellow knights," Celdron began. "You have all heard about the death of the royal councilman in Albakran. Although he was old, his death was unexpected. Many believe he was poisoned. And now, a young, charismatic nobleman named Maldock will take his seat. Most know little about his political allegiances, but the Order believes he secretly supports Pharon. As many of you remember, Pharon is the descendent of one of Albakran's former kings—of the Grelleck bloodline. He is also believed to be behind the royal assassinations years ago—in what many believe was an attempt at reclaiming the throne for his family."

"You mention Pharon for a reason, Celdron. Answer the question you know that we all want to ask," said a tall, bald man with a deep voice.

"Yes, Krevold," replied Celdron. "We believe Pharon is involved in the councilman's death."

The knights murmured among themselves as many turned in their seats.

Another knight spoke from his seat. "With Maldock now a councilman, that gives Pharon influence over a quarter of the royal council."

Celdron looked at him but did not respond.

"Isn't that right, Celdron?" asked the same knight. When Celdron failed to answer again, the knight added, "No? More than a quarter?"

An elder knight named Balkar stood. "There are three we know to be Pharon loyalists already on the council, but we've been watching Lord Mildren, who only recently joined the council. He was preparing to sell several of his manors, but, after a visit to Pharon's castle, a large sum of money was deposited into his accounts. He's managed to keep all his property."

Many knights vocalized their anger.

"That still is not all," said Balkar, putting his hand up to quiet them down. "Another councilman was also seen with Lord Pharon. We have strong reason to believe his allegiances have also been bought by Pharon."

A knight named Karamir stood. "So with this new councilman Maldock, that gives Pharon influence over half the council! Six of twelve are at his mercy!"

Balkar nodded as Celdron replied, "It is true. Which is why we must watch the six loyal councilmen and the king closer than ever. King Bardane does not have the majority of the council to back him anymore. As we know, since Rallden is not his direct heir, Bardane needs a majority to approve Rallden as his successor. With only six loyal to him, Albakran would be closer than ever to seeing Pharon seize control...should anything happen to King Bardane."

"You speak as if there is imminent danger to King Bardane's safety," said Krevold. "I know Pharon wants Bardane gone, but is that a real threat at this point? Killing an old councilman is one thing, but the King of Albakran...."

The elders nodded to Leandros, who rose and cleared his throat. "Unfortunately, Krevold, there is a real threat. The assassin who poisoned the councilman is part of a much bigger plot. At least two other assassins have been in contact with Pharon. One of our own, Pellonum, was tracking them, but he disappeared."

"You're saying that there is an active plot to kill the King of Albakran?" Krevold demanded.

"Yes," Leandros sighed. "Against the king and probably at least one more of his councilmen."

"When? Where?" one knight shouted.

"How can this be?" cried another.

Celdron answered them. "We believe Pharon has been working for years to plan this carefully, but we know very little about the plot. There may be more than two assassins, and we don't know exactly who their targets are—but we can guess. As for when, we suspect the summit...the Western Albantrian Alliance Summit next month."

"Pharon is more powerful than we realized," said Karamir, "To have repopulated the council so efficiently, to time everything just right...."

"Yes," said Celdron slowly. "But he did have help. He has a powerful ally."

The room fell silent.

"Malakron," said Celdron ominously. "Several of the Emperor's agents were seen crossing into Albakran. They met with one of Pharon's men. The Malakronians would do whatever they could to see Albakran overturned by civil war, and so they are helping Pharon seize the crown."

"It is no surprise to any of us that the Emperor has been plotting something," Leandros said. "We did not know what, however."

"Not until now," said Krevold, shaking his head. "They are making their move."

"Yes," said Leandros. "We have seen more dragons in the west. You heard that they are nesting here in the mountains of Geldar, and that Amaran has slain two. The increasing presence of dragons in the western lands is one of the signs from the Prophecies. Next comes a long war in the east as Malakron invades its neighbors. Lastly, Emperor Nalldron and his armies will come for the western kingdoms. He has already started an effort to weaken the strongest kingdoms in these lands with his plan to help Pharon. It will make his invasion all the easier when war reaches Albakran."

"What can we do about it?" asked Krevold. "What is our response?"

"That is the question we all must answer today," said Celdron.

"So it is decided," declared Leandros once the Order had agreed on its plan. "With the information we have, we do not know who we can trust in the king's inner circle. As such, we will discreetly position some of our own in Balankor. Balkar will arrange for those chosen to accompany the Geldarian Ambassador, Galfarr, to the summit. As his guests, they will search for the assassins and keep watch over both King Bardane and the Royal Councilmen. They will try to find and kill the assassins before they are able to kill the king."

The seven elders met behind closed doors to discuss which knights would be best for the mission. Shortly before sunset, they reached a consensus. Leandros walked toward the doorway and called to Amaran in the hall.

"Amaran," Celdron began, once Amaran entered, "your first mission as a Knight of the High Order has been decided by this council of elders. You will accompany Leandros to the capital of Albakran. It will be your responsibility to do whatever you can to protect King Bardane and to find and kill the assassins. Though you will not be able to be everywhere at all times, we feel that having you both there as eyes and ears of the council will give us our best chance at finding the assassins before they strike. There will be other members of the Order in the city, ready to come to your aid should you need it. There are also several inside the palace with whom we have close ties."

Overwhelmed, Amaran looked around the room. "How was it that you chose me over so many others? I have only just recently become one of you."

"For one," said Balkar, "you are more familiar with the Balankor Palace than any of us. And this council has every ounce of faith that you and Leandros will be the best to see the task is done. The summit begins next month, so you will leave three weeks from today."

After he was dismissed, Amaran made his way to the courtyard, but saw how crowded it was. Knowing he would be bombarded with questions, he opted instead for a quieter retreat. Before he was noticed, he slipped out of sight of the other knights and walked toward the shade garden on the far side of the manor to think about the return to Balankor.

To go back now after all this time, thought Amaran, pacing back and forth along the path. *I'll see Rallden again, and Murken…and of course I'll see her, too…..*

By nightfall, the banquet room was mostly empty. Only Celdron, Leandros, Balkar, and Amaran remained.

"As we hear anything more, Leandros," Celdron said, rising from the table, "we will send word to Prennek, and he will relay it to you."

Balkar added gravely as he stood, "I hope we succeed in finding them before they find the king."

Before leaving with Balkar, Celdron added, "By the grace of our Creator we will succeed. And for the sake of all of Albantria, we must!"

As the two elders headed to their rooms, Amaran noticed Leandros' look of worry. "You and the others seem troubled, Leandros."

"There is still so much that is uncertain, Amaran. Pharon was so careful in devising his many plans. It has been nearly impossible to find out certain details. We know only about the two assassins, but there are most likely more. We also don't know the exact time of the strikes, who they will strike first, or which councilmen they might target."

Amaran opened his mouth and put his hand to his head, as if suddenly remembering something important.

"What's the matter?" asked Leandros.

"I don't know why I didn't think of it before," Amaran said. "Why didn't I think about him?"

"What? About who?" Leandros pressed.

"You need to know more about the intricate details of Pharon's plan. I know the perfect man. I've told you before about my slave friend named Harron. I guess I never told you that he was connected to Pharon—indirectly. He was hired by one of Pharon's men to track Bardane's brother and his family and learn some of the royal councilmen's darker secrets. He knows about Pharon, and might even still know some of his agents. He is an expert at ferreting out information, even from places like Pharon's castle."

"Do you trust him?"

"I do. With my life."

"Can you find him?"

"If he is still alive, maybe."

"The other elders and I will want to meet him. Do whatever you can to find him."

Chapter 35—Harron is Rescued

Amaran arrived in Kelishran several days later. He went from one end of the city to the next, scouring every worksite where slaves were present. He found no one who looked like Harron at any of them. About to give up, he started back to his lodging for the night, angry at himself for ever thinking Harron would have survived after all this time.

When he passed one last worksite, he stopped momentarily to watch them make their way towards the slave wagons—a routine he had once been all too familiar with. One of the men looked strikingly familiar. His heart jumped into his throat. He could hardly believe his eyes.

A skinny, white-haired man with leathery, bronze skin turned to face Amaran. Amaran knew instantly it was Harron. Amaran approached him, but before he walked more than several yards, he heard a voice he recognized well.

"Get going!" shouted a tall, muscular slave driver as he raised his whip. "Move now or you'll feel the sting of my old friend here!" A slave, worn from a day of harsh labor, had fallen on the way to the wagon.

"Bellok," said Amaran with disgust. The slave driver that had haunted Amaran's nightmares for six years was still finding satisfaction in his persecution of slaves.

It was obvious the slave Bellok shouted at was too weak to stand. Even if he could, he would be of no use to anyone. Regardless, Bellok's whip flew. First there was the loud crack, then the scream. Instead of standing, the man fell forward, his face landing in the sand. Amaran could still hear the slave's cries for mercy even though they were muffled by the sand.

When Bellok prepared to strike the slave a second time, Amaran grabbed and held his wrist back. Surprised, Bellok pivoted round with a fierce-looking expression, ready to pummel the slave bold enough to stop him. He was confused to find a stranger looking him defiantly in the eye.

"What the hell do you think you're doing?" Bellok demanded.

"Whipping him again won't do anything," said Amaran firmly. "He's nearly dead."

"What's it to you?" Bellok growled. Turning his back to Amaran, he added, "Mind your own business."

But when Bellok raised his whip again, Amaran grabbed the whip itself and pulled it back so hard it yanked Bellok backward. Livid, Bellok swung his huge arm straight at Amaran. Even though Amaran was less than two feet from him, he missed. Amaran easily leaned out of his reach.

"I don't know who you are, but you have no authority here," Bellok sneered. "Get lost before I tear you to pieces."

The slaves watched with intense interest from the wagons as the other two slave drivers approached Amaran.

"You may not fare so well," said Amaran calmly.

"Is that so?" Bellok snickered. "You might not fare so well yourself."

With that, Bellok started to turn, but before he had taken a step, he turned back around in a blur. His fist came flying at Amaran fast and hard.

Amaran simply leaned back, grabbed Bellok's wrist as it narrowly missed his face, and used the huge slave driver's own weight against him as he threw Bellok into the side of the wagon.

If Amaran thought Bellok was furious before, he would have been mistaken. Bellok grabbed onto a loose sideboard from the wagon and ripped it off with his bare hands. Nostrils flared, he started towards Amaran, who was still standing as calmly as before.

The slaves were watching with restrained excitement, afraid to cheer for this unknown hero. The other two slave drivers watched with bewilderment, unsure whether they should jump to Bellok's aid or watch the finale of this fight—and what was sure to be a painful end for the foolish stranger.

Bellok moved swiftly toward Amaran and swung the broken board. Amaran ducked out of the way of the first swing, and caught a glancing blow of the second. Before Bellok could strike again, Amaran was behind him. The brawny but clumsy slave driver turned, only to find Amaran's fist landing squarely in his nose.

Bellok's eyes watered, but he wasted no time in picking up the whip at his feet. With the board in one hand and the whip in the other, he glared at Amaran. When he swung the board, Amaran yet again dodged it, and when he swung the whip, Amaran was too fast. Amaran had come up underneath Bellok's swinging arm and caught hold of his wrist. Twisting Bellok's forearm until he dropped the whip, Amaran brought Bellok to his knees. He then shoved the slave driver's head toward the dirt.

"What do you care about them?" groaned Bellok, his cheek pressed to the sand. "They're just slaves."

"Because I was once one of them," Amaran answered. Then he rose to his feet, releasing Bellok. "You deserve far worse, so remember the mercy I showed you the next time your raise your whip to another one of these men."

The other two slave drivers who had contemplated helping Bellok took a step back as Amaran approached them.

Amaran pointed to Harron as he said to them, "I'm buying this one." He tossed a bag of coins at the slave drivers' feet and added, "There's enough there for your masters to buy two just like him— and for you to keep a large sum for yourselves."

The slaves and slave drivers looked on with utter confusion, but no one was more stunned than Harron.

When they had gone two blocks from the worksite, Harron broke the silence. "Who *are* you?"

"Who do you think I am?"

"How should I know?" laughed Harron. He studied Amaran's face closely before adding, "You do look a little like...Ha, it couldn't be! Right age I suppose, but that would be...."

Amaran cracked a smile. He couldn't keep the secret any longer. "Harron, my friend, it is me, Amaran!"

Harron smiled back, but his eyes were still riddled with doubt. "Amaran? How can it be? I don't understand."

"There is too much to tell here and now, but we have a three day journey. There is a lot to explain."

"I don't care what the reason is. You've saved me!" Harron exclaimed.

Chapter 36—The Return to Balankor

Back at Leandros' manor, Celdron prepared Harron for what he would look for in Pharon's castle. Meanwhile, Amaran and Leandros departed for the Geldarian capital to meet Ambassador Galfarr. It took them five days to reach the Albakranian border from Ambassador Galfarr's home.

When Amaran first saw the walls of Balankor, he could scarcely believe it had been seven years since he had left. Once through the main gates, Amaran looked all about him, taking in the sights that had once been so familiar to him growing up. Some things were just as he remembered them as a boy, yet at the same time they seemed somehow altered, like in a dream. He saw the street that led to the barracks and the street where he and Rallden had met for their fishing trip more than fifteen years ago.

When they reached the Balankor Palace, there were ambassadors, noblemen, and dignitaries everywhere, milling about the main foyer and banquet hall.

Leandros leaned over to Amaran and said, "Let's walk about a bit. This way."

Amaran followed him through a set of glass double doors onto a small balcony.

"Remember that here you will go by the name of Korin," said Leandros. "You're my nephew, a nobleman from the Southern Province of Geldar."

"I remember," said Amaran. "You needn't worry."

"We must keep an ever watchful eye on everyone here, Amaran. Just as *we* were able, any of the assassins may also have been able to enter the palace under false pretenses. We do not know who is to be trusted or who may have ties to Pharon."

"Agreed," Amaran answered. "As for Prennek, how will he—?"

"He'll find us if he has news for us."

That evening, as the sunset colored the western sky, the greatly anticipated banquet began. This feast marked the official beginning of the Alliance Summit. Dozens of dignitaries poured in, each taking his seat at one of the extravagantly decorated tables.

Once most of the seats in the banquet hall had been filled, everyone turned to find Albakran's royalty entering. Amaran saw Rallden right behind King Bardane. Rallden's face was very much the same as it was years ago. His tall, lean, and strong frame was also as Amaran had remembered. However, he had a different air about him, reminding Amaran more of a king, and less of a young prince.

Nearly all the guests turned to gaze upon the next royal figure to enter. The elegant and beautiful princess Elle moved gracefully past Amaran's seat towards the royal table.

Amaran tried to focus on the conversations around him but his eyes always shifted back to Elle. Distracted, he missed the first two calls for his attention from Leandros. Now shouting into Amaran's ear, Leandros said, "I say, Korin!"

Only just then recognizing his new name, Amaran shook his head to clear his mind and looked at Leandros.

"Korin, the ambassador wishes to know more about our business in Kelishran this past year," Leandros said.

"Yes, Kelishran," Amaran answered. He then told the ambassador everything he had rehearsed with Leandros earlier on their journey.

Once he had satisfied the ambassador's questions, a nearby nobleman caught Ambassador Galfarr's attention. Amaran meanwhile turned again to see Elle. Having just finished a conversation, she was turning towards Rallden. As her head moved, her eyes naturally caught Amaran's gaze.

Amaran looked away as soon as their eyes met. He scanned the rest of the table, hoping to convince her that he had merely been surveying the guests along each side of the table. But out of the corner of his eyes, he could tell she was still looking at him.

Had she recognized him? It was impossible, he knew. Amaran was aware he looked far different from the boy she knew once. She would never recognize him because she would have never expected to see him.

This combined with his Geldarian attire should have been enough to convince Amaran that his secret was safe. Yet, dwelling on the way she had stared at him so curiously, he was not convinced she had been fooled. When he looked back at her briefly, he watched her lean in towards Rallden and whisper something to him.

She did recognize me! he thought to himself. *She's telling Rallden now, and he'll rush over to me. Who knows what sort of scene will follow....*

Nothing of the sort happened. After Elle spoke to Rallden, she took one more sip of her wine. Rallden resumed his conversation. Amaran then watched as she stood and excused herself from the table. Looking somewhat pale, she walked quickly out of the room.

Minutes later King Bardane rose to address his guests. "Gentlemen, I formally welcome you to another Western Albantrian Alliance Summit. It was my hope that this year we would once again have the privilege of hosting the summit here in Balankor. I trust your travels were good, and that the hospitality has been acceptable thus far."

The men began to cheer and applaud. Seeing their response, Bardane offered a broad, warm smile before continuing with his welcome.

After a restful night, Amaran spent the morning walking about the palace grounds and hallways, waiting for the first meeting to start. He wandered about the halls in the eastern wing, reminiscing about his days as a Balankor guest. Eventually he made his way onto a balcony. He leaned on the railing and looked down at the central courtyard. There were rectangular fountain pools edged by evergreen hedges, and potted plants carefully shaped to look like horses and knights and towers.

A small, dark-haired girl no older than three suddenly ran out from under the balcony. She was a beautiful, bright-spirited child. Something else about her face startled him. As the little girl pranced about gleefully, he marveled at how much she looked like the young Elle he knew many years ago, even though this girl was much younger.

He watched her smile and twirl in a circle and then say, "Mommy! Here!"

Elle soon appeared. "I'm here, darling! Here I come, Arellia!"

Amaran stared down as Elle ran towards the girl and picked her up. Hugging her tightly, she twirled the little girl around and kissed her on each cheek.

Amaran smiled sadly at the scene. The girl he had once loved with all his heart now had a child, a lovely daughter whose father was the heir to the throne of Albakran. He watched Elle smile gleefully as she danced about with the girl.

It was a bitter reminder to him of what he had once wished for but knew could never come true. It also reminded him of his utter loneliness. He suddenly found himself longing to be with Laila again—to hold her in his arms and tell her how much he missed her.

He watched the little girl run into her mother's arms again. A wide smile formed on Elle's face, one so loving and pure it caused him to realize something. She may or may not have ever truly loved Rallden, but she loved this precious little girl, and her daughter loved her in return. He watched as they continued down the walkway hand in hand.

216

Though he had moved on in his life and was no longer in love with Elle, Amaran's heart still hurt knowing that there was no longer room for him in her life.

A voice from behind startled Amaran. "I wasn't sure where to find you."

Leandros stood next to Amaran and looked down at Elle and her daughter playing in the courtyard.

"I had just begun to forget her, you know, Leandros. Seeing her and Rallden here, it brings so many memories back. Elle has made a new life for herself...and so have I. I just wish that I could have found happiness like she has. To have lost Elle as I did so long ago, and then to lose Laila, too...it is cruel. I must never fall in love again. If I were to lose anyone else in my life...."

They then heard the sound of doors closing and looked behind them. A number of men made their way past the glass doors that separated Leandros and Amaran from the main hall.

"They're heading to the banquet hall. It's time for the meeting to start." Leandros followed Amaran towards the banquet hall.

Chapter 37—The First Assassin

The first meeting of the summit lasted four hours. After the midday meal, everyone returned to their rooms to rest before the afternoon's main event—a grand parade marking the official beginning of the summit. The parade, complete with many fantastic sights, was a chance for all of Balankor's residents to celebrate the occasion. Amaran and Leandros saw it in a different light: a supreme opportunity for the assassins to strike the king.

Once back in their room, Leandros unrolled a map and showed it to Amaran. "The parade will follow this route." Leandros pointed to the bold, zigzag line on the map.

Amaran studied it closely. "I can tell you that there are very few places for hiding except within the crowd. It would be difficult for an assassin to not only conceal his weapon, but also to get a clear shot from the crowded curb. Here, though, is where we'll need to be especially vigilant." Amaran pointed to a spot on the map about halfway through the planned route. "There are several alleyways running perpendicular to the main street that could be used as hideaways. Around here there are a number of high buildings with excellent vantage points—windows, small balconies, and the like. Although there will be guards everywhere, it will be impossible for them to keep an eye on every window looking down on the king's carriage."

"Ach! What were they thinking?" Leandros grumbled. "This will be a nightmare. Don't they care about the safety of their own king? Anyone could be waiting in the buildings overlooking the parade route. It'll be target practice!"

"Leandros, what can they do? They can't cancel the festivities because of possibilities—possibilities that they know less about than we do."

"I know they don't know what we do, Amaran, but still—a parade is risky enough no matter the circumstances."

"The parade is a tradition whenever the summit is held here. The people expect to see the king. With guards everywhere, it might be enough to protect the king...and to deter the assassins."

Shooting him a dubious glance, Leandros replied, "You don't think the assassins know this already? We cannot afford to assume anything other than that they are ready to strike today at the parade. We must remain as close to Bardane as possible and watch the streets with the eyes of an eagle."

Two hours later, a long procession of horses and carriages rolled one by one through the main city streets of the capital. People were crammed together along the edges of the streets, anxious to see the sights. Leading the parade were two massive grallgen, stomping thunderously upon the ground. The animals were so tall their shaggy heads were level with the second floors of most of the buildings they passed.

Standing on top of the grallgens' backs were vividly dressed jugglers and musicians. Behind them rode two dozen royal guards in full battle gear on snow-white horses, as triumphantly as if they had just returned from a glorious victory. The first line of foreign nobility and ambassadors came next, waving to the crowds. Some even threw gold coins.

Behind them, powerful workhorses in colorful cloaks pulled a huge stage on wheels. Towering beams rose from the stage, and ropes connected one beam to the next. The audience roared as acrobats balanced upon the high beams, ran along the ropes as if on flat ground, and then catapulted themselves from one high platform to the next, flipping and turning in midair.

More knights followed the acrobat stage. Behind them was the royal carriage. At Leandros' request they rode on horses alongside Ambassador Galfarr's carriage, which was only two behind the king's carriage. Both Leandros and Amaran looked out into the crowd with unwavering eyes, Amaran to the left and Leandros to the right.

After some time, they neared the spot Amaran had mentioned earlier. With a nod and wave of his hand, Leandros assured him he remembered. They looked not only into the crowd, but up at as many of the hundreds of windows high above them as they could. Just at that moment something caught Amaran's eye. He cocked his head and stared intently up at a small balcony on a nearby building. There, a figure hid in the shadows of the corner. He was crouching, but moving into a standing position. He held something, but what it was exactly Amaran could not tell.

"Leandros, look! Up there! Do you see him?"

Leandros turned abruptly to look where Amaran pointed, and then immediately thereafter shouted to the king's royal guards just ahead of them. The figure made a sudden motion towards the balcony's railing, sensing that he had been spotted. He leaned over the railing holding what was now easily identified by Amaran as a crossbow.

The crowd, sensing something amiss, began to stir, many looking about excitedly. One of the royal guards aimed his bow for the assassin. Seeing this, the spectators knew there was danger. Panic began to spread as many dashed for cover.

When the carriage driver swerved the carriage to the right, completely removing the king from view of the assassin, the nearly hysterical crowd became even more excited. Guards moved in front of King Bardane to prevent any boldly curious spectators from rushing across the street to meet him up close.

Once additional guards reached the carriage, the captain sent some of them to apprehend the attacker. Amaran was about to follow the guards on his horse, but stopped when he noticed Leandros still behind him, not even looking in the direction of the assassin at all.

"What are you waiting for?" Amaran yelled.

Leandros scanned the faces in the crowd. "It doesn't add up. He was too careless, too visible."

"You don't think—" Amaran started, but was cut short by Leandros' cry.

"Protect the king! There, on the roof!" Leandros yelled to the guards.

He pointed frantically toward a nearby townhouse. A man was sprawled flat on its roof, aiming a crossbow directly at King Bardane.

When a royal guard saw this new assassin pull the trigger on his crossbow, he lunged forward to shield the king. He reached Bardane just in time. The bolt struck him in the shoulder. The crowd shrieked as they saw the injured guard fall, blood on his upper arm.

As the other guards closed in tighter, another bolt flew. Missing all of them, it landed forcefully into the carriage door—only inches from where Bardane was crouching.

Amaran spurred his horse towards the nearby alleyway below the second assassin's perch. Six guards followed Amaran, and about ten more went to the other side of the same building.

When Amaran turned the corner at the end of the alleyway, he stopped his horse beside a pile of crates stacked along the backside of the townhouse. He climbed onto the mound of crates. From there he jumped to reach the base of a tiny, second story balcony. Amaran held on to the iron bars of the railing and pulled himself up. After planting himself momentarily along the outside edge of this balcony, he jumped over to a nearby stone ledge. From the ledge, he clambered up onto another balcony. The guards below him, unsure of how to help from their position, watched helplessly as Amaran slowly pulled himself up and over the roof's edge.

In the time it took Amaran to scale the rest of the wall, the assassin had retreated from view of the king's guards. He had already started running along the roof by the time Amaran reached the top. At the edge of the roof, the assassin leapt onto the top of a neighboring building.

Amaran wasted no time in racing after him. Nearing the edge of the rooftop, he accelerated his pace. With a forceful explosion of his legs, he hurtled through the air and landed with a thud on top of the next townhouse.

He crouched to absorb the impact as he landed, and took off running once more at full speed, gaining on the fleeing assassin. When he reached the end of that roof he jumped over the gap between two neighboring buildings.

Now on the same roof as the assassin, Amaran raced after him, his arms and legs moving in a blur. Sweat soaked his skin. Amaran neared the edge soon after the assassin leapt. Once there he realized he had reached the end of the row of townhouses. There was a thirty-foot gap between him and the next building's roof.

He saw the assassin below, rolling off an awning below and landing in the street. Amaran used his strong legs to propel himself as far as he could jump, kicking his legs to give himself a little more distance to his leap. He began to fall, and was just barely able to grab hold of the awning the assassin had used to break his fall.

With feline precision Amaran landed on the ground on both feet, ready to begin a mad dash down the street after the surprisingly agile fugitive. Amaran pushed his way through pedestrians, keeping his eye on the assassin as best he could.

The assassin jumped up onto an oncoming cart. Using the cart as a temporary stepping stone, he leapt onto the bottom frame of a second story windowsill. Pulling himself up, he quickly disappeared into the open window.

Amaran looked about, figuring how to get into the window, for the wagon had already rolled out of position to be of any use to him. With several quick moves, he half-ran and half-scaled the wall of the building, using a flowerbox, an iron lantern, and several protruding bricks to reach another second-story window.

Amaran slipped inside, and raced through the room into the hall. Upon hearing a loud thud, he turned and saw the assassin burst through a door only several rooms away. Both men dashed for the nearby stairs, Amaran several yards behind him.

The assassin flew down the stairs, leaping several steps at a time, while Amaran froze at the top of the stairs, studying the spiral steps winding below him. He put his hand on the rail and swung his body up and over the railing, plunging downward onto the steps that curved back into his path below.

He landed on the step right behind the assassin. Amaran then pounced on him, causing him to crash into the wooden railing. Both men rolled onto the floor below.

Somehow the assassin ended up on top of Amaran. With little time wasted, the assassin drew a knife with one hand while holding Amaran down with locked knees and his left hand about his neck.

But Amaran was not trapped for long. He quickly brought his hand up to stop the arm with the knife. In one rapid move, he brought his other hand across his chest and into the man's outstretched arm, freeing his neck from the assassin's grasp and throwing him off balance. Amaran thrust his left leg sharply into the man's ribs, knocking him onto his back. Amaran sprung upon him, seizing the assassin's hand that still grasped the knife.

The man flailed his free arm and legs to release himself, but Amaran punched the man hard in the face. Then Amaran picked him up and threw him into the wall. The assassin slumped to the ground unconscious. Amaran wiped the sweat from his brow and turned to face the wide-eyed and speechless caretaker standing behind him.

"Go find a guard, and tell them what's happened. There should be one nearby."

The man nodded and sprinted out the door.

Chapter 38—Another Strike

Later that night a celebratory banquet was held in honor of the king's escape from danger. It was yet another cause for entertainment and fun for the distinguished guests, and they loved it.

"To the men who were so vigilant and courageous—Lord Leandros who spotted the second fool who wanted me dead, and to his young nephew, Sir Korin! What bravery, my lords!" announced King Bardane during his toast. Then he added in a much more serious tone, "I owe you my life. I do not know how I shall ever repay you."

Everyone applauded when the two heroes of the day rose from their seats. As the evening continued, many men came up to talk with Amaran, or Korin as he was known there. Councilman Haldegran was one of the first. Putting his hand on Amaran's shoulder, he said, "My boy, you should be proud of what you did today! Put the king's guards to shame, though! Ha ha!"

Soon after Haldegran left him, he heard another familiar voice. "I wanted to personally thank you for your brave and selfless act today, Sir Korin," said Murken.

Amaran bit his lip when he realized who it was. "Thank you, but I assure you it was—" Amaran saw no point in continuing as Murken slipped away before he had finished his response. He had seen Murken only several times before this week and that was from a distance.

Leandros found Amaran a minute later. "Two down, but we have more to find before the week is over."

"And no idea when or where they will strike."

Leandros shook his head.

"No word yet from the outside? No word from Harron's findings?"

"Nothing. Prennek knows where to find us if he discovers anything. Until then, since we have only so much access to the king, we must watch closely when we can. Always, no matter where we are, keep our ears and eyes open for anything suspicious—especially as we near the banquet at week's end. Everyone will be there to hear the final resolutions of the summit. It would be a supreme opportunity—even if royal guards will be everywhere."

"I suppose you're right."

"Until we hear more, that is what we must assume. Watch and listen and wait."

At dinner on the fourth day of the summit, a particularly heated debate continued past dinner and well after the dessert plates had been cleared from the tables. One by one, those who had grown tired of arguing left for their rooms or to walk about the halls. Amaran suddenly noticed that Councilman Haldegran was no longer in the room. The king and all the other councilmen were there where Leandros and he could see them, yet neither had seen Haldegran leave. Signaling to Leandros, Amaran left the room, in search of the councilman.

Knowing he often walked in the gardens at night, Amaran made his way out onto the balcony which overlooked the gardens. They were illuminated by only a few small torches lining the paths. There was also a passing shimmer of moonlight, visible through the slowly moving clouds above. Even in the dark he could see the meandering paths that formed conjoining figure eights. The huge white moonflowers bloomed on vines that scaled the far walls of the garden.

He saw no one there, but something caught Amaran's eye just as he was about to leave. There was movement in the corner near the servants' entrance to the kitchen. Seeing nothing at first, he thought he had imagined it—until he saw something move again in the shadows. After his eyes adjusted to the darkness a bit more, he saw a figure hiding under a tree branch. It was a person.

Uncertain whether this person had seen him or not, but curious to understand his purpose there, Amaran dared not make a sound or sudden movement. Since the person was still hiding, and moving enough to be noticed from up above, Amaran assumed this stranger had not seen him standing on the balcony.

Why would anyone be hiding like that, and there of all places? Amaran thought. *Surely up to nothing good....* He had not ruled out the fact that he might be one of the assassins.

Just then the figure retreated further into the shadow, trying to disappear altogether. A moment after that Amaran heard a door shut. Below him, a man walked onto one of the main garden walkways, moving towards the center fountain pool. Amaran almost immediately recognized the familiar gait of Councilman Haldegran.

Amaran looked back into the corner, but had trouble spotting the mysterious figure in the blackness. Then something shimmered. He realized with horror that it was metal, reflecting the moon's light upwards. The ambusher was holding a dagger!

Amaran knew then that this man meant to kill the councilman. Without a second's more hesitation, Amaran swung himself over the railing of the balcony and dropped ten feet to the ground. At the sound of his landing Haldegran turned on his heel, obviously startled.

"What are you doing?" the councilman demanded.

"Behind you!" Amaran blurted as the assassin rushed straight towards Haldegran.

"What?" Haldegran glanced over his shoulder, flinching once he saw that there *was* someone—someone charging towards him with a blade in his hand. He stumbled backwards, tripping and falling hard onto the ground.

Amaran lunged at the assassin with his sword.

"Get out of my way, fool!" he growled to Amaran, dropping his knife and drawing his sword. "You don't know what you're up against. I'll kill you!"

Amaran did not step back.

Their swords clashed. The stranger was quick and fierce with his swings. In a series of swift, powerful strokes he managed to back Amaran up a few steps. But from there Amaran held his ground, keeping up with him swing for swing.

Amaran moved his challenger backward several steps. Feeling more confident in his rank, Amaran swung harder to push him even further back. Caring less about his form and more about the power of his blows, Amaran continued his relentless assault, moving the swordsman even closer to the garden wall.

Just when Amaran felt as if he had established himself as the better swordsman, the man darted to the left and lunged toward him with several rapid strokes. Amaran was completely surprised by the maneuver. He lost ground quickly, moving several feet back as he desperately fought to keep the dangerous rapier at bay.

Not realizing how far he had moved backward, Amaran's next step caused him to fall into a large bush. He lost his concentration for a split second, enough time to see a strong and vigorous blow come straight at him. He had only time to turn his body to block it.

Pain sliced through Amaran's shoulder. The wound stung, but it was not deep.

The attacker followed through with a second blow. Out of desperation, Amaran rolled out of the way. With free space around him, he managed to scramble back to his feet. His embarrassment at being fooled by the swordsman angered him, but his disappointment with himself over his careless swings made him furious.

With a rush of determination and renewed confidence, Amaran felt strengthened despite his fresh wound. Amaran backed up his opponent slowly but steadily. Taming his newfound strength, his swings were smooth, disciplined, and precise.

A crowd gathered. Several guards hurried to guide the councilman away from the danger. Leandros rushed out once he heard what was happening, but stopped just inside the courtyard, seeing Amaran skillfully wield his sword just as he had taught him.

Amaran moved the assailant closer and closer to the corner where he had once been hiding. Ever so gradually, the swordsman became more winded and his swings slower. Finally, the attacker made his mistake, leaving his right side open. Amaran thrust his blade into the assassin's side. The swordsman gasped for air before collapsing onto the ground, his sword clattering away.

Chapter 39—Elle

Amaran waited with his sword point hovering over the assassin's face until several guards came and seized him. It was not until several noblemen came to him, remarking about his victory in spite of the wound, that Amaran suddenly remembered the pain in his shoulder. Wincing, he searched for a place where he could sit. A servant came to him, pressing a cloth over the wound to stop the bleeding.

As the onlookers shifted from the balcony and doorways to the center of the garden, Leandros moved away from the crowd and sat next to Amaran. "A skillful swordsman, wasn't he?"

"Yes, and he almost had the better of me."

"Almost, but did not," Leandros finished for him.

"Overconfidence made me careless," Amaran said, carefully moving his shoulder to reposition it.

Once the servant left them, Leandros changed the subject. "How did this all happen? How did you find him?"

Amaran told him about spotting the figure in the shadows and then seeing Councilman Haldegran. "The man was highly skilled. He is one of them, without a doubt," Amaran said.

"I agree. We knew that any of Bardane's supporters on the council could be targets," said Leandros thoughtfully. "Since the attempt on the king's life was foiled, there must be at least one more assassin at large in the city. I'd bet my life on it. There is no way Pharon would have allowed his plan to fail so easily. He is not naïve."

"Pharon won't stop until the king is dead, will he?" asked Amaran.

"I fear not. The fourth assassin may already be here in the palace. Whether he strikes during the summit or not, we don't know, but we must continue to watch closer than ever."

"The king's guards will be even more alert to danger after these two attacks, especially with this one at the palace itself."

"True, but which of his men can be trusted?" Leandros asked. "We will do whatever it takes to ensure the king and councilmen are protected. The High Order will not let Pharon seize control of Albakran and put the stability of the whole region at risk."

Amaran looked at him thoughtfully. "What if the councilman and the king had both been assassinated? What then?"

While looking off into the darkness, Leandros answered in a low voice, "Then there would be chaos. Pharon could sway the council's vote in his favor and consequently hurt Rallden's chances as successor. Pharon could take control, and then...then the future of Albakran, as well as all of Albantria, would be in jeopardy."

"Leandros, wasn't this extraordinary...that I found the assassin just as he was about to attack Haldegran? What are the odds? We can't keep watch over the king and the councilmen every hour, yet I had a feeling that I should try to find the councilman. The attack could have just as easily happened sometime when we were not around."

"But it didn't. We have stopped all of them so far, exactly what we intended to do. It certainly makes you feel protected, watched over, as if we are not alone in this, doesn't it?"

Amaran raised one eyebrow at Leandros. Just as he was about to respond, there was commotion behind them. A frantic voice called out from the large doorway that led into the gardens.

"Father! Are you all right?" It was Elle. Her mother was beside her. They both ran towards Haldegran, tears streaming down their cheeks.

"Someone said that you were attacked!" Haldegran's wife cried.

"And that you had been wounded," added Elle.

"Wounded? No, no. Attacked? Well, not quite—thanks to this man!" He pointed at Amaran. "He is quite the hero, is he not?"

Elle threw her arms around her father's neck and kissed him. After this she turned towards the two Geldarian noblemen on the bench. They both stood as she approached them.

"Sir Korin," she started, "I want to thank you for your bravery tonight. I cannot show my appreciation enough, but you should know that—"

Amaran stopped her. "My lady, I am glad I could be there to save the councilman's life, but you need not thank me more than you already have."

"You are wrong, Sir Korin. You deserve more...and also proper attention to your wound! A rag to stop the bleeding will not be enough. You must have this cleaned properly."

Taking the wounded arm delicately into her hands, Elle gently repositioned it to examine his injury. She spoke in such a caring manner that Amaran could say nothing to contradict her, despite feeling the need to protest.

"Come, Sir Korin. Follow me. The wound needs to be cleaned and bandaged, and I will do it for you."

"My lady, I cannot allow you to do this. It is nothing a servant couldn't—"

"No, there is no refusing my offer. It will be done." She responded almost indignantly. "This way."

In a small room just inside from the courtyard, Elle ordered the servants to bring in supplies. Amaran sat down as he had been instructed and watched as she knelt beside him and soaked a cloth in a bowl of warm water. Ringing it out in her small hands, she brought the cloth slowly to his upper arm. He watched her eyes move over his shoulder as she wiped away the blood. Then she placed the blood-stained rag back into the water.

As she brought the cloth to his shoulder again, her eyes looked up into his. After first darting away from his stare, her eyes slowly shifted up again to look at him. Although he should not, he wished he could tell her who he was.

Her gaze had since fallen upon his wounded shoulder, but he could tell that her mind was greatly troubled. Desperate to understand her, he studied her expression as she continued wiping away the blood. What had drawn her gaze to him and then caused such distress seconds later?

Breaking the silence he asked, "Is this too much for you? The blood and the wound, do they bother you?"

"No, no," she said softly. "I am sorry if I seem distraught. It is just that you remind me of someone."

There was a long pause.

"Someone I once knew who was very dear to me. But that was a long time ago...."

He knew she had meant him. And with that realization, he could not help but wonder if she still had feelings for him.

Laila's face appeared in his mind. He missed her terribly. Could he ever heal from her passing? He craved companionship and love. But he knew he could never love anyone again. He couldn't risk it.

As Elle moved her hand past his face, he noticed the exquisite jeweled ring on her finger—her wedding ring—a blatant reminder to him that she was married to the future king of Albakran. What a lucky man Rallden was!

With that thought, Amaran began to feel sorry for himself. While he was arrested and sent to the desert to become a slave, Elle had married and started a family. She had once assured him that she would love only him and that she could never be happy by marrying Rallden. But she had married Rallden nonetheless. Though he had found a new purpose in life with the High Order, he was still alone and without love. Why did everyone else find joy and contentment in life? Didn't he deserve those things too?

Yet seeing the sadness in her eyes made him wonder if she was actually satisfied with her life. He sensed something—a hint of despair deep down inside of her perhaps—that made him question her happiness. He did not understand why she might be so troubled, but assuring himself that he was not imagining it made him a feel little less alone in the world. Perhaps he was not the only one who had suffered after they parted ways all that time ago.

Chapter 40—The Banquet

On the final day of the summit, the deliberations had come to a close. It was time for the grand banquet. After the attack on Haldegran, the number of guards had been doubled and entry into the palace had been greatly restricted. The king was surrounded by guards everywhere he went.

When the sun set, Amaran and Leandros accompanied Ambassador Galfarr into the banquet hall and found their seats. Soon after that, the twelve members of the Royal Council entered. Maldock, the newest councilman, was last in line.

A minute later, an announcement was made and all fell silent. "The Albakranian king, King Bardane!"

The trumpets announced the king's entry. Flanked by two dozen guards, he made his way to the royal table. Up front, he welcomed everyone before signaling the feast to begin.

While everyone ate, the musicians played and court jesters entertained on stage. Towards the end of the last comedic performance, Amaran happened to turn towards the back door. Prennek was there, trying to get his attention.

Amaran motioned to Leandros. They both quietly slipped away from the table, making their way towards Prennek at the door.

"I have news, just in the last hour. I came as fast I could," Prennek said hastily.

"Well, what is it?" Leandros asked impatiently.

"Harron found something." He paused for only a second and with a most serious tone continued, "There is one more assassin and he will strike tonight. Two men, both here tonight, arranged it."

"They are both here?" demanded Leandros.

"Yes. One is a friend of Pharon's." In almost a whisper Prennek said, "Maldock."

"Maldock." Leandros' jaw tightened. "There was always little doubt in my mind as to his allegiance to Pharon, but I didn't know he would be involved to this extent. Who is the other?"

"Druin," Prennek muttered.

Amaran looked at Prennek and then at Leandros. "Druin. I know the name."

"Of course you do," came Leandros' foreboding reply. "Druin is Captain of King Bardane's Royal Guards."

"Druin could bring anyone into the castle," Amaran whispered.

"And place an assassin anywhere," said Leandros. "There is no telling where this assassin is now or when he'll strike."

"What can we do?" asked Amaran.

Leandros shook his head. "We can do nothing but watch for danger. We'll run to Bardane's aid as soon as we see something, but we won't be allowed any closer than we are now."

"We have to warn him."

"Who would we tell?" asked Leandros.

Leandros tried to walk calmly back to his seat, but Amaran could sense the trepidation in his step. Joining in the applause for the jesters' performance, they brought their hands together to match the rhythm of the rest of the audience. As they clapped, they scanned the perimeter of the room.

After the applause died down, the Albakranian ambassador stood. Raising his hands to command everyone's attention, he announced to the guests with his booming voice, "Chosen representatives, the ambassadors of each nation voted on nearly a dozen proposals today. Now it is time to hear the results of those votes. Please welcome Ambassador Rodaren who will bring us those results!"

As the guests applauded the ambassador, Amaran and Leandros studied the king's position. They watched each of the nearby guards—especially Captain Druin. He was off to one side, standing near one set of steps leading up to the stage. Meanwhile, the king's guards were positioned at either end of the royal table as well as surrounding the raised platform where the king would soon speak.

"I can't imagine an attack could even be possible," whispered Leandros to Amaran.

Ambassador Rodaren of Crescocia, a short, stout, bald man, took his place up front. Gathering his notes, he cleared his throat and looked out upon the crowd. "Thank you! Now, I first will begin by...."

As he continued, Amaran and Leandros kept their hawk-like watch over the room. All remained quiet and peaceful throughout the ambassador's speech. As the ambassador left the platform and returned to his seat, King Bardane rose to take the Crescocian ambassador's place up front. Several royal guards positioned themselves to flank the king.

When King Bardane moved to the podium, even Amaran and Leandros had trouble seeing him through the line of guards, despite being seated close to the front. Anxiously they watched and waited, but the transition was a smooth one—there was only calm and quiet across the room.

Standing tall with his arms stretched outward, he began in his loud, commanding voice, "Men of Kallendria, of Crescocia, of Geldar, and of Baldoran; men of Mardaria, men of the Valencian Empire, and of the Hekrelian Islands; men of Fleur, and my fellow Albakranians, I applaud you for your undying commitment to seek and maintain peace in the region."

A standing ovation followed. Nodding, Bardane continued, "I share your joy—"

And then it happened. Leandros saw it first, and Amaran a second later. They jumped to their feet but could do nothing to stop the royal guard who rushed across the platform. The attack had come from such an unexpected location. The guard drew a blade in the charge and thrust it forward with palpable force. One, two, and then three more times, it plunged straight into the king's stomach and chest.

Bardane stumbled backward. Blood was everywhere. He slowly reached for his belly, his mouth open wide and his eyes glazed. Then the king collapsed onto the floor.

The entire attack lasted a matter of seconds. The guards finally seized the attacker. Dozens of men from the royal table, including Rallden, scrambled to the stage to help Bardane. It was impossible for anyone else to see through the dense human wall.

The banquet hall erupted into chaos. While the guests watched with horror. Amaran, straining to see the stage, noticed Rallden now leaning over the king, saying something hastily to one of the others beside him. Elle had just come to his side. Stunned to silence, her eyes fell upon the king.

Amaran felt helpless, but he could only stand and watch. It didn't feel real. How could it be? As he contemplated the horrific tragedy he suddenly realized that they had failed. It had been their duty, their obligation, to prevent this, but they had not.

If only we had known sooner, Amaran thought.

Yet, it was all in vain, for such thoughts accomplished nothing. There was nothing they could do now. Amaran looked at Leandros, who was standing quietly, his eyes fixed upon the stage.

Doors opened. Several physicians made their way to the king's side. More guards entered and moved into position at the base of the platform to keep the riled guests at bay, allowing room for the king to be examined. Amaran and Leandros made their way together through the confusion to the stage, looking around them for Druin or another assassin. Pandemonium everywhere, it was an opportune time to strike another of the councilmen.

238

On the platform, Rallden leaned over Bardane and said, "Uncle, Uncle! Can you hear me? We will take care of you. Be strong!"

Bardane's eyelids twitched and slowly opened, though only partway. "Rallden," he managed in a frail, hoarse voice, "you—were like my own son. I hope that—"

"And you *are* like a father to me," Rallden answered in a quavering voice. "I could never have asked for a better man to teach me how to rule a kingdom. But rest. Save your breath."

Bardane continued, ignoring Rallden's plea. "I must—speak. I—"

"Uncle, rest! Save your strength!" cried Rallden.

Bardane feebly shook his head. After a long pause, he continued, "Rallden, you must—be a good leader—as I have taught you. Be strong—love the people. Do not...trust anyone without first...."

"Uncle...."

King Bardane's mouth opened to say more, but no words came. He gasped for more air, and then—nothing. His breathing stopped and his shoulders fell back. Though the king's eyelids did not shut, his eyes dimmed, the life slipping away from them as he breathed his last.

The men who had been by the king's side slowly stood and retreated to allow the lady Elle to join her husband's side. Amaran knew well what this meant. The King of Albakran was now gone. After drawing in a deep breath, Amaran looked to Leandros, who had his hand to his forehead.

When Bardane's chief advisor announced that the room must be cleared, no one protested. Slow to move, but cooperative, the guests left one by one, catching one last glimpse of the terrible sight from over their shoulder.

Looking up at Rallden as he left, Amaran felt sincere pity for him. Rallden stood silently over the king's lifeless body with tears in his eyes.

A short while later, Amaran and Leandros shut the door to their quarters. "Leandros, what do we do?" he asked.

"There is only one thing to do now, Amaran. Pharon must not be allowed to assume control of the council. Protection of any who supported Bardane is vital, especially Haldegran and Rallden. We must keep them safe."

"That is quite an undertaking for only two men—and our invitation into the castle extends only until tomorrow. If we could not protect the king, how will we—?"

"As I said, there is only one thing to do. It will require the other Knights to help us, but it must be done swiftly. We must start tonight."

Amaran looked at him with questioning eyes.

Leandros answered, "Pharon and his associates must die for what they have done."

Chapter 41—Eye For an Eye

A short while later, Prennek knocked on their door, summoned at Leandros' request.

"Come in," said Leandros.

"I am here. What do you need from me?" Prennek answered as he hastily slipped inside.

"I need you to send a message as quickly as you can to the elders of the Order and to any knights positioned near the city. We'll need at least ten men tomorrow night. The others should arrive by this coming week's end, when I would assume the funeral will be held."

"Of course, Leandros."

"And Prennek," Leandros said in a low voice, stopping the eager Prennek from opening the door. "This is of utmost importance, so see to it that this is done quickly."

With that, Prennek gave a quick nod before slipping through the door.

"You and I have work to do tonight, Amaran. Taking down Pharon himself will take more men than we have now, but we can start tonight with some of his men."

"Druin and Maldock," said Amaran.

"Yes. The king trusted Druin with his life, and Maldock got his seat on the council only because the old councilman he replaced was poisoned by Pharon's men."

"Maldock is leaving tonight. I overheard him talking with some of the others. If we must take him down tonight, then we must act immediately."

"Yes, agreed. I will find him, and you, Druin. Are you ready?"

Guards were posted everywhere in the palace, especially outside the king's chambers. It was here that Rallden and Elle mourned behind closed doors.

Amaran walked down an empty corridor. Disguised as a guest in want of something to drink, he moved along the hallway with apparent purpose and an empty mug. He turned to his right at the end of the hallway, heading to the dining rooms. When passing two guards at the next corner, he willingly announced he was searching for some ale to help him sleep after a much too eventful night. The guards nodded indifferently and on he went.

Once out of sight of the guards, he made a sharp left turn at the next corner. He moved down this narrow passageway, but he was stopped by a guard at the end of that hall.

"What are you doing, sir?" the guard demanded. "No guests are allowed down here."

"I am sorry," Amaran started, still walking towards him, "but you see I was on my way to—"

Amaran did not finish. At that very second he reached out with his right arm and wrapped it around the guard's neck. Pulling tight, he let the guard slump to the floor, unconscious. He dragged him into the shadows of a doorway that was set back several feet from the hallway.

Amaran emerged from the doorway soon after, dressed in the Albakranian guard's uniform. Amaran's victim was now wearing his robe, curled up in the shadows, and with an empty mug in his hand. The disguised Amaran went around the corner, passing several more guards who paid him no attention.

Meanwhile, Leandros made his way through another corridor of the castle, this one leading out to the side entryway where carriages came to retrieve passengers. Here there was a driveway that came right up to a stone archway. Two guards waited by a carriage.

Leandros walked quickly out to them. "Is this Lord Maldock's carriage?"

"Yes it is," replied one of the guards. "But he is not here yet."

"When is he leaving? I need to ask him an important question."

"He will be leaving shortly, so if you wait here you might be able to speak a word with him."

"Thank you. I will find him now, though," Leandros replied abruptly.

Leandros turned from them and walked back through the door. The hallway was entirely empty except for a man turning the corner and heading his way. It was Maldock.

Leandros subtly grasped the hilt of the knife that was tucked into his belt, and then started directly towards the young councilman.

At first Maldock did not seem to notice. It soon became obvious, however, that he was slightly unnerved by the fast-approaching nobleman. Cocking his head slightly, he opened his mouth to question Leandros.

Instead of speaking, however, he gasped. In one fluid motion Leandros had pulled the knife from his belt and stabbed Maldock. His knife went through the useless tangle of arms that Maldock had thrown up to block the assault. He quickly withdrew the knife and stabbed him again in his gut. Maldock's eyes widened in anguish.

Leandros pulled out the dagger, but still held it tightly as he watched Maldock fall to his knees. He brought the blade rapidly across the front of the nobleman's neck. Maldock's lifeless body fell prostrate onto the ground.

Leaning over the body, Leandros took the point of the blade and carved the letter T on each cheek, marking for any who found him that he was a traitor. He wiped the dirty blade on Maldock's robe, then sheathed it. Moving swiftly away, Leandros headed for the stairs at the end of the corridor.

In a dark room in another part of the palace, a door opened to allow in only a small beam of light from the hallway. A dark figure entered. He lit some candles to light the room before shutting the door behind him. The man made his way toward an open door on the far end of the room. He was none other than Druin, captain of the king's royal guards.

Druin had taken off his outer gear and boots, and was now removing his tunic. Underneath was a layer of chainmail. Unhooking the protective mail vest at its sides, he carefully pulled it off. Then he went over to the table to pour himself some wine. With glass in hand, he grabbed a large envelope from the desk next to him. Aware only of his wine and the envelope, Druin failed to notice something behind him. An Albakranian guard—or rather a man dressed in a guard's uniform—emerged from the shadows.

The unwary captain tilted the envelope towards the light of the candles so he could see while he used his letter opener. His eager hand reached deep into the envelope and pulled out a wad of paper money and some gold coins. Sipping his wine, he dropped the money back inside.

Just as he put the glass back down, he jumped. He had just felt an arm come from behind and wrap around his neck. Amaran's grip was strong. Even Druin, a large and powerful man himself, could not break free from its hold. Clawing at Amaran's arms and writhing violently, the captain desperately tried to escape, but the arm-hold became only stronger. His face began to turn a bluish purple. He kicked his legs frantically, trying to plant a heel into the shin or knee of his captor, but he was quickly losing control—and was weakening fast.

Amaran spoke in a low voice. "Just as you have done, you also shall be killed. Only you will not die an innocent man like Bardane."

The captain tried to shake his head in the hold, but Amaran did not let go. Instead his hold shifted so that he now grabbed the man's jaw. Violently, quickly pulling on it, he snapped Druin's neck.

With a thud, Druin slumped to the floor. Amaran took out a knife and carved a T on either side of his face, and then placed the envelope full of money into the man's outstretched, lifeless hands.

Chapter 42—The Castle of Malkhaven

News of the murders of Druin and Maldock spread to every corner of the kingdom. There were dozens of rumors and theories regarding the mysterious deaths, but no evidence was found, nor any suspects named.

Soon after the bodies were discovered, Rallden, Murken, and Councilman Haldegran gathered behind closed doors.

"After meeting all day with the rest of the council," the councilman reported, "all I can tell you is that little progress was made. Those who support Pharon refuse to give in on anything, and others are indecisive and unable to commit with full support to anything that Councilman Lapellium or I have put forth. We must reach some sort of a consensus on appointing Rallden as the next king."

"And it seems unlikely," said Rallden.

Haldegran turned to Rallden with a serious look in his eye. "Yes, very. There is also the matter of deciding what to do about the twelfth councilman. Albakranian law says we must have twelve to vote to approve Bardane's successor, but—"

"But there is no time to follow the usual protocol," interrupted Murken.

"No time!" exclaimed Haldegran. "Albakran needs her next king this week, not next month!"

"Who might Maldock's successor be?" Rallden asked.

Haldegran replied, "There is no telling at this point. All of the noblemen would need a chance to nominate and then vote for the candidate of their choice, but we have no time to spare."

"If I am correct," Murken said, "in such a circumstance the council can vote to temporarily bypass the usual protocol. Could this not be the only option at this point?"

"Is that true?" Rallden asked, turning to Haldegran.

"Yes, but I don't know how we will—"

Murken quickly interjected. "You are the longest serving member on the Royal Council and you're very influential. You must propose this as the only choice and then you must persuade them to accept it. The voting cannot be delayed any longer. We should have the majority needed to appoint Rallden if it's decided with only the current eleven councilmen."

"A slim majority yes, but I agree," said Haldegran.

"Will it be possible to persuade the others on the council to go along with this?" asked Rallden.

"I will do my best," Haldegran answered, shaking his head.

Then Murken cleared his throat and said, "Until then, Your Majesty, you must be kept safe. We do not know how many more assassins there are or who else they plan to kill. If it is as many are assuming—that it is Pharon who is behind it all—he will stop at nothing to succeed."

"Regardless of who was behind it," said Haldegran, "Rallden needs protection. Your Grace, come next week, you will be the new king of Albakran."

The Castle of Malkhaven, Lord Pharon's home, was a forbidding sight. Sitting on a high cliff, the shadowy outline of its tall towers jutted upwards, standing in stark contrast to the clouds drifting slowly behind it.

After it had been dark for several hours, eleven men emerged from the woods below the cliff. With no moon visible that night, they could see very little, but there was no mistaking the sheer cliff that rose high above them. One of the men put his hand up, motioning them to gather closer. It was Leandros.

Harron stepped forward and made his way to the base of the cliff. He had a rope fastened to his back and some spikes in his hand. Having already infiltrated the castle once, he was asked to lead them in that night. With one swift, fluid motion, Harron climbed onto a boulder. From there, he drove a spike into the cliff and fastened some of his rope to it. He climbed higher up the cliff, driving in more spikes and tying more of his rope to them along the way.

When Harron reached the cliff top, he hid behind a boulder near the base of the castle wall. One by one, each began his ascent up the rope Harron had left for them.

When the last of them reached the top, they hid with Harron at the base of one of the rear towers. From the ground, they saw two guards moving at the top of each tower. Harron gathered his climbing equipment and moved into the shadows. He then started scaling the wall. The other knights looked back at the tower guards, who were at full attention, but completely oblivious to Harron below them.

Once Harron reached the top, he pulled his body up and through the space between two of the crenellations before tossing down the rope. That being the signal, Beltron carefully aimed his bow at the unsuspecting tower guards above. With unwavering focus and a slow, steady pull on the string, the young archer honed in on the guard farthest to the right. The arrow sat tense upon the string, ready to fly. With a quick release of his fingers, the arrow was loose. It hurtled through the night sky straight up into the tower, landing in the guard's chest.

When he heard the sound of the arrow behind him, the second tower guard whipped around. His eyes lit up with fear when he saw the arrow in his companion's chest. Before he could utter a single word of warning, however, an arrow plunged deep into his own chest. The guards in the neighboring tower fell moments later.

When the last tower guard fell, the knights started up the wall. The first two to reach the walkway went to the right and the next two went to the left. They assumed their positions in the towers, replacing the guards who had been shot by Beltron.

The rest followed Harron along the top of the wall until they stood across from the castle keep. There was a six foot gap between them and the outer wall of the keep. Harron leapt across first, landing on a ledge of stone protruding only a foot from the keep's wall. For security he reached up and steadied himself by grabbing hold of the stones above his head. He shimmied along the valance carefully, heading for a window.

The others followed Harron's lead, first jumping over the gap to land on the ledge, and then following him to the window. After poking his head in and looking to either side, Harron crept through the window. The knights did not move inside until he gave the word.

"Pharon's quarters are that way," Harron whispered, motioning to his right. "Take two right turns and you will find him. Be careful, though. There are many guards in this hallway."

Leandros led the way down the corridor. The others padded quickly behind him in the dimly lit passageway. They slowed when they reached the end of the next hallway, knowing they were nearing the entrance to Pharon's bedchambers.

At the corner, Leandros had his back flush up against the wall so that a simple turn of his body would put him in the adjacent hallway. Hand on the hilt of his sword, he closed his eyes briefly before reopening them. There was no mistaking the intensity in his eyes. Behind him, three knights drew their swords. The last in line, Laidan, loaded his crossbow with a bolt. He moved to the wall opposite the others so that he would be the first to have a clear shot of any guards on watch.

When Leandros nodded, Laidan moved into the hallway with his crossbow ready. He unleashed one bolt and immediately prepped another. There was first one thud and, seconds later, another. Two guards lay dead in the hallway.

Before the third guard was shot, he managed to shout, "On guard! Intruders in the—!" The frantic warning was cut short by Laidan's shot. Nonetheless, the damage had been done: their presence was known and their mission had become exponentially more dangerous.

They charged down the hallway and turned left into a smaller passageway, this the hall leading to Pharon's chamber. There were two wooden doors at the end of the hall, about twenty feet from them. Four guards stood in front of this entryway, three of whom rushed for them with swords drawn. The fourth lingered back with a loaded crossbow.

The bolt from the guard's crossbow flew through the air half a second later, directly towards Laidan. Laidan dove out of the way, landing on his side at first, but quickly rolling back to his feet. Now kneeling with his crossbow pointed towards his enemy counterpart, Laidan pulled the trigger. Pharon's crossbowman stumbled back as the bolt blasted through his chainmail. He clutched the end of the bolt protruding from his chest, trying in vain pull it out.

The other knights had since charged forward to meet Pharon's swordsmen. While the hall echoed with the clashing of steel, Leandros, Amaran, and Karamir each dropped a guard with ease. Amaran seized the keys from one of the dead guards' belts and opened the door.

The lord of the castle was nowhere in sight, but thanks to Harron's information they had detailed knowledge of the layout of his quarters. Leandros raced into an adjoining room and tried to open a sturdy oak door at the far end. It was locked. Knowing that the guards must have taken Pharon through this back passageway, he looked for something to use as a battering ram.

"Help me with this," Leandros said, pointing to a heavy chest against the wall.

Three of them helped Leandros pick up the chest by its side and hurl it toward the door. The chest smashed into the thick wood. A second hit ripped the door off its hinges.

As soon as the doorway had been opened, more guards appeared. Leandros and Karamir raced after Pharon, while the remaining knights challenged the guards in Pharon's chambers.

After only two of Pharon's guards remained, Laidan called out to Amaran. "We can handle these last two! Follow them. Help find Pharon!" Amaran turned and sprinted through the doorway.

Meanwhile, Leandros and Karamir rushed along a winding corridor, guided only by a flickering torch that Karamir had ripped off the wall. As they moved in the darkness, they sensed a faint, lingering smell of smoke and lantern oil.

"They extinguished the flames behind them as they went! It'll be hard to see them, but at least we know we're on the right track," Leandros said to Karamir.

They raced around a sharp curve and found a long flight of stairs that disappeared into darkness below. Both men raced downward.

Suddenly Leandros noticed the faint light of Pharon's torch in the distance. Before he could warn Karamir behind him, he heard something fly past him. He turned just in time to see Karamir's torch falling down the steps. As it tumbled downward, Leandros caught a brief glimpse of Karamir stumbling forward. He froze on the steps until he saw Pharon's torch disappear. Knowing he was in the clear, he grabbed the torch off the bottom step and held it over Karamir's body. An arrow protruded from his chest, and he was not breathing.

Leandros could not linger. He held the torch up momentarily to light up his path, then dropped it as he moved along in the darkness, hoping to catch up to Pharon unnoticed. Leandros eventually reached the doorway near where he had last seen Pharon. Out of breath, he swung the door open and moved into a lighted room. He gave his eyes a moment to adjust and soon saw the door on the opposite side through which Pharon had fled.

But as he moved towards the door, he felt a sharp blow to the head and fell to the ground. Desperately trying to stay conscious, Leandros pushed himself off the floor as the room spun violently around him. He knew he must recover his balance soon if he was to survive. He saw movement out of the corner of his eyes.

The guard who had ambushed Leandros was directly behind him. He kicked Leandros in the ribs as he raised his sword. He swung down at Leandros, but Leandros rolled out of the way just in time. He rose to his feet and drew his sword. Before the guard could spin all the way around, Leandros stabbed him. The guard grunted, spit blood from his mouth, and fell forward.

Leandros took several deep breaths as he reoriented himself. Wasting not a moment more, he raced through the open door and down a small flight of stairs. Two men were passing through a door just ahead of him. The first of the two was Pharon, and the second was Pharon's guard. The guard drew his sword and waited.

Leandros charged with full force at him. Right before he reached him, he pulled his sword back and took a quick step to his right. With an uppercut, he slashed his blade across the guard's torso and up through his shoulder and neck.

With this last guard out of the way, Leandros set his sights on Pharon. He passed through the next door, but stopped suddenly as his body grew cold and his legs became weak. His breath left him. Looking up, he saw Pharon standing not twenty feet from him. Then he felt the pain rip through his body.

Leandros moved his eyes downward to find the sturdy hilt of a large dagger sticking out of his chest. Pharon had released it the moment Leandros passed through the doorway. Despite resisting with every last ounce of his strength, Leandros fell to his knees. As everything began to spin, he managed to focus upon only one image: Pharon heading for the nearby stairs.

Chapter 43—The Duel

Amaran ran through the passageways, holding a lit torch in one hand, and his sword in the other. He turned one curve then the next, following the dark corridor to a stairwell. He was just starting to wonder whether he might have missed a turn when he found Karamir's body at the bottom of the stairs. He leapt over Karamir as he sprinted towards a curving wall ahead. Finding several doors to his right, he went through the open one. He found first one lifeless guard, and then another in the hallway beyond. When he moved through the next door, Amaran froze.

Forgetting everything, including their mission, he fell to his knees. He turned Leandros over to see his face. "Leandros!" he cried, lifting his head.

Leandros' breathing was shallow and his face was pallid. With obvious effort, Leandros' eyelids first twitched and then opened halfway.

Amaran looked down at him, unwilling to accept that the man who had once rescued him and given him a new life, was dying.

Leandros' cheeks moved slightly as his lips parted. "Amaran, you—you must—" Leandros uttered each word with great effort. He gasped before continuing, "You must—find Pharon. He cannot—get away. You are now the only one who can get him. Go!"

Amaran was reluctant to leave, but he accepted that Leandros was right about stopping Pharon. "Leandros..." he said in a shaky voice.

"Go!" Leandros said, mustering all his strength into one command.

Amaran looked one more time at Leandros before pulling himself away. Grabbing his sword, he ran up the staircase where Pharon had escaped. As he leapt up the steps, he could not shake the image of the wounded, helpless Leandros from his mind. He still saw the dagger in the great man's chest.

On he raced, quicker with every step, a look of fierce determination fixed upon his face. At the top step he had to make a choice: either follow a narrow passageway or ascend a spiral staircase. He chose the staircase and began his climb, continuously peering around the bend of the helical pathway before him.

As soon as he neared the top of the stairs, he saw Pharon. He was waiting with a sword in his hand while staring down at the ground. The lord of the castle then slowly moved his eyes up until he met Amaran's stare, lifting his head so that he stood tall and proud above his young challenger.

"You will not give up your pursuit of me, will you?" Pharon's cold, deep voice echoed. "Let me on my way and you will live. Take another step forward and you will die. You are no match for me. I will kill you."

Amaran did not break his stare. He continued his slow ascent up the few remaining steps. Knowing he held the lower ground, he positioned himself to prepare for an attack from above.

Then with a flash, Pharon's sword came slicing through the air straight towards the young knight. The duel had begun. With each thrust of the blade, Pharon turned his wrist to alter the angle of each blow. This was the work of a master swordsman.

Amaran successfully deflected each blow, but was unable to go on the offensive. As Pharon took swing after swing, Amaran saw the unmistakable confidence on Pharon's face and the ease with which he executed each perfect swing. As Amaran's breathing quickened in his efforts to keep up with his challenger, he felt beads of sweat form upon his forehead.

Then Pharon swung down with one particularly powerful and direct blow. Amaran not only had to concentrate on deflecting it with his sword, but also on regaining his balance as he stumbled down one step. Another blow followed the first, this one even more devastating.

With little time to reposition himself, Amaran saw yet another quick flash of metal fly towards him. He thrust his sword out to his left as quickly as he could to counter the swing. The blade came crashing into him again, pushing him down two more steps. Amaran then blocked a strike aimed for his neck and was forced down yet another step.

Pharon pushed Amaran further and further back, a step or two with almost every stroke. Amaran's enemy was relentless now, his face as fierce and unyielding as the repeated blows. Amaran feared he might not last much longer against the experienced swordsman.

Amaran was sweating and grunting as he kept up with Pharon's violent swipes. The next strike knocked Amaran's sword from his hands. He completely lost his footing and tumbled down half a dozen more steps, landing on the floor below.

Pharon was immediately upon him after jumping down the last few steps. He swung his sword to strike his now defenseless opponent. Amaran rolled out of the way just in time. He had avoided a fatal blow, but winced as he put weight on the shoulder he had wounded several days before. Amaran turned just as another blow came straight at him, but he was slower in avoiding this swing. It sliced his side, exposing a gash along his rib cage. He let out a stifled cry of pain as he retreated.

There was no time to think about the pain. Pharon advanced to kill.

But it was here that Pharon made his mistake. Pausing briefly to admire his success in this duel, a faint but growing smile spread across his face. "My boy, I did give you fair warning. Now you will suffer the same fate as your old companion." Then he raised his sword for the final blow.

Amaran saw a brief image of the pale and helpless Leandros on the floor where he had found him. It was then that something happened inside of Amaran—something that sparked a second wave of strength so great he felt unconquerable. He was furious in his grief, and he was determined.

His sword lay only several feet from him, and he moved with a flash toward his weapon. Unaware of his pain, he grasped the hilt of his sword and quickly sprung to his feet. He stared deep into his challenger's eyes as his sword smashed into the blade of his opponent.

It was not the sudden recovery, the surprising resilience, or even the seemingly unbreakable spirit of the younger swordsman that affected Pharon; it was the wild and fierce look on Amaran's face. Amaran was seething with anger and his eyes were ablaze. It was this that destroyed the confidence of the older swordsman.

The deafening sounds of the swords filled the empty hall. Amaran went on the offensive, swinging viciously but still with precision, as his repeated blows slowly moved Pharon back. Every time Amaran's sword came at Pharon, the great lord thrust his sword outward to deflect the incoming blows.

What Pharon was reluctant to acknowledge and Amaran was too consumed in his relentless attack to notice was that Pharon was tiring quickly. Pharon's repeated strikes on the stairs had demanded much energy. Now he was doing his best to defend himself against the onslaught. Amaran continued to deliver the skillful but crushing blows, backing his opponent closer to the wall only a few feet away.

Then one extremely powerful swing from Amaran forced Pharon's weapon from his hand. The panicked lord looked desperately at Amaran and then to his sword.

"This is not the fight of gentlemen," Amaran snarled. "This is war and justice served. Now, Pharon, you will die."

Pharon made a sudden move for his sword, but decided instead to scramble backward from the approaching Amaran. Then he simply stopped and stared, frozen as Amaran advanced.

After a slight pause, Amaran tightened his grip on his sword. He raised it, took a deep breath, and then thrust the blade into Pharon's chest. It landed almost exactly where Pharon's knife had struck Leandros.

His eyes wide and his mouth agape, Pharon's face quickly lost color. Amaran withdrew his blade just as Pharon began to double over. With a powerful and even stroke, he sliced through his neck. The body crumpled to the ground.

Lord Pharon was dead.

Chapter 44—The Procession

Peasants, merchants, and nobility mingled together on both sides of the street that ran from the palace to the main gates of the city. The large crowd was silent, and no one moved about or fidgeted, save the occasional restless child.

Albakranian flags blew majestically, rippling in the wind. Hoisted atop towering white poles along the length of the street, they reminded everyone that a king was about to pass through. Flower petals blanketed the cobblestones. They were from the Delurian plant, native to the southern slopes of the Aldaran Mountains, and known for their everlasting blooms. They were a common sight at royal occasions, weddings—and funerals.

The gates around the palace opened. Nearby spectators simultaneously turned their heads to watch. Four knights dressed in extravagant tunics, all bearing the colors of Albakran, rode on splendid white horses. They moved slowly onto the petal-covered road ahead of them, starting the procession. Behind them rode the members of the Royal Council. As the solemn march passed by, two men on a nearby roof watched.

"I am sorry that Leandros could not have had the funeral he deserved. He was a man of truly good character—of the highest caliber. Though I know you knew him well, you do not know everything about him. He was unlike any other. He will be missed sorely, just as King Bardane will be missed by his own people."

The man who spoke wore a black tunic with a yellow winged horse emblazoned in the center.

"Yes, I know, Celdron," Amaran replied.

"He would be proud of you and what you did, Amaran." Celdron placed his hand on Amaran's back.

"The mission is done," Amaran said in a low voice, "but I wish he were here to take pride in our accomplishment. It is incomplete without him. It almost does not seem a victory."

"The victory is not yet ours, Amaran. This was only one mission of many." Looking down at the procession, he continued, "Look. Here comes the carriage of the king."

Amaran watched the funeral carriage that now passed. The snow white caisson rolled past them carrying King Bardane's body for all to see. He was dressed in his royal robe and his open casket was covered in Delurian petals. The onlookers bowed until the lifeless body had completely moved past them.

Riding behind Bardane's carriage was the new crowned king, King Rallden. His wife, Queen Elle, rode by his side.

Amaran had noticed Rallden for only a moment, instead turning his attention towards the queen. Her long hair was not flowing, but instead braided and gathered, its locks held together by flowers and pins garnered with precious stones. Even on such a solemn occasion, her face radiated with a beauty for all to admire; but none marveled at it more than Amaran, whose gaze was fixed upon her. He watched her pass by until she had completely disappeared from view.

Then, trying to clear his mind, he said to Celdron, "What does the council wish of me now?"

"The Malakronian Empire will strike again. They were without a doubt behind Pharon and the plot to overthrow Bardane. This will be only a minor setback to them. They will not stop until Albakran—and the entire region—collapses. The next time they strike, it will be much more severe."

Amaran looked back at him. "You think they may already have another plan in the works?"

260

"I would not be surprised if they had another plan even before this one had begun to unravel. There are many of King Rallden's men we know little or nothing about. As such, we know not who can be trusted...or who may follow in Captain Druin's path. There are some who could have been in possible contact with agents of the Empire and we must know who they are. This will be your next mission."

"You wish me to stay in Albakran," Amaran said.

"Yes. The Order wants you here. With Albakran being one of the most powerful kingdoms in the west, Malakron will surely try again to cripple it. If Albakran falls, there is one less army to stand in the way of Emperor Nalldron and his soldiers."

"What will I do? How can I be of help to Albakran?"

"You will be a set of eyes and ears for the Order. Remaining close by, within arm's reach of danger, you must watch over the eastern roads leading to Balankor. The Emperor will grow still more powerful, and he will soon prepare his armies for the Great War. The dragons which have awakened will continue to multiply. Your role will become more important than ever. And as you protect the new king and his people, your identity must remain unknown, just as with all of us. If anyone were to discover who you are, it could compromise our mission."

"Celdron," Amaran started hesitantly, "Where will I live? What will I do? Until now, Leandros looked after me. The other knights are established and successful men, but I—"

"Leandros has left you all that was his. Before the mission he spoke to me about it. His estate, his accounts, all that was his is now yours."

Amaran tried to speak, but could say nothing. The lump that formed in his throat did not subside.

Reading Amaran's expression, Celdron continued. "You will not have to worry about providing for yourself ever again, for you have all that you could ever need. Leandros was a very wealthy man as you know."

"I will do as you ask—what the Order asks of me. It will not be easy to move on without Leandros, though. He was more like a father to me than a teacher. It is unfair that I have lost so many dear to me."

"I understand how difficult your life has been, but you know how important your role is, Amaran."

Amaran sighed. "I know what Leandros would have wanted me to do. I assure you that I will do as the Order asks, to the best of my ability."

Celdron nodded. "Good."

"How do we expect Malakron to strike next?"

Celdron sighed. "The Malakronian Empire is powerful and their influence great. Before the Great War nears Albakran's doorstep, Malakron will likely try to get men inside the new king's inner circle. Perhaps there already are such men close to Rallden."

As Amaran listened, he looked off in the distance to the streets below. Turning onto a new curving road to their right, he could once more see the elegant Queen Elle riding next to Rallden. And there was someone else, someone whom he had not noticed earlier who was riding right behind them: Murken, King Rallden's new chief advisor.

Celdron continued, "It is for these reasons, imminent dangers already lurking inside the palace, that your mission is of utmost importance to not only the Knights of the High Order, but to all peoples of the Albantrian Continent. It was this very evil that was the ultimate cause of Leandros' demise. Avenge his death. He can't have died in vain."

After the funeral procession had completely disappeared from view, the crowds slowly thinned. Even after Celdron left, Amaran remained on the roof, alone, looking out upon the city. He looked over at the streets leading to the barracks where he had once lived. He turned to his right to look at the main gates through which he and his father had first entered the city some fifteen years ago. He then faced the palace, sitting on the hill high above the rest of the city, where he had met a young girl named Elle.

Amaran stared upon the palace for some time before he finally turned to leave. He retrieved his horse, swung himself up into the saddle, and then waited a moment. Though he felt alone, he was unwilling to give up. He knew his mission was important. It was for this reason that he still found purpose in his life.

Then the last of Celdron's words to him resounded in his head once more: 'Avenge his death. He can't have died in vain.'

Slowly raising his head and looking past the western wall of the city, Amaran said aloud, "I will do all I can to protect Albakran from the evil power that lies to the east. If for no one else, for Leandros. I *will* avenge his death. He will not have died in vain."

With a triumphant "Onward!" to his horse, he tapped its sides with his heels. The hooves pounded upon the cobblestone as they picked up pace. As they neared the main gates, a guard motioned for him to stop, but then jumped back and out of the way once he realized Amaran's intentions.

Amaran raced across the drawbridge, turning onto the road that would lead him out of the city. Instead of following the road, he turned his horse to the right, into the western fields where he had ridden so many times before.

Amaran then paused one last time, turning to take another look at the city. He caught a glimpse of the majestic North Tower, rising high above the rest of the palace. And though he did not know it, someone was standing in a window high up in that very tower. This person noticed Amaran's pause and the way he gazed at the city, then watched as he took off again at full speed.

His cloak flew wildly behind him as the wind rushed against his face. He rode through the meadows of golden grass and rolling hills, past the valley with the stream and the old tree, and beyond the last patches of forest. On he rode into the distance, leaving the familiar landscape behind and riding fast towards the vast sea of grass that lay beyond Balankor. As the bright orange sun slowly descended in the violet evening sky, horse and rider grew smaller with each passing minute, until they disappeared into the distant horizon.

THE END

The Story Continues in
Legend of the Dragon Slayer: Rise of the Empire

About the Author

Inspired by stories like Tolkien's The Hobbit and Lord of the Rings, Jonathan Dorr always wanted to create interesting stories based on his own fantasy world. The result was Legend of the Dragon Slayer, the first book in a series of five, which follows Amaran as he grows up in an enemy's palace, falls in love with the wrong girl, and discovers fate has bigger plans for him.

Jonathan Dorr has a degree in secondary biology education and currently teaches high school science. He has a collection of exotic pets and makes frequent trips to zoos, and enjoys watching wildlife wherever he can, from the swamps of South Carolina to the Adirondack Mountains of New York. His love for nature has inspired many of the habitats and creatures in his Dragon Slayer series.
Jonathan Dorr lives in North Carolina with his wife and son, and their two dogs. Connect at jonathandorr.com.

Made in the USA
Lexington, KY
16 August 2015